Being Romeo's Daughter

Being Romeo's Daughter

Liz Green

88 Palmtrees Publishing

CONTENTS

CONTENTS

To the man who taught me to live my dreams...
and the man who showed me *how*.

1

Being Romeo's Daughter

Real life ain't even begin for me til' my eighteenth birthday when I awoke to an unlocked bedroom door. With an hour to get to court, I crept downstairs and found an empty house. Our grand piano had gone missin', artwork snatched off the walls, and big spots on the rug where a couch, chairs and ottoman once been. I ain't seen no maid, no butler, no cooks. There weren't no men wandering with guns, in suits and shoes with spats neither. I was alone, finally, but damnit I was free. Six years in this lock up, pacin' round Millionaire's Row, without my pops permission to leave simply cause Romeo Romello's precious wife had to up and die. Yes, ya know, that day I felt like startin' a little trouble!

Regina Louise, Lord rest her, always been on the level with me. She told me the truth as far as she knew it whether I got hurt feelings or not, but it taught me to be one tough son-of-a-bitch like she. Regina was tiny, five foot one, and I grew only two inches taller than that. She had a fur coat and ice that weighed more than she did, but they fit me just fine. I dressed myself that morning in her gear cause she weren't using it where she was, and I were practicing that look in the mirror she used to kill. For a high society dame, she sure was one cold bearcat, I swear. They had a rags-to-riches story they did, Regina and my pops. They was born out of the city slums, the poorest area where even the rats are starving and try to eat ya. She'd been destined to stay in that heap of filth if it weren't for my pops and his big ideas, his wheelin' and dealin.' He swore to get them outta there soon as he could, and he did cause Romeo Romello's the finest man ever lived! He's how we landed in this house, this big house, my big elaborate prison.

Their marriage was a bargain of sorts, yes, it was. Regina kept her end up, runnin' the household and in return pops made sure she ain't want for nothing. She had the best of everything; expensive makeup, loads of jewelry, decorative pots and plants with fine bone china to entertain with. A wardrobe lousy with dresses, hats, coats, marbles, you name it she got it. There was maids that cleaned everything from our diapers to Regina's outlandish chandeliers. Even had them opaque Russian eggs and satin upholstered furniture in rich purples and deep blues, us kids weren't never allowed to sit on. She had a parlor, a sitting room, a breakfast nook, perfectly set dining table, and a swimming pool for a bathtub in her master bedroom with floral wallpaper.

Old ladies would come in, them old ladies that knew old money and could teach it to the likes of us. They came for tea with stacks of books on etiquette couldn't Regina ever read. They'd tell her to do this and that, dress this way and that and she'd do it cause for as much lack of schoolin' she had, well, Regina had this way of mimicking' down to a tee. All she wanted, her whole life's dream she wanted, was to hob knob with high society in New York and she could have if it weren't for that big mouth of hers. The most vulgar, guttural language came out of it and she had some type of high shriek shrill of a voice, you'd shutter to hear it. In silence, she got away lookin' like class, and that upper crust would know no better.

The shame of it all was that no Romello, woman or otherwise, could keep their mouth shut but for so long and wasn't the whole block gonna know it! Didn't matter all the cars and money and power, them rich fancy folks was still gonna stay away like the plague with Regina being the only one out of our gang that gave a heck!

One of the maids found her, all slumped over in the bath, a bottle of that damn bootleg hooch empty between her legs. The meat wagon come to get her, the fuzz in and out of things. They was asking question after question to my pops while he laid his head in his hands pretending not to listen. My brothers had bloodshot eyes, chain smoking in the parlor room, playin' casino and gin rummy till night turned into another night. The newsies put us all over front page and if Regina had been alive the scandal woulda killed her for sure. Pops buried her in an all-white casket with shiny new diamonds and price tags on fur pelts. A horse drawn carriage pulled her lifeless body down Park Avenue. He insisted having cursive carved scripture on a white marble headstone that took days to perfect. Some goons even schemed to dig her up and rob her grave, but pops had em' clipped.

Now don't start thinkin' Regina were a cruel, wicked stepmother or none of that fairytale junk cause my life were far from no fairytale. If my story were to start with once upon a time, then once upon a time my pops had a terrible reputation chasin' skirt. He'd dodged the stork so much I'm sure that old bird was grinnin' some sort of smug and satisfied carrying me to their doorstep in a dusty crate for a bassinet. My real old lady weren't even old, something like fourteen or fifteen when she lammed off, left me with them. Some jazz club they met at in Harlem, my ma, the little hoofer and pops was hooked. She tried playing some badger game on him and it ended with me nine months later, at least that's how Romeo lies about it. Truth is no Romello would fall for no badger game, well maybe except my dumb cluck brother William. Anyways, the story is pops followed my ma round like she was candy and wouldn't leave her alone until it was his idea.

Regina said she didn't know I was colored until I got older. Pops hid that fact from her and rightly so, in them days. I had loose curls, little light brown spirals all over my head, but to have Regina tell it they were jet black and the kinkiest coils she'd ever seen on an Italian baby. All them old women told her she'd have to pass me, bleach my hair blonde and there wouldn't be no problems. Every other Sunday, I'd be sitting with an apron around my front, smelling god-awful, but things was just easier to play along and make her happy. I was the one girl in a house full of boys -- Romeo's only daughter. Regina dressed me in frilly clothes and saddle shoes with little lace socks and truth be told I liked gettin' all spruced up. There was tutors and piano lessons and people that come to the house just to look at me. They always saids how beautiful I was, my eyelashes longer and lips fuller than pin ups. 'Put her in pictures', they'd say and there was a gleam in Regina's eyes when she presented me like her little porcelain doll. When it all stopped, kinda sudden yeah all kinds of sudden, that's when I started in the life. There was a turn-about when I was five or six, she just told pops if he wanted to keep me that was fine, but she 'weren't no babysitter.' To this day don't even know what I did.

From then on I started goin' with pops everywhere, cept' if it were someplace I couldn't at least sit in the back and wait. It was just facts, life as we knew it, and that's why I'd been out earlier than any of my older brothers. Ended up learning everything from pops, I did. All the conversations, all that knowledge, plenty of schoolin' for a life in the mob. Learned how to cook books, bet on horses, fix fights, mix drinks, con mugs. Pops told everybody I had a photographic memory and a keen ear so watch what they was doin' and sayin', round little Cece. It made them goons get real particular with me in the room, treatin' me like some sort of snitch and they was right. I was reportin' it all back to boss every word and every move they made without fail. There was men who didn't like it but they was also men who got the bump off. Ain't nobody threatenin' a Romello specially a little one with spiral curls and didn't matter how big and tough they were, they weren't gonna scare me no how!

All my life, I've been tough, yes real tough but also smart. Those fools been eating out of the palm of my hands since the days of sittin' on pops' shoulders and barking orders from six feet in the air. The Romello name gives the feeling of power and being feared. Pops swallowed every room he walked into whole and so did my big brothers. It was like a wave over me, that thing about my family, it were bubble wrap keepin' me safe. If my life were a fairytale, it would have started with once upon a time, a princess sat high on top of her own fire breathin', gin swillin', gun totin' dragon!

When Regina died pops decided, and all types of sudden, to lock me in my bedroom and throw away the key, but it was far too late. Locked bedroom door or not, I was formed, I was a Romello, and I'd shout it from my open window to the world down below. I had already had that taste of power and I'd learned the con. I knew how to be a mug and I were the best mug cause I weren't no mug I was a girl. Being Romeo's daughter meant I had to be tough as a guy and they'd think I wasn't cause I weren't no man, but I were the manliest dame on them streets apart from lookin'!

All them times following pops, it was no more dresses, no more bows in my hair. No, more tutors or lessons or setting tables, practicin' piano. I was soon good as the rest of them, spitting and fighting, clawing, wearing suspenders and dungarees all hitched up to my waist like a boy. Pops wouldn't hear of manicures or smelly bubbly baths cause ya gotta put all that con aside, when you're a girl dealing with men. Pops said, ain't no respect for all that ritz and them frills when you're tryna make rank, and I sure did want to make rank.

My eighteenth birthday meant just that, heir to the Romello throne. Romeo had picked me over all his sons, cause the business ran better with me, and my brains then it did with 'them hoods barreling in with their bean shooters ruinin' our best laid plans', he said. I'd be high in the organization, higher than pops maybe one day, and nobody would say nothing bout me being a woman because I was Romeo Romello's daughter and if he said it, it was law. At eighteen I'd be a made woman, a woman of honor, and that was my destiny.

There was something else about my birthday and that door opening for me so willingly, standing there in full makeup, blonde curls, wearing Regina's coat and jewels. It wasn't the heavy behind our name I felt. It was other feelings... urges. I was a woman now and I was gonna act like it, walk like it, speak like it. I could picture the broads dancin' down the speaks, the way they moved, the way they dressed. They swung their arms and hips around so provocatively, all sights on em.' Those dames would be dancing and drowning in free drinks, fresh flowers, and attention from men all googley-eyed like they'd just done something as big as a war hero or bringing world peace. Just moving their legs round the bar, it was like no other bim in the world could ever repeat it. For those women, like my mom, the men came calling. Not ordinary men -- big powerful men much like my father who had a lot to offer and big houses with maids and diamonds and trinkets to fill their time.

I shed the boy's clothes for something softer, frillier, more female, cause damn it if I weren't gonna have em lookin' all googley-eyed at me as well. It was a hot city summer, and my skin stuck to the fur round that coat like glue, but I still wore it as a rite of passage. I was walking down the streets of New York hailing cabs and strutting in kitten heels I'd had no right to wear. My curls were set, perfectly pinned, bangs falling over my eyes and a bedroom stare. My shoes were polished, stockings with no holes in em', and my dress with the high slit to keep em' guessing. The newsies ate me up.

Is that Cece? That sure is, that's Cece Romello! Cece give us a smile dolly – yes show us some leg – Duckie finally goin' up the river? No more duckin' con college, huh, your old pops? Blow us a kiss Cece! Yes, blow us a kiss! You're beautiful!

It was a long walk, up the courtroom steps, and I was making it longer by turning and giggling and pretending, hamming it up for flashbulbs. Every time they clicked, I turned like I were on stage. There it was again, the flood, the overwhelming warmth through my body when I was being Cece Romello, and the attention that came with it I reveled in. I ain't never been addicted to booze, drugs, or sex, I'd leave that for pops and my brothers -- Regina even. But I did love the fame, and the fact that when we moved as a family the world noticed -- though I'd always been angling to move alone. I wanted to be seen out of the shadows, to matter as one, see?

"What the hell ya doing, little girl?"

Jewels was the only man who ever had the nerve to rake me over the coals about anything and to reprimand me when pops didn't. That wrinkly old bastard been attached to this family longer than I'd been alive and he outranked me just on principle. Pops didn't make no moves without that fool's advice... *well his and the fortune teller's.*

"You know better! Actin like some little chaser for the cameras! Aren't your pops in enough mess?"

"Ah kick off ya old bastard!"

Jewels grabbed me by my elbow, forced me to the top of the steps and out of the limelight. The cameras stopped clicking as that audience disappeared. It was just me, Jewels, and his cheap old shoes up against my hellcat fury. The infamous Jewels, lots of soup jobs got him that name. It was respect he had, respect and a wooden leg. But he weren't gonna get none of it from me.

"Get off!"

"Me get off? You get off! You actin' like a little tramp and you better put some sense into your head or I'll knock it into ya!"

"Who you think you're roughing up? Not Romeo Romello's daughter, I know that!"

"Romeo Romello's daughter yeah, where was he when I was changing your damn dirty diapers and reading ya at bedtime, tuckin' ya in!"

"You ain't do that. You're connin'."

"Connin'? You crazy – how many meals I made ya huh? How many clothes I washed for ya? How many times I clean your up-chuckin' when you was sick?"

"You ain't never done it."

Truth was he did, that olive-skinned son-of-a-bitch did. He was nice to me, Jewels was. Them days traveling with pops weren't all great. I was shivering most nights, wrapping myself up in anything I could get my hands on to sleep. Jewels always made sure I got home safe. Jewels always made sure I didn't go hungry. Jewels made sure when the rest of em didn't. Jewels was good people he was, but being good people ain't make him any less annoyin'.

"If you were my daughter –but ya ain't my daughter, praise be to God," he'd start, "I'd do what your pops shoulda done, woulda done years back 'cept he was too busy knockin' guys lights out."

"Oh, yeah? What?"

"I'll tell ya what! He should have give ya what for! The old one-two!"

Now his old body's creakin' as he's squarin' up. I'm laughin'.

"Oh yeah?"

I wrapped my arms round him, smilin', the old softie. I really did care about him and his terrible temper, but it was one of them tempers like old folks get when they see you makin' the same mistakes they did, and they just want to beat it out of you so you'll stop. The crimson round his neck eased, his blood pressure went down, but he was tryin' to hide it. I laid my head on his shoulder, smellin' his familiar aftershave and stale cigarettes. I laughed as he kept up ramblin.'

"*And another thing* – there's more clown paint on your face than they got leanin' down the lamppost! And a whole chinchilla 'round your neck to boot! More chinchilla than cheesecake!"

2

Being Romeo Romello's Defense Attorney

Romeo Romello never been to no prison. Yes, jail, a night here a night there and always for fighting or getting caught with giggle juice during Prohibition, but ain't never no Sing-Sing. And all them charges they laid at his feet, well, they never had quite enough evidence to book him on– nothing substantial -- as Anthony Romello called it. Anthony was the only one out of the six of us that went to university, but pops weren't doin' him no favors. Romeo sent Tony, his third oldest son, for his law degree cause it was gonna *'help the family'*.

Only for Regina's sake did he attend the most prestigious school their two-hundred pound henchmen could force him into. Tony would register as Anthony McAllister *just for the records,* using Regina's maiden name. Cause what good school would dare let a Romello in -- even one as sheepish and sensitive as Tony? Not the type of school Regina would be proud to say her son went to! Not one that would be good enough for Regina's favorite boy of all five boys. Tony was the one who never got dirty playing with others, with his nose stuck in books all day and skin pale cause it never seen one ounce of daylight.

Folks thought this was it for my old man, yes, there were actual charges this time he couldn't talk hisself out of -- charges with some meat on em. We're talking 'tax evasion', which had put so many others in iron bracelets that the rumors of his fate made it all through the underground, scarin' the life out of the other mugs. For months, Romeo sat behind bars waiting for trial and while he was away, they came with a big truck and took his fortune nearly one stitch of furniture at a time. Took em six days to do it and they was moving real slow too like they had some type of enjoyment out of it. Or maybe it was because three of my brothers and all his kings men were posted at the door frame with pockets in the shape of guns, checking inventory. They'd call to me, and I'd have a pencil and paper jotting down notes, sticking my head out my bedroom window and nodding.

"Write down what you see leaving that house, Cecelia," Tony ordered, "you write down everything– don't miss one item!"

And there was a laundry list of items! I brought it with me to court just in case and it was deep down in my coat pocket, my fingers tightening around the paper, so it didn't fall out. Pops looked piti-ful, staring straight at the wall. Jewels and I slid into seats in the back row. Pops didn't see us, but I sure saw him, sweating like a pig.

There was also this thing about Duckie, he was always sweatin', nervous of not, and it was his doctor called him out on it. He'd walk around with big sweatstains, pools of wet all on hisself and no ma-terial or type of clothes could hide it. No matter the season, weather, temperature in the room, pops was an overflowin' faucet and this time he'd looked rung out like a linen sock. This was a man who al-ways dressed immaculately, took three showers a day and had nearly four wardrobe changes, but they didn't have them type of luxuries in prison. Poor pops was just sitting there in his striped pajamas cling-ing to him so he didn't have no secrets. Bracelets bound his wrists together so tight the poor old soul couldn't barely reach to wipe the stream of sweat pooling on his forehead drippin' into his eyes. His face so sorry and sad that I stood up to help him, but got stopped in my tracks by that big, bossy bailiff.

"Court is now in session, Honorable Judge Braylin presiding,"

Recess was over. Jewels grabbed my arm and bailiff's glaring, so I stayed put. Pops already had Tony pouring a glass of water and William whose job it was to give him baby powder so he could dry hisself out.

"Tony's set to pay every dime of that schoolin' back," Jewels mumbled to me, "God hope he'll get this right. We don't need Duckie goin' away, not right now. Too much to do."

Jewels done his own stint in the big house. He told me about it once, that it was cold and lonely, his own voice echoing off stone walls. There's a whole bunch of grown men cryin' and carryin' on, he said. *But you's all in the same boat so nobody cares to hear ya, cause what makes you so special?* Jewels was lookin' real depressed rememberin'.

"They ain't bookin' him," I assured, "not Duckie."

"You live in a little girl's dream world," he spit.

Sometimes Jewels eyes went all dark reminiscing on those five years of hard labor out in the desert somewhere. Every so often he went right back out there digging holes with chains on his ankles and I had to remind him that he weren't out there no more. This time he didn't wanna hear nothing, especially from the girl he changed diapers for.

"William, would'ya gimmie that talcum?"

The whole courtroom could hear pops suffering.

"Stop hoggin' that talcum, damnit!"

He reached for the bottle from William with his big meaty, sweaty hands all cuffed and bound working as one. William weren't paying no attention when he got wind of me and Jewels sittin' way in the back. He started peerin' without his glasses trying to figure if it was really us and why was we sitting so far anyway.

"Oh that dumb son of a –"

Jewels saw it before any of us -- the bottle squeezed and sprayed everywhere! Powder went up all in the air and all over Tony, Pops, William and the row behind him. They all waws just covered in talcum and coughing up a storm. Tony was asking take another recess cause of William being stupid.

"No, we will NOT take another recess!"

We heard the Judge yelling, at his wits end. The people from the front row that had to leave and clean up did so, but Pops, Tony and William were ordered to stay put. Through the clearing of talcum fog, they set their sights on me and Tony motioned to come closer. I figured he needed the paperwork, the inventory sheet, so I rushed right over careful not to get no talcum on my nice furs.

"Princess," Pops pleaded, "princess wipe my face would ya? Take the towel and wipe my face. William, move over and let her have that towel to wipe my face!"

Pops wasn't somebody who said please, but he made up for it with his sigh of relief.

"Thanks princess, that's my sweet babygirl."

And then there was Tony interrupting.

"Where have you been, Ceceliaaa?"

My biggest beef with Tony weren't that he was so smart thought he was smarter than all the rest of us cause all that school he had the right to act all high and mighty. *If I'd had the same schoolin' I'd probably most likely very surely act the same way.* My issue with Tony was a simple one. When I looked at him, his blonde hair all slicked back neat and his eyes piercing, his voice high and shrill, I thought of Regina. He was the spitting image of his mother, if not for the fact he had a penis, I'd wonder.

"Well?"

And that 'Ceceliaaa' was what I had listened to everytime Regina had a visitor and wanted to show me off or wanted me to practice piano or help set the dining room table. She'd go, wrong side of the dishes Ceceliaaaa, you know where the forks go, the glasses go, put it right Ceceliaaaa and don't get anything on that nice new dress Ceceliaaaaa----

"Ceceliaaaa? You ready?"

I took the list out my pocket and passed it towards him. Tony looked confused, annoyed even.

"Don't you listen?" He asked.

"Not to you."

"Well, you'll get yours when you take the stand."

"Take the stand?"

"Oh, so now who's listening?"

But that was Tony, always getting my nerves up. I had to sit there, front row of a courtroom after been finally freed myself, on my eighteen birthday, sweatin' bullets underneath all that fur. He had me sitting awaiting like I was on trial too!

"Take the fur off Cece," William insisted.

"Mind your business."

"It's makin' me sneeze, please take the fur off Cece."

"That's the talcum William, ya damn palooka."

"Nah, Cece I'm allergic to chinchilla."

"You ain't no allergic to chinchilla."

"Yes, I am I swear to it, pops ain't I allergic to chin—"

"—hush!"

Anthony is warnin', making that face like Regina when us kids was bothering her, running round her perfect dining room table moving forks and knives the wrong way round.

"Do you solemnly swear to tell the whole truth—"

That's the baliff, coming over asking pops to swear in. Romeo put his palm on the good book and it left an imprint all soggy and I don't think you supposed to get the bible wet, it might be a sin even. He was takin' a couple of deep breaths.

"—I solemnly---"

"—Excuse me Judge,"

That's Tony again. This time he stands and Judge Braylin, well we could all tell the reason for his anger, annoyance, it all was cause of my brother.

"What now Mr. Romello?"

That man's voice was so hoarse from yelling, he took a big gulp of his own water and fanned hisself under his robe. And didn't he look familiar from down the speaks?

"Any more objections? Found anything in the fine print of that law book of yours that you'd like to bring up now instead of at the most inappropriate times?"

Tony's straightening his tie, approaching the bench innocent as a little child gonna ask for a second helping of ice cream.

"I just ask Judge —is that a King James Bible?"

"What?"

"I'm just trying to make sure it's the King James version—"

"—son it's fine, let's get this over with—"

Pops is struggling, he needed somebody to wipe him down again, but Tony raised a hand.

"No father," Tony insisted, "we must really be sure of it being a King James."

The judge leaned over, and I'm sure in his head he was ripping Tony's ears off and feeding them to that big lug of a bailiff, but instead a cough came out, some talcum and he shook his head, nearly defeated. Poor judge didn't stand a chance, Anthony Romello had a reputation of playing around in his trials, spinning prosecutors and judges round on his pinky. Tony was a Romello through and through, even though he acted more Regina than Romeo he was still a mug, and he still enjoyed the con.

"Mr. Romello, if either you or your defendant ask another silly question, I'm going to dismiss you from court and Mr. Romello will have to represent himself, is that clear?"

"Crystal clear judge,"

"Thank you, continue,"

"I was just trying to make sure it was King James –"

"—well it is!"

"Actually if I could just take a peek at it to be sure –"

The judge stood. Tony didn't back away he was firm, he was respectful, but he was smiling, smug. All of us kids had this smug smile and it got us into a lot of trouble, I'll tell ya.

"I know what you're doing and it won't work with me! Maybe with Mason, maybe with Jenkins but NOT Judge Braylin! You understand the severity of the state's claims? Your father, if found guilty of these charges, will go to prison for a very long time and you will get yourself disbarred if you keep up these asinine antics!"

Tony adjusted his suspenders, his eyes wide with disbelief.

"Will you disbar me, Judge Braylin? Not even Judge Mason or Judge Jenkins could do that and trust me there were many inquiries. Many files being shifted around from one department to another. An awful lot of paperwork. Too much really."

"I can have you arrested for contempt."

Pops and Tony laughed. Jewels laughed from the back row.

"Now that would be a badge of honor, Judge, since I am the only son of my father's who hasn't been arrested for contempt. But out of anything to be arrested for, I guess I'd rather it be for contempt."

"Get em', Duckie's boy, get em'!"

Someone called out.

"But I've done nothing contemptable your honorable honor,"

Tony smiled wide and put his hands on the loops of his suspenders, strutting back and forth in his pin striped suit, teasing the Judge like a caged animal, poking him with a stick every so often. That's how he had them in the end, my brother, fit for the loony bin, finger to lips wagging up and down, crazy.

"I haven't been impolite either, my client was brought up devout Catholic and the poor man can't swear in on anything other than a King James bible. I'm advocating for my client's rights as a God-fearing Catholic, that's all and if that's categorized as contempt then I'm sure we can bring in somebody who'll explain that to me—"

"—is that a threat Mr. Romello?"

Judge's eyes darted back and forth following Tony's every move like he were trained to do so. Tony shook his head, assuring it was not a threat. Judge Braylin knew it was.

"You're about to lose your representation,"

Judge looked squarely at pops and raised his gavel.

"Judge no!" Pops pleaded, "he's been doin' that since he was little, ya know, it's like a nervous tick it's annoying and ya think he's playing and – I solemnly swear to tell the whole truth and nothing but the truth so help me God on this King James bible – so yeah like I said he was always getting' into trouble because of his big mouth, it's just nerves ya know?"

"Funny thing about nerves is –" Tony started, but pops was on a roll.

"–He was always lookin' goofy with his big glasses and books tucked up under his arm and I told him one time, I told him, Tony I swear if I'd been your age and seen you out there while I was playing you'd have gotten a big fat lip from me –"

Pops is laughing.

"Ain't that right Jewels?"

"Damn straight! Four eyed fool."

"—*Funny thing about nerves is* –" Tony continued, "nervousness runs in our family your honor. Look at my father! Is that the sweat of a man with nothing to hide?"

"What?" – Pops

"Are you trying to help the defendant or the plaintiff, Mr. Romello?" - Judge

"If you'd let me finish Judge, that's very rude to interrupt by the way but I see your point from earlier – anyway I'd like to say that my father, the defendant and my client, he has an overactive glandular disorder that causes him to sweat uncontrollably even on the coldest of winter days. Isn't that right Mr. Romello?" - Tony

"He sweats like a pig!" – Jewels

"The court will have silence!" Judge presided, "Answer the question Mr. Romello."

"Well yes I suppose I get a little sweatier than most –" - Pops

"—most coal miners," – Tony

"I hope it ain't that noticeable but yes I do sweat a lot for no reason but that don't mean I'm nerv—" - Pops

"—Just a yes or no will suffice." – Judge

"Yes."

Pops was gonna kill Tony if he ever got home.

"And this uncontrollable sweating," Tony went back to pacing, "which I have a doctors note for as exhibit C, has that medical diagnosis ever hindered you in any way during your...how can I put it...business meetings?"

"Huh?"

"Speak English!" Someone yelled.

The district attorney, who already looked like he'd resigned to his fate, shot up in his chair this time,

"Objection! That was never entered into evidence prior to this trial. There was no exhibit C."

"Overruled."

"Judge?"

"I've had quite enough of this, now finish Mr. Romello, yes or no to...well that Exhibit C."

"I don't even understand the damn question." - Pops

"Then I put it to you this way father, I mean Mr. Romello, has your sweating ever caused a problem for you during these meetings, negotiations with partners?" - Tony

"Well..."

"And please remember you did swear under oath."

"Um...it's hard to say"

"On a King James Bible."

"Yes," but it was the tiniest squeak of a yes, so nobody actually heard it.

"What was that?" Judge asked.

"Pops?" Tony asked.

"Yes. It is hard."

"And why is that Mr. Romello?" Tony pressed on.

"Cause you can't have a poker face makin' deals when you're sweatin' bullets in front of mugs – I mean other business partners."

"So, would it be correct of me to say that you don't hide any-thing, because you can't hide anything, because there would be no point in you having secrets that you're medically diagnosed disorder, Exhibit C, would prevent you keeping?"

"Huh?"

"Objection – leading the witness." – District Attorney

"Sustained, don't lead the witness Mr. Romello," Judge sighed, "Please get on with this. We get it, the defendant doesn't bother with secrets because he can't hold his cards."

"I objects to that!" Pops stood.

"Sit down!" the Baliff barked.

"But Judge Braylin, the tax returns," the D.A. started, "'exhibit A, returns from 1921, 22 and 23 all understating Mr. Romello's earned income by thousands of dollars! We aren't talking sweating or secrets – none of that is relevant, there's the simple fact that we have this – hard evidence! No amount of double talk can get around that."

"He has a point Mr. Romello –" - Judge

"—hence why I was just getting there," Tony glared at the prosecution, "Mr. Romello, did you ever complete your own taxes?"

"Yes."

"What year?"

"I did them all the years."

"Let me elaborate – I mean complete as in fill out and mail in yourself, not simply review the work of another."

"Oh – why didn't you say -- 1920."

"And you have not completed your own taxes since then?"

"No."

"Oh yes, blame the accountant!" – the D.A.

"So, you have hired and paid, someone to complete these returns the years following 1920?" - Tony

"No." - Pops

"No as in you haven't hired someone or no as in you haven't paid them?"

"Well I..."

"Please remember you are under oath."

"Your honor, the defendant knows full well he is under oath I object to wasting the courts time" – D.A.

"Sustained," Judge Braylin, "Mr. Romello stick to relevant questioning."

"Have you paid them?"

"No – well I give her a house to live in –"

Pops turned to me and there was the hot seat.

"I'd like to bring up my last witness, Judge."

"You have no more witnesses to call Mr. Romello."

"Yes, I do, I'd like to call my defendant's daughter to the stand."

Tony and I locked eyes for just a second. He could see the frightened expression on my face, but he was gonna press on, nearly ripping me from my seat with his glare and making me take the stand.

"Come on Ceceliaaa. Judge Braylin doesn't bite."

He might not have bitten but he sure wanted to and I know it from the way he was watching me swear in I knew it. I had to sit pretty closely indeed to him, especially when the District Attorney was raising cane talking bout not being able to cross examine. Judge Braylin, something like in his sixties, but he was still all googlely eyed lookin' at me.

"Tell your story my dear," Judge smiled, and I realized he was missing teeth.

Court weren't really nothing to a Romello. Growing up we went to court more times than to church on Sunday but me, I'd never been a witness to nothing. They'd always say I was too short I couldn't look over nobody's shoulder and I never heard nothin', they'd say. I guessed that was part of growing up too, eighteen, finally on the witness stand like they had trusted me with all this. Pops life was in my hands and it was sudden, yeah all kinds of sudden.

"Does the defendant use an accountant?" Tony asked me.

"What defendant?"

Tony's eyes lowered, "our father."

"Oh yes."

"Does he use a certified accountant?"

"Certified?"

"Oh, come on," Tony huffed.

"You elaborate for the witness!"

Judge Braylin insisted then turned back to me flashing his eyelashes. Maybe he had been in them speaks watching broads dance and throwing coin. That was him, wasn't it?

"Certified as in licensed to prepare and complete taxes," Tony explained,

I drew a blank. He sighed and continued.

"licensed as in was given a license by the state of New York to complete taxes after a series of courses finished and certificates obtained thereafter?"

"Speak English Tony!" Pops yelled.

"Yes or no?" Tony asked me.

"No, I ain't got no certifications."

"And who is Mr. Romello's acting accountant?"

"I am."

"I am trying to establish a timeline for the court. Miss Romello, were you Mr. Romello's accountant in 1921?"

"Yeah I guess so."

"1922?"

"Sure."

"1923?"

"Geez Tony, yes! What about it?"

"How about 1920?"

"Nope."

"I bet you are a cute little accountant, aren't you? Very efficient," Judge whispered.

"Okay Ms. Romello now I'll ask you a personal question, when were you born?"

"You know when I was born Tony."

"For the courtroom please, Ceceliaaaaa,"

"August the 8th."

"What year?"

"1910."

"And what would that make you today Miss Romello?"

"Eighteen."

"Oh -- Happy birthday Princess!" Pops called out.

I knew better than to believe that. He *was tryin' to hide the fact that he forgot.*

"How old were you in 1921, Ms. Romello?"

"Eleven."

"And 1922?"

"Twelve."

"And 1923?"

"Thirteen."

"Can you please review exhibit A, tax returns our D.A. is most proud of, the returns from 1921, 22 and 23. Please tell the court yes or no is this your handwriting?"

"Yes."

"Look them over, inspect them – can you be one hundred percent sure of your answer."

"Yes."

"And is there anything in particular that stands out to you on these three tax returns that makes you sure that this was your handwriting and not that of your fathers or a licensed, certified, adult accountant?"

I looked them over one last time.

"Yes…I draw smiley faces in my zeros."

"Oh how sweet," Judge smiled sly.

The courtroom laughed, but Tony didn't.

"Smiley faces, your honor, and if you don't mind me saying -- *kid stuff*. Miss Romello, please turn the tax returns around to the blank side of the pages. What do you see?"

"My name in cursive letters."

"How many times is your name in cursive?"

"A lot."

"What is a lot Ms. Romello?"

"I don't know I haven't counted."

"Count them now," Tony ordered.

"One, two, three –"

"Oh, this is ridiculous!"

The district attorney ran towards the bench. Tony ran after him and their both arguing back in forth in front of Judge Braylin who's looking confused, half on me half on them. They was arguing about how many hands touched those tax returns, nobody saw no smiles or cursive writing before this day, how could it be on official documents, how could it have been gotten by everyone, I was just a child, *blah blah, blah*. Pops did eventually get out that same day cause of Tony and his arguing and me and my high slit dress that Judge liked. For sure there was a few things I didn't like, two things really. One was that Tony made me look like a little kid up there on the stand like a little fool he did. Last thing I didn't like and this was the worst, it was that my own Pops ain't even remember my birthday or that I was eighteen, the big eighteen!

3

Being Mackie's Lackey

Romeo Romello didn't like birthdays, cause he didn't like gettin' old. All my life he never made a fuss over nobody's birthday, except Regina's, but it was my eighteenth so he knew I was gonna want something special or scream! But for all that trantrum I was throwin', first thing pops wanted to do when he got out of jail was get a shit and a shower, he said. Then he was going down to visit his precious bangtail — a race horse, Lovely, he called it. She was a dark-haired Egyptian mare and he loved that damn horse more than any other female. When he went to visit Lovely, he always insisted goin' alone, so the rest of us had to kick rocks!

For as much as Pops didn't like birthdays, he loved homecomings, and we'd had enough of those to go 'round. Enough opportunity for hooch and a big spread, cause of my brothers goin' in and outta the pen. Our dining room was filled with more food than should be allowed for one family. In all the day's commotion, I'd forgotten that August the 8th, 1928, my eighteen birthday and the day Duckie got off on tax evasion charges, was also the day set for my least favorite brother to get out of lock up hisself. I say least favorite brother because nearly a year in the big house and I would have forgotten he was still even breathin' if it weren't for all those letters he wrote me. They was all mushy with his sloppy handwriting and I'd take my matches and light those babies up without a care.

Joey, Joseph Romello, was Romeo and Regina's youngest son so we was the closest in age. I could throw a stone and catch up to him, we was nearly a year apart. Joey was spoiled rotten — just spoiled rotten he was! He was youngest of five sons, with dimples on his cheeks that made him get away with murder. Romeo tried to rough him up, teach him the ropes with me, but he weren't having none of it. He'd been the only one of the Romellos to take full advantage of a life on Park Avenue, real obnoxious type all running round with his friends throwing pops' hard-earned dirty money down the drain. Pops even had enough of it one day, this was after Regina died of course since she was the main reason for his spoils. One day pops told him to shape up or get out, so he got out — got right to con college.

Now by thirteen my oldest brothers, Romeo Jr. and George (my favorite of all) they had already carried guns, went on jobs with pops, but they had also grown up before the good old days we had. They were in them slums, Hell's Kitchen, running around street corners and stealing food to eat. When it came to Joey, his older brothers ain't want much to do with him, so they wouldn't teach him a thing about connin'. He also had no sense enough to come to his younger sister, no sense and too much pride, so he was on his own. He picked up football, and he was actually good at that, but he didn't go no pro or nothing cause that would've taken more work than talent and Joey Romello weren't in the habit of doin' no work.

"Hey Doll."

I got back home and he was already there, a knapsack by the door and the same clothes he went in with that were much smaller on him now. He had that voice I hadn't heard in a year and barely remembered who it were, if not for the nasally, annoying heavy breathing that went with it. Joey never could breathe normal, he always sounded like he needed to blow his dumb damn nose. It hurt his football career he claimed, maybe he was asthmatic or something, but didn't stop Pops from barreling out onto the field while they all did drills, asking why Joey hadn't thrown enough guys down in the mud. 'You get him next time Joey! You get him, you knock him down and ring his neck! You ring his neck or I'll ring yours!' I never seen Pops so damn proud of somebody as I did when Joey was playing football and I guess if I were Joey not playing football no more, I'd be upset too.

"Hey – Doll! You listenin'?"

"Who you callin' doll?"

The sorry sight of Joey Romello in front of me almost made me run for it, but I didn't. Romeo Romello's daughter ain't yellow and she sure ain't afraid of no dumb son of a bitch with all his heavy breathing, who she always thought of as her least favorite brother. He'd looked older than I last saw him, but not like he aged natural, more like forced aging. He didn't have that baby-faced grin no more, that clear skin, or that devil may care attitude. He still had them dimples though.

"You gonna keep treating me bad?" he asked, "I thought all that was behind us? Old days? Kid stuff?"

"That ain't no kid stuff. I don't like ya, never will cause you ain't no good and you're never gonna be, now kick off!"

"You gonna tell Joey Romello to kick off?"

"Yeah and how!"

Joey's arm was in a sling and he was one of those men, those grown men, who anytime they had just a little paper cut or something was ailing them they had to whine about it or sit down over it, you know take a knee, take a rest. Well his whole arm was *'throbbin and hurtin* -- why was I so mean as to not see he was in pain?'. But he still had the other free arm to pick his yellow teeth with a match. He still was coming towards me wanting a hug, but I dove the other way.

"Yeah, so what? So, what ya been injured?" I said.

"So, aren't you gonna ask why?"

"I know why. Probably doin' somethin' you ain't supposed to be doin' to get ya injured. Probably sayin' something you ain't supposed to be saying to somebody who knows better."

"They didn't care durin' my bit, ya know? George and Junior told me once, they said there's respects in there, respects cause we're Romellos. But I ain't get no respect in there. Nobody cared."

My beef with Joey was that he were always comparing hisself to George and Romeo Jr., but he weren't even half — not even a third — the men they was so why would he keep comparing? It's like putting a couple of apples up next to a rotten orange. No, Joey didn't get no respects from me or none of them in the lock up, far from it.

"You ain't get no respects nowhere," I spit.

Joey was just plain stupid and I turned the habit of being real mean to him from a young age, cause he was always just a big lug. Joey was all muscles and over six feet tall, taller than pops and all our brothers, but they was always tearing him down too so his height didn't mean nothin'. It made it worse even, going on jobs with the punk, and everybody would run away when they seen him coming, this big linebacker heading towards the door – if they only knew he was carrying a gun with no bullets and didn't know how to use it neither!

"Remember when I used to put ya high on my shoulders and run ya 'round like a Coney Island ride? Remember? You liked me then, didn't you? You sure liked me then."

"You ain't never put me on your shoulders, quit lyin'. I do remember you locking me in closets and scaring me with rubber spiders."

Joey liked to pick his teeth so hard he made his gums bleed and I couldn't watch it. He also didn't use all those muscles for nothin' good, just defendin' little guys. You gotta be dumb, the way I sees it, to use all them muscles to defend little guys only.

"Just to think — I been missing ya something awful in that joint! And I ain't lyin' bouts that!"

"Yeah, we'll it's only cause you ain't have no moll or old lady to miss, so you started missin' me."

"Whaddya mean?"

"I mean, I don't forget ya watching me in the bath ya damn pa-looka. Why'd you think pops locked me in my room all them years? It was to protect me from those big meaty hands of yours! You ain't never been no good to me! You ain't never earned no respect with me!"

"Joey Romello never watched no sister of his in the bath, especially being young!"

"Yeah, you did and that dumb friend of yours was doin' it too, that no good Mackie Jones!"

"If Mackie Jones was watchin' you in the bath that's his problem, but I swear on my ma's grave I ain't never watched you in no bath and that's the truth!"

"Yeah, well, says you."

"Maybe I'll just go die!"

Joey was all drama, wouldn't hurt a fly unless he was defending little guys doing it. And like I said he didn't scare me any, he was just my least favorite brother and all. No, the only person I think I might have been scared of growing up was that Mackie Jones. Mackie Jones should've never been friends with Joey. The match never quite made sense to me. He was William's age, about two years older than Joey, but mean through and through. He weren't no Romello. Romellos' have class.

Story was Mackie Jones still lived in Hell's Kitchen and he'd heard all the stories, yes, underground chatter floating around of the Romellos' and families like 'em. Romeo Romello might as well have been a superhero to Mackie. Any excuse to get into the family, any excuse at all, as far as I seen it. George never had time for him, he was too grown, doing his own thing. Romeo Jr. was at war 'round the time Mackie came started coming over and when he got back he ain't talk to any of us, much less this new guy in the house. Tony was in school and had no time for people dumber than him. William had no time for people smarter than him. Last choice was Joey.

I blame myself, pops, and the whole family for giving Mackie Jones some type of purpose in our lives. He took Joey under his wing himself, to teach him the ropes and prove something to Romeo. We was all fighting for Romeo's attention, his love and respect, but you get that sometimes right off the bat from your parents, ya know? We was his blood, a reflection of him, so we couldn't be that bad. Mackie on the other hand, he was sleeping on street corners, basically an orphan when he met Joey and our house looked like a palace compared to that. To Mackie, our pops was number one and he was gonna stick around until he was his bonafide son.

"Who'd ya take that rap for anyway?" I asked, "You took it for Mackie didn't you? They was right about that, wasn't they?"

"They wasn't right."

"Don't lie. You're just plain dumb, you are."

"You always callin' me dumb. I got feelins' ya know! It's a sad day when a guy gets all spiffy to come home, but his own sister don't have nothin' good to say to him."

"Yeah well, ya always been dumb! Takin that rap for a little guy, that damn Mackie. That's all your life is — defendin' little guys! You coulda been playin' pro ball down the leagues. But instead, you defend little guys and they get the dough for it!"

"I couldn't play no pro ball," he kicked his feet around, sulking.

"Yes, you could have, I was real proud of ya at one time — real proud and so was pops."

He gets this big shit-eating grin on his face and his toothpick falls to the floor.

"You was proud of me? Honest Cece? Real proud?"

"Don't make a federal case out of it."

He hugged me and it was alright cause he's still family. I didn't say I hated him, just said he was my least favorite.

"Well, since we're all made up now, you'll be happy to know I'll be staying here for a while. Pops said I can get myself sorted out before I find a place of my own."

"Alright."

"And Mackie too."

"Mackie?"

"Yeah, Mackie."

"He ain't allowed in this house!"

"You ain't allowing it, pops is, and he wrote to me 'fore he got locked up, so I got paper evidence this time. Too many people in this family want to start going back on their word. Where's all the furniture? I wanna put my feet up."

"Pops ain't want him here, pops don't even like him. He's just stuck with him like the rest of us, for years, just coming over bothering everybody cause his parents didn't want him. The lucky bastards shoved him off on us."

"Is that my Cecelia?"

Mackie Jones wandered out the kitchen, a chicken leg in one hand and his other, greasy, outstretched trying to grab me. He smiled when I shrieked. He said many times he liked the sound of women screaming. He got some type thrill from it, which was one of the reasons he liked watching me take my baths. I'd scream and hide my face in the bubbles until he was gone.

Mackie thought he was the most handsome guy in town, handsomer than George even, and maybe like he ought to be in pictures. That was a laugh! I couldn't see what other dames did, I just saw a snake hissing with his eyes all black and his face all scrunched up, skin leathery. How he managed to eat chicken and smoke a cigarette at the same time...he was no good. No good Mackie Jones.

"I like the looks of you," he smiled.

He always said that too, followed me around like a puppy, wanting me to sit on his lap and stuff. He'd follow it up with, 'I like the looks of you' and this time was no different. Except this time, his eyes grew, like he remembered my birthday. Out of anybody to remember, it had to be him.

"You're eighteen today, ain't you?"

Now I'd been fine if the torch he carried for me, or that he said he carried, was genuine. But, he had another thought to think if the idea hadn't left his head already – Cece Romello was not making Mackie Jones no son-in-law of Romeo's. From little, he'd kept asking me to marry him, making me promise I'd be his wife. When I was little, I didn't know no different. He was handsome to me, with his big blue eyes and his crooked smile. I used to like to run my fingers through his hair, cause it was floppy kinda and I'd flip it from one side to the next. It waved out at the end and I'd curl my fingers around it. I cringe to think of them days and how naive I was.

"Yeah, you been growing up and all, haven't you?" Mackie said, "how's about me and you go out?"

"Why?"

"Cause I got some sugar now and I wanna spend it on you."

"He's telling truths Cece," Joey started, "guy owed us some spinach 'round the way and we stopped fore we got here to collect. Mackie's got a stack. Let him take you out nice."

Joey always piped in when it had something to do with that fool. It would be his wet dream for us to marry, for Mackie to be his brother-in-law, a true brother who wouldn't fool him around — who might respect him even. I'm not sure who was rooting for us to get hitched more, he or Mackie, but it would be a cold day in hell!

"I ain't goin'."

"Why you always been so mean to me? I always been stuck on you, you know that?"

"You're stuck on any woman that moves."

"That ain't true and that ain't nice," he laughed in my face, "I did ask ya to marry me, didn't I?"

"Yeah, when I was six and I said no."

"And then I asked ya again."

"Yeah, when I was twelve and I said no."

Mackie even wrote me multiple letters, from the big house, all claiming the same. He'd wait for me to be ready, he said. He wanted to make sure I'd wait for him too. The letters were so romantic and sappy. I liked them, but only cause of them being romantic it gave me something to read and focus my attentions on, but not cause of who was sending em.

"You never wrote them letters yourself, did ya?" I asked.

"I did! Every one of them!"

"Nah, your connin'."

"You know how many broads out there trying to see me since I got out? How you gonna turn me down? I want to spend time with you, not them, savvy?"

"Awe, Cece, go out with him," Joey sided.

The whole time we're talking, and we're standing because Pops ain't got the furniture back yet, Mackie's sliding closer to me. He had this way of inching closer and closer until he was standing so close over top of me. And before you ask if I was breaking down, susceptible to his pleading and his promise of a good time, well no it wasn't for that reason. I was breaking down cause of his expression. Prison had made his eyes darker, more intent. I didn't think of playing with his hair or kissing his lips cause, I weren't attracted that way, but it's just one of those things for us females. Sometimes we say yes to stuff, cause it's just easier than if we say no. Don't make it right just easier, easier than fightin' and arguin' with dumb men ain't never gonna see any side 'cept his side no how. Still don't make it right.

"Yeah, fine I'll go out with ya."

"When?"

"I don't know — sometime. I said I would didn't I?"

Mackie cracked a smile,

"Yeah okay, just tell me one thing...after all these years...you still a cherry, ain't you?"

4

Being in the Family Way

I remember my oldest brother's wedding. It was over the top and fancy, planned by Regina Louise herself. The match was pre-destined, years in the making. Romeo Jr., the oldest of the Romello clan, was to be betrothed to the only daughter of Salvatore Santini Jr. The news printed it half mockingly as they always did our family, cause ain't nobody really know how we all got so much money so fast and they was jealous. To hear Romeo tell it, his fortune had come from various businesses. *Just between us* it was; loan sharkin', gamblin', bootleggin', prostitution and a Sicilian pact.

The Santini name meant more in Sicily in the early days than America. They had a what was described to us kids as a castle back in the old country and Big Sal, Sal Sr., ran it all. He'd decided to send his only son over to America at ten or eleven with pockets full of money, an English translation dictionary and a few names to call on. He'd be the golden boy, taken care of by the underground, because it weren't nothin' but a trip over the water and Big Sal wouldn't hear of nobody hurtin' his boy. The plan was to establish some sorta business, some sorta presence in this country and for all the talk

Big Sal did with his guns and his old money, Salvatore Santini Jr. wouldn't have gotten nowhere without my pops protection.

My pops was a few years younger than Santini Jr., but knowin' the streets might as well have made him his older brother. Sal, on the other hand, was a stranger in a strange land. He was scared when he got over here. He'd been spoiled rotten in Sicily, not a tough bone in his body until he was made to get in scrapes and get hisself out. But, regardless of the tough guys out to get him, he still loved America. America and American women. He learned English as fast as he could. He started dressin' what he thought was American instead of them Italian threads. Couldn't be from the old country no more. Had to be and act New York and he loved my pops cause pops was the same. He was just as patriotic as the rest of 'em.

Land of the free, they said, and in America you could do anything, so they was doin' crime and they was doin' it big. Pops needed cabbage to do it and Santini had plenty of it. Together they had security, financially and otherwise. At fifteen, Regina was knocked up and Romeo had to make big moves real fast. The syndicate officially started. He and Sal made the trip back over the water to see Big Sal. Sal Jr. told his pops just how Romeo Romello had saved him time and time again. He told him just how my pops was there for him all those years and how he was gonna start a family with nothin'. The Sicillian pact began.

Big Sal would give my pops money, but only if he promised that our two families would be inseparable. This started with a marriage. If pops had a first born son, he would have to marry any daughter of Sal Santini Jr. This would link the families in blood straight through into the next generations. They'd always be connected — never to fight, rift or break the bond. The two boys were officially made men, ritual completed, and they returned richer than they'd ever even imagined. Every red cent of Big Sal's money was poured into the businesses that would put us all on the map.

For Sal Santini Jr. to burst through my father's front door years later, the front door of his personal home — the home he felt safe in and toiled over and fought blood sweat and tears to get — well that just weren't regular. He knocked our ezeielas over too, the nice ones in pots at the sides of our walkup. His big fat feet knocked into 'em as he flew in, enraged. We ain't seen Sal in months, and maybe it figured quite right he'd come calling now that his alleged best friend had just dodged con college, but he ain't come there for all that. Sal was lookin' for a fight. He was out for blood and it was all over his face, big googley eyes crazed like a mad man.

"Sal!" Pops shouted happily.

"Where is he?" Sal said.

Sal's grabbin' air and swingin' his arms, trying to bulldoze through our party talkin' in a heavy Italian accent. My pops is drunk and pouring more drinks, excited to see his old friend. Sal's seethin', angrier than I'd ever seen any human, yet Pops is oblivious, just ramblin' on...

"—How's the wife? How's May? How's business treating ya? That weather this summer — hot ain't it? Evaporates the hooch it does, yes it does. See that bad rap they give me, they tried to get me, but my son, my good Tony, Tony got me out of it he did. That's that schoolin'. That good schoolin' I tell ya. How's Santini's boy? Saw 24 and 1 on the books. He's got another good year in him I'd say. I keep tellin' ya I'll go down the stables with ya and check him out. You gotta look out for the whites of his eyes, I say. How's about a drink? You want a drink? How's about some food? Yeah, you'd like some food wouldn't ya, ya big fat lug!"

Pops is pouring more liquor into two tall glasses and handing one over to Sal. He's still ramblin', but Sal ain't smiling and let me tell you why. When Pops gets drunk, he gets blind drunk and he focuses in on one or two things. That's all his brain can handle real drunk like that. I think it was a way to forget, a way to unwind. He weren't no angry drunk. He weren't no sad drunk — just emotional.

"This ain't no pleasure trip Romeo," Sal said, taking the drink, "where's that son of yours?"

"Which one?" Pops asked.

By now, everybody gathered; pops, me, Mackie, and Joey. Jewels was by the kitchen, the smell of tortellini pasta and gravy wafting from the stove. He'd leaned in the doorway, and even with a pink apron on what used to be Regina's when she wanted to fake domestication, he still looked intimidatin'. Tony's face peeked 'round the corner at the sound of Sal. His eyebrows perked up, but he had three cases he was working on, so he found a spot at the kitchen table and placed all his piles of paper on it, daring somebody to disturb him. Tony weren't one for confrontation. William was busy in the corner makin' a fire, the same fire he'd been makin' for the past hour. Sal looked around like he still hadn't found his target.

"I want that no good bastard that married my daughter," Sal growled.

Pops is absentmindedly making his way to our buffet table filling a plate, handing it to Sal.

"My son ain't no bastard, he's a war hero," pops said, "here."

Now Sal's holding a drink and a big plate of potato salad. He spit at pop's feet.

"Ain't no war hero, ain't been to no war in ten years!"

I was seven when Romeo Jr. was drafted. There was a big homecoming for my brother when the war ended, but he ain't never showed up. He was runnin', wanderin' the country for years. He came back at twenty, never openin' his mouth to speak. He married May like it was his duty. They got a house in a small, quiet neighborhood. He was pops muscle on jobs when he needed him, but other than that he kept his distance. Rumor has it they was tryin' to have kids, but May couldn't never get pregnant. I forgot even what my brother's voice sounded like and I think he did too. Just had this far away look in his eyes, he did, a far—far away look.

"He ain't here," I said.

"You speak when you're spoken to," Sal warned.

Sal Santini Jr. never liked me. I never met Sr., but Romeo says he would have liked me and all. Sal Jr. put up with me that's all, but he put up with most women 'cept his own daughter, his darling May.

"I ain't raised Cece to wait until she's spoken to," pops said.

"Yeah, well maybe you should have."

"That's how you raised May, but that ain't how I raised Cece."

"We ain't talkin' daughters, we're talkin' sons," Sal said, "I come here for Jr. and I come here for answers. May's three months pregnant and he ain't been home in a fortnight. Where the hell is he if he ain't here?"

"Maybe he's somewhere havin' thoughts," Jewels interrupted.

Jewels come out the kitchen in full view, wooden spoon in hand like he was gonna beat Sal. William reached up and took it from him, finished with failing at the fire and wantin' some tomato sauce -- the greedy bastard.

"Thoughts about what?" Sal asked.

Jewels shrugged.

"Maybe he's wonderin' whose baby she's havin'."

"Then he better have some nerve, come and ask me!"

Sal threw down the plate and drink. They crashed onto our tile floor, breakin' into pieces. Ain't nobody flinched. Pops looked down at the broken glass and laughed that maniacal laugh of his.

"If it weren't for your old man...may he rest in peace," pops said, "I would take this glass and break it over your fuckin' head."

Sal takes the gun he'd been hidin' out his waistband.

"Now boys," this was Jewels talking, "we gonna settle this nice now -- we gonna settle it like Kings, okay? Big Sal wouldn't like this, no fightin' amongst family."

"Settle it?" Sal groaned, "yeah I'll settle it with my .45 puttin' a bullet in that war hero's head, and I ain't leavin' until I do!"

"You wanna settle this proper?" Pops swayed, still feelin' the liquor.

He did as promised -- took his glass and broke it over Sal's head. Blood started coming out of the bald spot on the top. Jewels is signaling to Joey with his finger to his nose. Joey's reaching for the gat in the flowerpot near the door and puttin' it in his jacket pocket quick and slick. I backed away from the scene into the kitchen as I was always ordered, and Tony stayed sittin' at the kitchen table, still unimpressed, whisperin' some 'tell me when its' over'.

I swung my head around the doorway to look. Sal didn't yell and he didn't back down. He was shakin', tremblin' with anger. His pale face was stained that crimson red from his own bleedin'. The room got real still and Sal's voice got real low, but we could hear the stutterin' and stammerin' comin' out. That thick accent he'd tried to hide all his life was comin' back.

"I ain't leavin' til I put this gun gainst' your no good son's head and pull the trigger. That's a promise!"

Sal's Daughter, May Santini, well -- we didn't grow up with her, and rightly so. Sal did keepin' her away from the life. She wasn't like me who got stuck growing up in it. She had a chance for a different life when they sent her away to a nice boarding school up state. May were educated, refined, taught by the best to be the best. Sal always said, *she's gonna grow up and make something of herself -- marry a congressman, president, doctor, anybody but a goon!*

That Sicilian Pact made it so she had to marry my brother, but didn't mean Sal Santini Jr. had to be happy about it. The wedding had so much glamour that we almost forgot 'bout the angry Sal Jr. walkin' her down the aisle. I remember she's tryin' to pull away from her father's vice grip on her arm to stand beside my brother and say them vows what would bond them in holy matrimony forever. We ain't believe in no divorce. We ain't believe in nothin' but *death do us part.* The only way Sal saw he was gonna break the rift meant just that -- death. It would also mean the abrupt end of the pact and then maybe he could put a bullet through my pops head too.

"Don't ya think it's right," Pops said, calmly, "don't ya think it's better let em' work it out like married couples work out their fights? We ain't gotta fight our kids battles for em', Sal. Just let em' work it out—"

"—May!" Sal yelled, not listen', "May get in here!"

When she walked in we all froze, but only cause we was all lookin for that bump. She had that stomach stickin' out in a way you couldn't really tell, but they all warned me against happenin'. Her eyes was all red and puffy. Her hair was a mess. She had rings 'round her arm like somebody had ripped her from her bed and made her show up to our house. Sal loved his daughter. He'd kill for her, give her all the money she needed and all the schoolin' in the world, but he weren't much nice to her. It looked like it hadn't been the first time since he roughed her up, and it wouldn't be the last. My pops never laid a hand on me, Lord is my witness. Not one hand my whole life.

"She been cryin'!" Sal continued, "she been cryin' and cryin'. She's all upset over that bastard and it ain't doin' nothin' for the baby!"

He grabbed her wrist and drug her towards us. Jewels reached for his gun again when he saw how Sal was treating May, then eased up when pop's signaled.

"I'll make sure your husband comes home to ya May," pops promised, "he ain't like that, he's a man of honor."

Sal spit again.

"Ain't no man of honor!"

Pops glared.

"He got you out of enough scrapes to be one, didn't he?"

"Past is past."

"Maybe all past is past."

"Fight like kings," Jewels warned again.

"That pact shoulda ended with my pops dyin'," Sal said, "ya know it really shoulda. And you got this big fuckin' house cause of my pops and all. So, this house is mine too!"

Sal started towards the stairs. Mackie backed up but Joey stood in front.

"You ain't goin' nowhere in my pops house."

"Oh, so another son of yours tryna get fresh?"

Sal's wavin' his gun around, but Joey's a statue. He stood up to him and made us all real proud that day, yes he did.

"That's it,"

Pops had enough and he's reachin' under the table.

"all you little boys runnin' round with pistols. Ain't no pistol never settled no fights or ended no pacts."

That's when he lifted up his automatic -- that machine gun he saved for special occasions. He pointed it towards Sal, truly meaning every bit of the focused expression on his face. Let me tell ya about made men...ain't none of em' scared to die. Sal was wearin' a grin on his face wider than I'd ever seen on anything human.

"Been waitin' decades years for this," he said.

Sal's gun looked real small in comparison, but now they was gonna duke it out and let everybody see. May's cryin' harder, nearly hyperventilating. I'm just shakin' my head cause pop was gonna ruin the walls with his bullets and Sal with his flesh and blood. We all ducked when Sal and pops turned to focus on the top of the staircase. Romeo Jr appeared on the landing, looking down at everybody with a hardened expression. His two guns were strapped in shoulder holsters on his sides like the damn Wild West and a rifle across his chest. He's smokin' his cigarette real slow and makin' a way down, his old dusty cowboy boots scuffin' the floors. May runs towards him and hugs her husband. My brother embraces her with one arm and leads her down the stairs to Sal. Pops lowered his gun, but Sal didn't.

"Listen Sal, I told ya let the kids work it out themselves that's all. I mean, look at em'," pops started, "look at em' bein' in love."

May looked at my brother like he was the love of her life, like there weren't no other. But when Sal saw that, it angered him even more. He tried to grab her arm again, tugging her towards him, but my brother weren't havin' none of it. Romeo Jr. took one of his guns out hisself.

"You tell him to put that gun down or I'm finished with the Romellos, pact or no pact, baby or no baby," Sal said, "I'll tear that beast right out of her myself!"

This only made my brother madder and now he's walkin' and pushin' Sal's big fat stomach with the end of his gun.

"Honey stop," May said to her husband, "I'll go with my father. Daddy, please don't hurt him -- I love him. He'll come home. I promise he'll come back home."

She put her hand on her own stomach and with pleading eyes started towards the door. Romeo Jr. let go of her hand, however unwillingly, then turned and walked back up the stairs. We all saw him drop his gun, as if it weren't worth it. When my brother knew it was over, he knew there was no fight and didn't want none. But then there was that big mouth Sal Santini, that no good Sal Santini, who couldn't leave well enough alone.

"Yeah that's right you run away you coward. A real man fights for my daughter!"

We heard Sal's gun cock once more and he's pointing it at the back of my brother's head. Ain't no Romello never pointed no gun at a man's back. He was the coward.

"Baby or no baby – pact or no pact!" Sal yelled.

A ringin' shook the room. Everything moved in slow motion for me, 'cept the bullet making a beeline for Romeo Jr.'s skull. My brother ain't never even seen it coming.

5

Being a Caville

Bein' born a Romello ain't mean we had an automatic spot in the family business. We had to carry out what pops called our *'special mission'*. It was somethin' that proved loyalty to him and the rest of the family. If we completed that successfully, we'd be rewarded with respect and plenty of coin. If we failed — well, that meant we couldn't never be trusted, see? That meant we wouldn't never be no real Romello, even though we was blood. Pops would tolerate us, sure, but never respect us.

My brothers completed their call to action and got to made men status, but everybody was different. Tony had his law degree, even though he went through school kickin' and screamin'. George had his prizefightin', so pops made money off that from years of bettin' on him. Romeo Jr. was fifteen takin' pops' own draft notice and goin' to war in his place. All my life I'd been waiting for my mission, even if it had to come on the boot heels of William failin' his, that was fine to me. It all started for me with a hit out on this guy named Caville.

Harry Caville weren't no good guy. He was a well-known sharper — some real boozehound that owed spinach to every boss in the city, including my pops. William was called for duty, just supposed to go and shake guy up, to finally earn that respect after years of tryin'. When he gets to the apartment, William sees Harry's crying poor with his son watchin'. William always got real emotional 'round men and their sons. *'No rough stuff in front of the boy'*, was William's motto, so he walks Harry out onto the ledge. Now that drunk was swayin' somethin' awful and tipped hisself over about ten flights of stairs. William swore they was talkin' only, and that he didn't push him. And truth be told, the Romello clan had no gain from killin' him cause we weren't gonna get our cabbage from a dead man! It was Harry's son, Henry Caville, that spilled the beans to the judge. He told the truth, from what he seen, that Harry's death weren't no bump off. *'Just an accident'*, he said, and good thing too cause William woulda probably hanged for it. Even all Tony's fancy double talk and dancin' around that Judge couldn't help my dumb cluck brother, since the prosecutor had William damn near false confessin'.

Though young Henry Caville had done our family a favor by takin' the stand and savin' William's skin, he'd still hate the Romellos. That weighed on pops, it really did, and he even took the boy over some money personally, but Henry refused —threw it back in his face. Pops said this Henry guy was real particular, didn't want no parts of us, but he obsessed and stewed over the reasons why. Now don't get yourself confused, my pops were one of the toughest guys you'd ever meet, but this hit him different. I think cause Pops grew up poorer than poor with no parents and now so was Henry. To him, this Caville kid was his kryptonite.

That's when pops asked me to see Henry that evening. He wanted me to talk to him in a way only a pretty woman could really get the point across. And in no way was he selling me out like some pro skirt! He just knew if anybody were able to get through that thick skull of Henry's it was me and I'd been happy to do it. My eighteenth birthday present was completing my special mission for pops. It was a big step and I'd have to do a good job completin' it and not mess up like William.

I showed up to Henry's house, *not knowin' what to expect to be honest.* I were wearing my nice dress, heels and Regina's ice while standing in the hallway of his apartment building. It was all dirty and dingy, with paint chipping off the walls. There was people walkin' by eyein' my jewelry, but I'd give em one look and it was over. I'd be clutchin' my pen knife in one hand and my handkerchief with the Romello emblem in the other. They'd be scurryin' off without any more bother.

"To what do I owe the pleasure?"

I turned, surprised at the voice that was callin' at me. A door creaked open.

"What?" I asked.

"*Who are you* and why are you here?"

Henry Caville was only nineteen, but even then he looked like an old man. He wore old-fashioned britches with suspenders hanging 'round his waist and his white silk undershirt was all wrinkled up. He had some thick round cheaters on that made him look fifty. I could tell he was very different from those other mugs. He didn't have that look about him like he was out to get somethin', steal somethin', or lie about somethin'. Even with a scowl, Henry had innocence drippin' all over his face and to a Romello...that was shark bait.

"Well?" he asked again.

I was lookin' real spiffy, I must say so myself, but he didn't even look me up and down like most guys. He just looked passed me, kinda. He looked like I weren't nobody special, or maybe like I were just plain botherin' him. I was used to being looked at like a Romello, so they always had to have some sort of gleam in the eye or die. This threw me. I was all kinds of confused and found myself just starin' at him. Maybe I had some kind of googley-eyed stare like those men in the speaks when they seen a lady hoofin'.

"Well I –" I'm stammerin'.

I was seein' his jet black hair was all mussed with little ringlets coverin' his eyes and when I looked passed him into the apartment, it was some sorta wreck. I felt bad cause he looked like he didn't have no woman there carin' for him or his place. Maybe even then I wanted to care for him as soon as I saw those dimples on his cheeks and those dishes in the sink. I knew I were keen on him for sure, since he had me thinkin' of doin' dishes and I ain't never touched a dish in my life cept' to eat.

"Come on, hurry up, I'm busy." He snapped.

"Um...I'm here to see...Henry Caville. Is that you?"

He was holding a big book in his hand and he waved it in the air as he looked 'round.

"I'm the only one standing here, aren't I?"

My eyes darted around like that was gonna help me get my thoughts together or somethin'.

"Yes — oh yes — well I just wanted to be sure, cause I was supposed to come call on a Henry Caville and I wanted to make sure you were him. I wanted to be real sure, that's all."

"Why?"

"Why what?"

"Why'd you come calling on me? Who put you up to it?"

I was trying my best, but he was trying my patience. I had gone to the finishing school of hard knocks and everything I knew about being a lady I was using up in this very moment. Henry knew no better, but I was about to say the hell with it and rush him. The only thing stopping me were my new high heels and pantyhose, cause I didn't want to trip and tear em'. Henry took a good look at me in my sparkly short dress with Regina's jewelry danglin' from my wrist. His eyes grew wide.

"Hey, you can't stand out there with those on," he warned, "you'll get roughed up!"

He yanked my arm quick, pulled me towards his chest, into the apartment and slammed the door. Now I was standing real close to him, smellin' his cologne while he was holding onto me still. He was looking down at me so I was makin' big doe eyes and his expression softened.

"Where'd you get those?"

"Get what?"

"The jewels?"

"They're mine."

He was lightly touchin' the silver dangling 'round my neck and his fingers brushed against my skin makin' me shiver. I was hooked.

"You steal em?" he asked, "Come on — I won't tell."

"Of course I didn't steal em'!"

"Yeah, alright."

"Don't *'yeah, alright'* like you don't believe me. I don't care if you do believe me, cause I don't need to steal!"

"Yeah, alright."

My high society act was slippin' and that's when I had no choice but to start showing the real side of myself. I pushed away from him, lookin' around the apartment makin' sour faces at the laundry on the floor and the dishes on the table.

"This house is a holy mess, ya know that?"

"Well, what're you doing here then?"

"I'm just visitin' ya and I'd think you'd straighten up for female company."

"I don't even know what female you are, so excuse me if I ask you to leave so I can finish my studies."

"Studies?"

"Yes," he pointed to that same book in his hand.

"Whatcha studying?"

"Don't worry about it! Who sent you?"

"What?"

He rolled his eyes, wise to my con.

"That goon that did my father in...did he send you?"

"Who?"

"I really didn't think he'd be that desperate, but if he already paid —well anyway...did he?"

"Did he what?"

"How much did he pay you to come over here?"

In the cab ride earlier, I had some sorta speech written that I thought I memorized, but now I couldn't remember. Something in Henry's eyes made my mind go blank. It was the soft features of his face and those goofy glasses. I could just imagine being his little chippy and that was sayin' somethin', cause Romeo Romello's daughter weren't no little chippy! In a minute I was carryin' a torch for him, I swear.

"Did who send me?" I blinked.

"Romello."

"Who's that?"

"Romeo Romello."

"Never heard of him."

"Oh. Sorry, I just thought—well there's been some people coming to my place recently and I'm not havin' any of it. I'm just trying to finish my studies."

"Oh, what do ya study?"

"Acting. You never told me who you are or why you're here..."

"Can I sit down?"

"No, not at all. Not until I find out who you are! I don't just let strangers sit down in my house."

"Maybe just for a little?"

I'm twirlin' my hair and pouting my lip, just so's he couldn't resist.

"Yeah, well that's alright I guess. But I don't really have a place for you to sit and it's been kind of rough around here lately, so I'm sorry if I don't have coffee or anything for you either and...what am I saying? I don't even know who you are!"

"That's okay, I'll just sit right here," I smiled.

I went over to the chair and dare I say it, I folded some clothes and made a space for myself. I didn't tell nobody that he had Romeo Romello's daughter foldin' clothes, but I tell ya' I was mighty keen on him.

"So...who are you?" He asked again.

I patted the seat next to me so he could come near.

"Listen, I don't have no money if you cost," he started.

"Cost what? I ain't no prostitute!" I snapped, standing up again, "I was trying to have you come over here so we could have a nice sit and maybe talk a little, that's all!"

"Okay, okay!"

"I ain't opening my legs for nobody!"

"Okay! I'm sorry," he put his hands up to the sky, "I'll sit with you, don't get sore."

"Thanks very much, that's much better."

We sat down next to each other with this big book between us, this 'Learning the Art of Method Acting'. I imagined his handsome face and smooth voice in the talkies.

"So, what about this acting stuff?" I asked.

"What about it?"

I'm lookin' at him wild like he's already famous or somethin'. He kinda laughed all nervous like no woman had looked at him the way I was lookin' and he didn't think he deserved it.

"Well, what are you gonna be in pictures or somethin'?"

"Only studying," his voice cracked.

"That's a big book."

"Um..."

"You learn a lot from that?"

"Yes, I suppose I have."

"You like to read?"

"I suppose I do."

He's checking the clock. I kept gettin' closer and he kept inchin' further away. He's tightening his grip on that book like it's a safety net.

"I suppose it's late," he said.

I swear I couldn't stand him supposin' and playin' me for some fool, cause I was gonna get him in the end. In my mind, I wanted him and it was good as done.

"Oh yeah? What else do you suppose?"

I fluttered my eyelashes, fingernails tracin' his collar bone, makin' him even more nervous.

"I suppose you don't know a thing about me and you're sittin' too close."

He's backin' up a bit, but I keep getting closer.

"I suppose I know plenty, like how your old man was a booze-hound. I mean, your pops was stuck on the sauce."

Now he's mad and leaps to the other side of the couch, far away from my clutches.

"So what? A guy whose father was a boozehound can't like to read? He can't be trying to better himself or become something of himself? A guy whose old man was stuck on the sauce is destined to be stuck on the sauce too?"

He's got his shoulders all puffed up like he's some big bird ready to fly away.

"No, I ain't saying that," I lied.

"Then what exactly are you saying, Miss...Miss..."

"...Cece."

"Cece?"

"Yes."

"Miss Cece. What's your surname?"

"Don't have one."

"Who doesn't have a last name?"

"Fine...it's Caville."

"No, no, no! Don't tell me you're some half-sister or something coming to collect the inheritance, cause there weren't nothing! I scrape by with my dancing which is just enough to keep this place. My old man didn't have a dime."

"No, no — I was foolin', ya know? It was a little joke."

"Well, I didn't think it was very funny. Besides, what are you here for then?"

I'm stalling, just trying to think.

"Well...I've seen you dance," I lied.

"You've seen me dance?"

"Yeah, what of it?"

"Where?"

"What?"

"Where have you seen me dance?"

"Where?"

There was a wrinkled pamphlet on the coffee table with *Moxie's Tea Room* written on it. I was surprised really. Didn't figure him for one of them places, with all those rich, old women payin' young men to dance with em'.

"Moxie's," I said.

"Lucky guess," he grabbed the paper and shoved it in his pocket, "that's not somethin' I'm proud of, but it's money ain't it?"

"I'm no judge."

"Your type shouldn't be."

"My type?"

"Yeah, the type of girl who comes over eight o'clock at night to a man's apartment, just cause you've seen him dance at Moxie's. And don't think I don't keep my dancin' to Moxie's either."

"No, you've got the wrong idea about me. I dance too, see? And I was thinking we could go out, ya know? Like, as a couple? I'd dance with you and you'd dance with me...and then you'd take me to dinner. Simple as that."

"So...you came over because you saw me dance and you wanted to ask me to dinner? Dinner that you wanted me to pay for? On this particular Tuesday night at eight o'clock—"

"—you're makin' too much of this."

"I'm tryin' to make sense of it!"

"Well, it's easy. I think you're the most handsome and interestin' man I've ever met, and I've just met you, so that's that."

"And how many guys you find handsome and interestin' this week?"

"Just one."

I moved so close that I knocked the glasses off his head.

"You ain't gonna kiss me," he ordered.

"I am."

"But —I don't even know your last name!"

"Yep."

"And you won't tell me?"

"Nope."

I must say I was closer to him in that moment than I had ever gotten to a man, cause Romeo Romello's daughter don't get so close. The fact that he was pulling further away was kind of like a challenge and that was making me ever keener on him, I swear.

"I'm not in the habit of kissing women when I don't know their last name," he said.

"Why's that?"

"Cause they might be married."

"Might not. I'm only eighteen."

"You can be married at eighteen."

"Not me."

"Why?"

"Not allowed."

"Not allowed to be married?"

"Wouldn't dare."

He paused and his eyes were fixed into a determined gaze.

"Are you Romeo Romello's daughter?"

I stopped dead in my tracks.

"Why'd you think that?"

"Well...I know he's got a daughter and I know he'd probably send her up here to talk to me and get me to forgive him. But I don't forgive him, so his daughter wouldn't be welcome in my house, much less if she were trying to kiss me."

"Oh yeah?"

"Yeah. But I ain't no sissy. I'd let her kiss me, but I'd never take her out to no dinner."

I let him sit for a second, trying to figure me out while I stalled to think.

"Well, that's somethin'," I said finally.

"What?"

"If I were Romeo Romello's daughter, you know how much trouble you'd get into for sitting so closely on this couch with me? For even accepting the promise of a kiss on the lips from me, whether I wanted you to or not?"

Henry gulped.

"Men have gotten killed over less," I smiled, "and if I were really Romeo Romello's daughter, why in the world would he send me over here alone? Huh? Don't ya think he'd at least send over some goons to stand guard outside? Don't ya think they'd be watchin' just to make sure his pride and joy is alright bein' alone with ya? Or do ya think he's just plain dumb?"

Henry's runnin' to the door and openin' it, looking this way and that. When he saw the coast was clear, he shut it back real quick. My smile's gettin' wider and wider.

"Or maybe not standing outside...maybe parked out front in a couple of bulletproof cars. Maybe their hangin' out the windows with their gats, just waiting for you to make the wrong move."

He's really sweatin', runnin' towards the window. He's peekin' through the smoke stained curtains tryin' to check. I saw the biggest look of relief on his face when there weren't no men, no cars, and no guns. I start laughing something fierce right from my belly.

"Well, are you or aren't you?" He asked, still nervous.

"Nah, I'm just foolin' with you. I ain't his daughter. Don't even know the guy just heard stories, but he sounds like a chump. You can give me the bums rush if ya want, but I ain't gonna leave till I kiss ya at least once."

"Oh yeah?"

"Yeah."

I had never kissed a man before in my life. The only time I'd kissed somebody back then was when I was a kid, just cause that sneaky slimeball Mackie Jones talked me into lockin' lips with him in the coat closet. Even then it was nothing more than a peck, cause my brother Georgie found us and beat the tar outta Mackie right then and there.

"Well..if that's so then let's just get it over with. Ya gonna kiss me or what?"

Henry was a little impatient, although he was lookin' like he ain't really kissed nobody neither.

"Well, actually," I started, *imagining what Regina would think*, "I don't kiss no man before he takes me to dinner."

"Oh," Henry looked more than a little relieved, "dinner where?"

"That depends...what can you afford?"

"I gotta fin."

"Eh—that ain't much, but I know a joint."

Johnny's Place weren't no place for a woman, which is why it were named after a man, see? They had paint chippin' off the walls, liquor bottles half-filled with water and dancers with see-through dresses and runs in their stockings. It weren't on the best side of town, but it weren't one of our family's speaks. It was the only place I could get away with not seein' one of my own, so it would do for now. I was about fifteen when I learned how to sneak out of my bedroom window at night and go explorin' the parts of the city my pops hid me away from. That's how I found Johnny's and I'd get all dolled up so no one were the wiser. Sure I'd dance a little, but all them men was so sauced by the time I'd get on stage that nobody recognized I was some sorta Romello. By the end of the night I'd be outta there, back up the fire escape, safe in my own bed by morning.

Taking Henry Caville to Johnny's Place felt good cause it were my little secret, ya know? I felt like I was showin' him this whole world I'd found that nobody else knew about. When we walked in, there was barely anybody sittin' and nobody dancin'. They was all gathered in the corner with drinks and the radio soundin' off reports of my brother's big fight. They was hollerin' and carryin' on, takin' their bets and smoking cheap cigars. They was yellin' that George Romello was gonna knock that other guys lights out for sure.

"Table for two, garson," I called out, real ritzy like. Didn't matter though—weren't nobody listenin'.

I walked up to the unattended bar and leaned on the edge, grabbin' a bottle and two glasses without nobody noticin'. Henry followed me skeptically through the emptiness of their back room.

"You must come here often," he said.

I ignored him and found us one lone table with a candle in the middle. Henry raised his eyebrows as I took the matchbook from my suspender belt, coolly strikin' it on my heel. I poured us two shots of the gasoline they called whiskey and we drank to our health.

"What's to eat around here?" He asked.

"Cold roast beef."

"I'll pass."

Henry held his stomach after the first shot and he were feelin' bad. I was pressurin' him, so I poured another.

"I don't drink too much," he said.

"You gotta have a drink, it's my birthday."

My eyelids fluttered again. I think he maybe mighta blushed.

"Yeah, okay."

Two-thirds of the way through the bottle and four cold roast beef sandwiches later...Henry's slurrin' his words and I'm sittin' on his lap like we're instant lovers.

"You know what happened to my pa?"

"What happened?"

"He died. The old drunk tipped over the railing outside our apartment window."

"Sorry to hear that."

"That's why ya shouldn't drink. Pour me another, would ya?"

"I think you've had enough."

He's all sloshing around hisself and I realized I had somethin' like a super power. I couldn't get drunk. Maybe it was all them years 'round the speaks. Maybe it was all them times helpin' make shine and bein' around those fumes. I guess I had more liquor in my pours than anybody could stand.

"Where are we?" he was fadin' fast.

"Johnny's Place."

"Oh. I know this joint. I gotta friend who works here."

"A lady friend?"

"Shhh," he's puttin' his finger to his lips, "she's a little blondie."

Now I'm mad.

"What about her?"

"No, no, no," he's shakin' his head like he ain't gonna spill.

"Henry, ya gotta tell me!"

I poured him another drink.

"I don't drink. How'd ya get me to drink?"

"I told you to try it. I told ya it was my birthday and I wanted you to try the whiskey here."

"It tastes like horse piss."

"Yeah I know – but you was tellin' me about the blonde."

He took his shot and nearly spit it back into his glass.

"I ain't never drank before cause my old man was always so soused. I couldn't stand the thought of it. The smell on his breath made me sick!"

"Yea? That's a shame. Who's the blonde?"

"He was on the booze somethin' serious but, at least he wasn't one of them big goons that offed him."

"I thought it was an accident?"

"Awe hell! Accident or not, they was there and they was re-sponsible."

"Well...if he hadn't owed all that money to those big goons than maybe...nevermind."

Henry weren't listening anyway, he was already over a barrel. He got up, leaning on the table real hard to steady hisself till it rocked this way and that. Pretty soon he was tipping over the glasses and knocking the plates around.

"Where you goin?"

"I'm askin' the lady for a dance," he said.

"What lady?"

"You lady."

"Oh I—"

"Didn't you tell me you like to dance?"

"Um, yea I do, I guess..."

"Well okay then, come on birthday girl. Dance with me."

He had his hands out waiting for me to stand up and come closer.

"But, there ain't no music?"

"So what? You stallin' cause you're scared?" he smiled, "Cece is scared."

"I ain't scared!"

I stood up and fell into his arms. He was drunk, but still twirled me around the little backroom cause he was so professional at it.

"How'd you do that?" I asked, pretty impressed.

"Years of practice."

"You're real good."

"When I was little, my mom used to have me stand on her feet. She'd twirl me around the kitchen to her organ music."

"Where's she now?"

"Nevermind all that."

The whole room seemed to float around us while we was dancin'. I laid my head on his chest and let him keep guiding me across the floor. For the first time since being with my pops and my brothers, I felt safe and secure in another man's arms. I felt almost like I belonged in em'.

"You been here long?" he asked.

"Where?"

"In New York?"

"Oh. Yeah, all my life."

"Me too. It's a dirty city."

"Dirty?"

"Yeah. Dirty and broken."

"Why'd you say that?"

"If you lived where I live and seen what I seen, you'd say the same."

"Oh."

I thought of our big house and felt mighty spoiled.

He's gripping me tighter, "ain't you ever wanted to get out of here?"

"Never thought of it. Where would I go?"

"Anywhere else..."

"You ain't thinkin' of leavin' New York are you?"

"Why, you wouldn't like that much?"

"No, I wouldn't."

He smiled.

"Yeah well...my old man is dead and my ma ran off a long time ago. What's left for me here?"

"Well...me for a start..."

"Yeah, that's okay for a start, but what else?"

"If you want to dance, there's always Vaudeville...Broadway. New York's the place for dancin'."

"I can't get on Broadway. Gotta know people."

"Well, I know people."

"Oh yeah?"

"Of course and they've got plenty of...connections. I can get us both a job—"

"—No, no. Don't ya hear me? I want out of this city! I want far away. I got big plans."

"What kind of big plans?"

He's lookin' around like he doesn't want to be overheard.

"What if I told you I was goin' to be in pictures?"

"I'd say you're drunk."

He shook his head.

"Drunk like a fox. The plan's already set. I'm going to California to be an actor. I'm goin' as soon as we get up enough dough."

"We? Whose we?"

"Me and the blonde."

I was gettin' real sick and tired of that mysterious blonde business, so I reached into my tights and dropped a wad of bills on the table. Henry's eyes got real wide and he's drunk, but he's still tryin' to focus.

"Kick the blonde and count me in," I said.

"You?"

"That's right me. That's enough there for your California. That's a couple of train tickets. That's room and board for a month somewhere."

"You want to come with me...just like that?"

"Just like that."

He's still eyein' the money, so I grabbed ahold of Henry and give him a kiss that changed his life. I just know it changed his life cause his glasses were fogged up and they weren't even on his face no more, ya follow?

I didn't have no problem gettin' Henry Caville, that was never a worry for me. I also didn't even care about that little blonde, cause with my dough she were out and I were in. But as I was busy feelin' the warmth of Henry's lips against mine, I thought about my only real problem which was my pops. It was tellin' him that all I was goin' to the other side of the country with this guy whose father was a boozehound, who was tryna get into the pictures on a pipe dream. My other problem, which was bigger still, was gettin' home at six in the morning. See, Romeo Romello's daughter weren't allowed to get home no six in the morning, eighteen or otherwise.

6

Being No Little Girl No More

I'm sure it weren't easy for George Romello, bein' everybody's favorite. Out of all my brothers and all of Pop's men in our organization, it was George Romello on top. He was the second born and beautiful. He was the gleam in his mother's eye and his father's chip off the old block. George came out the womb with a pair of boxing gloves on. All his life he'd been fightin'. He carried our family, our problems, and all our worries on his back, but he did it in stride. George was the one we came to when we was havin' issues, needed money, needed advice, or needed somethin' taken care of. Yes, I'm sure it weren't easy for George Romello, bein' everyone's keeper.

I could always tell George's penthouse cause of the broads comin' and goin' at all hours of the night. He didn't like sunlight and rarely came out in it. *It hurts my eyes*, he'd say, and he had these curtains that blocked out any ounce of day. William became his personal assistant and believe it or not, he weren't as stupid when he was working for George. We was all dedicated to our brother George, out of respect, see? Pops had to be respected cause he was our father and it was automatic. But George's respect was different cause he had earned it, even with our old man.

His building let me in as always when I'd show up too late to face my pops. The staff all absolutely loved George, the whole ground he walked on, so of course I got whatever I wanted bein' his little sister. *Go on in*, said the front desk. *Oh, let good ol' Georgie know he did great in the fight last night*, said security. *Isn't he the bees knees*, said the laundress. There was always some type of flowers, food or champagne *(yes they was sneaking it in all through prohibition, don't let em' fool ya)* bein' delivered up the elevator to his place. That's where I was going, while them broads was coming down. I wandered up 'round six am that morning, bumpin' into one of those ditzy skirts on the way.

This one was a brand new girl. I'd never seen her before in my life, although they all looked the same, with her drawn on eyebrows and a chiffon negligee. Most times they wanted to play gatekeeper, standing outside his place smoking their cigarette watchin' for others like 'em. It was my experience that bims like those worked in packs and stayed with their own herd, ya know? Much like the animal kingdom, they'd work on him together. They'd try to take good ol' Georgie for all he was worth. But this one was different, like she'd rather work alone.

"He's busy."

The words slithered outta her mouth as she was looking down at me tryna scare me off, blowin' her smoke in my face. Regina called all the women George went out with low class. She swore they'd be hoppin' from one goon to the next, not for marriage or nothin'…just for the take. *The older they get the more desperate they look*, she'd sneer. George didn't keep girlfriends long when Regina was living, cause if she'd have something to say about em', she'd just give him a quick bat on the side of his head and straighten him out so they'd be outta there. But this one were different, like I said, and I couldn't put my finger on why. She had somewhat of a look of refinement the others didn't, and maybe Regina would approve.

"You hear me? I said George is busy," she continued.

"Yeah, well, not too busy for me."

"Yes, you. Besides, he doesn't like bleach jobs."

Drawn on eyebrows weren't no threat to me. I'd seen em' all come and go, the pro skirts, and the hangers on. They followed George and my pops longer than I could even care to remember and I'd be dealing with them for years to come. I'd heard it all from em' and then I'd say to em',

"ain't too busy for his favorite little sister I said, so get a wiggle on!"

Now this chiffon negligee was shakin'. Her cigarette fell, stem and all. She trembled, openin' her pocketbook to take out some cheaters. She put em' on her big dumb face, lookin' at me all inspectin' like. If she thought them glasses was gonna stop me from swinging on her, she had another think to be thinkin'!

"Yeah, it's Cece," I growled.

"Oh my– I'm so sorry Cece. I didn't realize it was – oh, I'm so sorry!"

"Oh you're gonna be."

"No, I really didn't mean..."

"Just skip it."

Now in cheaters she looked smart, clever even. She was probably a little prettier too and my brother and pops actually liked women in glasses. It was an odd thing, but the honest truth.

"You're not going to tell George what I've – I'm Annabelle Dellafield...by the way,"

"Oh yeah? By the way...I don't care."

And I really didn't care. She's followin' me inside the penthouse suite, still not gettin' the message. The whole place is dark and I'm feelin' for a light while she's still talkin'.

"Of the Philadelphia Dellafield's."

"Interesting..."

"My father, he's real big in timber."

"Fantastic..."

I found the light. The place looked empty, but a mess. She started rushin' to clean it, moving robes, blankets, and shoes all around the house. She was wipin' off couch cushions and tabletops, clearing glasses and puttin' cigarettes away, playin' maid.

"May I offer you something to drink?" she asked.

Now I found it funny, cause no bim ever stayed more than one night with my brother Georgie, so why was she playing house like this was her place too?

"Oh, so you live here now?"

"Oh no," she laughed.

"Good."

She continued cleaning, a bra here and a sock there. She took my brothers boxers off the painting of a naked fifteenth-century woman. He and pops liked collectin' art as long as it were of women and as long as them women were naked. She's still cleaning and carryin' on about her family, but I ain't hearin' her. I was goin' to bed.

"I'm across the street – just visiting family – my auntie is away. I'm minding her place while she's on holiday. I just graduated from school. Alford. I don't have to be back at home until Thanksgiving, so in the meantime..."

George was my favorite outta all five brothers on account of he was real wise, like street smart. He was makin' a real good livin' knocking guys lights out for money. He was 36 and 0 and working for hisself, earning rank as a prizefighter. By twenty-eight he had his own penthouse with imported furniture and gold pieces all over, fancy artwork and such, and no tax evasion charges to be found. He were loansharkin', yes, and makin' plenty of money on the side bettin' on hisself. Cause of all that work, he ain't ask nothin' from our old man in years. When he got his place, he gave me a key to get in whenever I'd like. He even made me my own room with little pink curtains and a canopy bed. He'd have fresh flowers delivered to it everyday whether I came over or not and our pops were never none the wiser.

"...so we'll be seeing a lot of each other I'm sure," Dellafield's still talkin', "I just love winters in New York. So beautiful—"

"—winters? How long you plan on stayin' for?"

George was real swell and smart and everything else, but when it came to broads...that was another matter. I mean, if I had to deal with some gatekeepers or some drawn on eyebrows or some cheese-cake in negligee every time I came over then that was okay because I could ignore them to a point, but not this one. This Annabelle Dellafield of the 'Philadelphia Dellafields' with her pops real big in timber and talkin' like she gonna be staying here in George's house for the duration of a summer, the beginning of fall and now talkin' bout winters...that was a real problem for me. I couldn't stand by and take that, oh no, not with her trappin' my favorite brother and takin' away my refuge.

"Oh, well the rest of the year–"

"—you must got the wrong idea toots. Georgie don't spend no *rest of the year* with a woman. You must have some fantasy, but this is the reality sweetheart. He'll have your bags packed quicker than sayin' it if you keep talkin'. Or better yet, let me help you—"

But that's when I saw it, that great big rock on her finger. She flashed it towards me on purpose, just so the gleam off the diamond was shinin' right in my eyes. Why didn't I see it sooner? No wonder

George was dodgin' the family, cause he was out marryin' in the timber family. I was a little more than pissed off.

"Cece!"

George come in through his own front door, in all his glory. He had his silk robe and slippers and a big cocaine smile. He ran to me, holdin' me tight, picking me up off the ground as I wriggled around trying to fight him, still mad at the whole ring situation.

"You put me down Georgie!"

And then he was tickling me, and I was laughin', nearly forgetting there was this lady standing there with her hands behind her back waiting to be introduced proper. George ignored her. Just me and him was all that mattered.

"Happy birthday Cece!"

"Awe, thanks Georgie."

"I gotta present for ya somewhere, hold on – what did pops get ya that fur? Looks swell Cece, just swell on ya. Turn around so I can see ya! Nice jewelry too. Wait, isn't that my ma's?"

George never slept after a fight and you could see it. His eyes were bloodshot with big bags under em'. He had cuts and bruises everywhere and bloodied bandages on his hands. He had a big black eye and the left side of his face were swole, but he still looked handsome that damn George. I don't know how he did it, but he always had a face for pictures that George Romello did.

"Georgie, are you alright? Damn, did you take a beating or what?"

"You should see the other guy."

"How's about the fight last night Georgie?"

"KO'd in the third round, bastard took a chunk out of me though,"

He's lifting up his sleeve showing me a fresh bite mark. It was real fleshy and still bleeding a little.

"but he ain't know what to do with no Romello. Ain't no Romello ever lived to fight fair."

And I really wished I had seen the other guy. I held my hand out.

"That's swell Georgie, where's my take?"

He frowned, reaching into his pocket and pulling out a bank-roll. He took the rubber band from around the bills and snapped it towards me. I'm pouting.

"Not even a fin?" I begged.

"No baby sister of mine takes bets.""I been takin' bets off you all my life Georgie, what gives?"

"Nah, it's time you stay away from them tracks and those speaks and them kinds of books. I gotta get ya into school."

And then that Dellafield perks up.

"I been to school," I said.

"College," he corrected.

"Nah, don't have time for no college."

"You'll make time for it and all – but all that and beside, what desk clerk saying you come in here at this hour? What you doin' wandering the streets?"

"It's complicated,"

Dellafield perks up again. She weren't filin' them nails, she was listening.

"can we talk, alone?"

I'm signaling to the lady and George looks up like he forgot she was there.

"Annabelle, scram," he ordered.

"Yes George."

She obeyed without an if, and, or but about it. It was real easy to get her to listen, not like them other broads woulda done it— and she also didn't scram out the front door like the others too, she scrammed into his bedroom.

"Who is she?" I asked.

"Nevermind her, not yet. Let's get back to it. What's complicated?"

"Ah, George..."

"No, no...ya come and sit on my lap like ya did when you was a kid. Come on."

He stretched his arms and took off my furs, then he grabbed me and sat me on his knee.

"Okay, now tell me."

"Like I said...it's complicated."

"Complicated's one am. Complicated ain't no six am."

"I'm eighteen now," I assured him.

"You're what?"

He took the back of my neck and gripped it tight.

"What are you?" he asked.

"I'm eighteen Georgie," I whined.

"And that mean's what?"

"It means I'm a woman."

"Ya ain't no woman," he said.

He kept hold of my neck and I couldn't move. I was locked in.

"And then I'm hearin' you was down Johnny's Place last night."

"Where did ya hear that from?"

"I been hearin' it. I got eyes out there. People been sayin'."

"I like Johnny's Place. Georgie, ya hurting me now."

He let go and kissed the back of my neck real sweet. He was always real sweet, George was.

"Johnny's Place ain't no where for my baby sister. You don't need to be drinkin' down there, or dancing around for all them men to be watchin' you. When I think of them men watching you I –"

He was tightening his grip around my knee.

"Georgie, stop!"

He let go and patted my leg to get up. He lit a cigarette and rested back on the couch, putting his feet up on the coffee table.

"What's with the outfit?" he asked.

"It's new, you like? I thought it looked pretty. I been telling you I'm a woman now –"

"—yeah yeah, I guess I'll have to get used to that."

George looked me up and down and then put his cigarette out on his hand. He was always doing stuff like that too. Tough as nails, that was George.

"Come here...come closer," he started.

I was leaning in and he's inspecting my face, rubbin' the lipstick away.

"you been makin' yourself up like a clown with all that makeup."

"Them other girls do it..."

"They're coming and going girls, you ain't no coming and going girl!"

"I don't know—"

"—you do know! Cece Romello don't run around till six in the morning coming and going with a face full of makeup. Them kinda women don't get no respect, you hear?"

"Yes Georgie."

"So what, you come here to hide out? Hide out from pops?"

"Yes Georgie."

"Yeah alright, but I ain't gonna spare ya the lecture. I been hearin' what you been doing. And all that dancing. Your ma did all that dancing, so where'd it land her?"

"Don't be talking about my ma."

"I'll talk about her, cause all pops says about her was that she was a good lay!"

"You ain't never been mean like this to me before, Georgie. It's that lady that's who it is. That Annabelle Dellafield of the Philadelphia Dellafields."

"Don't be talking 'bout her. She's a lady and she was taught to be it. You gotta learn from her,"

I cried. George looked at me and his eyes softened. He ain't never yell at me before.

"oh I'm sorry Cece. Awe, I shouldn't have –"

"—oh, dry up," I'm snifflin'.

"No Cece, I'm really sorry. That's not what I meant. Look, can you come here for a second? Just for one second, can you come right here?"

I hesitated, but eventually sat down next to him. I didn't want to look at him or talk to him or nothin' cause I was really hurt. The morning after my eighteenth birthday he's goin' off on me somethin' fierce and I'm not thinking I deserve it.

"I got you something," he's pulling a box out of his robe pocket, "Happy Birthday."

"For me?" I smiled.

George nodded. I opened the box and it was a bracelet with big diamonds in it and it was all shining and beautiful. Nobody ain't never got me jewelry before and it was fancy and perfect and nothin' Regina had could compare.

"Oh, George, it's the most beautiful ice I've ever seen! Thank you!"

I slipped it on my wrist and gave him a big hug.

"Yeah, yeah okay don't make a case of it, it's just some jewelry," he laughed.

I looked suspicious like ya had to do with George.

"Hey, this ain't regifted one of your molls right?"

"No, of course not," he said, real serious, "I bought this for you Cece. My beautiful Cece, who's becoming a woman right before my very eyes,"

He took his hand and touched my cheek softly. George weren't normally so affectionate as he was this night, so it kinda threw me for a surprise. He just kept looking at my face and being all sensitive.

"I also did somethin' else for ya."

"What somethin'?"

"Got your tuition paid for Alford school."

"I told you I didn't want to go there!"

"No, you told me you'd think about it—plus they don't accept no real money till they do the entrance interview. It's to see if you're even Alford material."

"George I—"

Suddenly the front door opened and there was a man enraged. He flew into the room after me in the form of a six-foot tall Romeo Romello.

"Who's this then?!" He shouted, "that ain't my daughter!"

I'm all slinking back onto Georgie's living room couch cushion. I'm all slumped down cause he's already started yellin' at me.

"Oh, hell pops, you've scuffed up your own carpets pacing the room all night, but don't scuff mine! Let her be, she's alright, I told ya she'd be fine, I'd tell ya when I saw her," George was upset, "I already talked to her. Don't be yelling no more, she don't need it, she already heard it from me."

I started crying again. The tears normally made him stop but no, not this time.

"You ain't her father! What good did it do you yellin' at her? You sayin' you're her father now?"

"No, I ain't sayin' that, she's still you're little girl," George tried.

"No! She ain't no little girl a mine no more!"

"Yes, she is."

"No, she ain't! Not at no six am in the morning she ain't! And this is where she been hiding, huh? All them nights I thought she was safe at the house, she was running the streets and coming back here to hide out!"

"Pops why don't you sit down. You must be tired. You want a drink?"

George is trying to offer him some whiskey, but pops ain't having it. He's busy waving his big fat finger in my face like he don't see my tears falling.

"I don't want no drink!" Pops yelled.

His eyes looked bloodshot from bein' up all night and he's using all the energy he has to keep himself from keeling over in front of me.

"I'm sorry daddy."

"And after all this, you had me almost callin' the johns and you know we don't do that for nothin!"

"Oh, you weren't gonna call no johns," George waved him off, "have a drink and stop your hollerin'."

"I was gonna call em'!" Pops kept shoutin', "I don't want no drink—I want answers!"

My old man's head looked like it was gonna explode and I was just sitting on the couch tired, takin' it. I'd had a long night of drinkin' and dancin', nothing out of sorts. Truth was...Romeo Romello's daughter was still as innocent as she'd been when she got to Henry Caville's apartment that night, but I weren't gonna explain myself to nobody who thought I were loose. That type of explainin' weren't necessary, not even to my pops cause he should've known better! Even if I told it to him the truth of it all, he weren't gonna understand. Maybe George would, but Pops wouldn't. I know sometimes a girl just wants to kiss, but things was different with Henry. I was kissin' him cause I loved it, not cause I just plain wanted to kiss somebody.

"I don't need you coming to my house all pissed off talkin' about *Cece ain't your daughter no more.* The amount of times all us boys came home late after a date and all you did was pat us on the back, bein' damn proud of it. Now what?"

George is rolling his eyes and sittin' down next to me, putting his arm around me trying to give me some sort of comfort. I leaned my head on his shoulder to cry.

"Look at this Cece," he said.

He's showing me his gold pinky ring.

"won this last night bettin' on myself, ya know?"

"That's swell Georgie," I smiled through tears.

"Ain't anybody listenin' to me?" Pops asked, "what am I when I ask for an explanation? It's one thing when a son comes home late as hell, but a daughter is a different story – a daughter has to be a lady, know what I'm sayin'?"

"Ah shut it," George is waving him off, "you're still a lady, ain't ya Cece?"

I nodded.

"Good. We're done talkin' bout it then."

I loved Georgie.

"And what if I had called the cops?" Pops asked, this time pointin' at me, "if I had, there woulda been dicks all gumshoein' 'round our place cause *she* decided to be out till six in the morning! Whatcha think they woulda found, huh? They're just waitin' for me to call em' —just waitin' for me to go back to jail! Fresh outta lock up and gonna go right back in!"

"Sorry daddy," I said.

"Don't worry Cece. He weren't gonna call no johns," George said, "we don't do that for nothing."

"Oh, I was gonna call em'. Romeo Romello's daughter don't come home at no six am in the morning unless it's in a meat wagon! Why'd you do it Cece?"

"Sorry daddy," I repeated.

"Oh, there's probably an innocent explanation for the whole thing. Why don't you let her tell her story instead of jumpin' all over the place actin' nuts. You'll give yourself another stroke," George said.

"No, she's the one who's gonna give me a stroke!"

"You gonna give yourself have a stroke old man! She ain't done nothin'! Now...tell us why ya did it Cece..."

George was my favorite brother out of all my brothers cause he could spot the truth a mile away and he knew I weren't loose. He was also the only one of all the family that could keep Pop's from tearin' his hair out.

"Well? Why'd you do it?" George asked again, since I weren't answerin' fast enough.

"Well Georgie, I didn't mean to come home no six am," I started.

"Whatcha mean you didn't mean to?!" Pops yelled, "That doesn't just happen Cece! You was neckin' with that Caville kid, I know it!"

"Well I—"

"—Did he force you?"

"Hey! Let her talk!" George warned, "did who force you? Who's the Caville kid?"

George and dad both looked at me for some sorta answer and all I could remember was dancing the night away with Henry and it was all worth it, I swear.

"Well, dad were the one sent me over to Henry Caville's apartment in the first place," I whined.

"You sent her?" George asked, angry.

"Yeah I did, but, I didn't send her for no lay!"

"What'd you send her for then? Some petting party?"

That was William. He wasn't my least favorite brother, but maybe third favorite, ya know? Only cause he didn't have all his teeth and he was scary to look at.

"You think I'd send my only daughter over for some petting party, ya ugly bastard?"

Dad got in his face, cause he didn't like William too much neither.

"I don't know," William shrugged.

"What'd you think I'd send my only daughter over to some guys apartment for?"

"I don't know," William said, "but that's why you sent me over to that broads apartment that one time when I turned sixteen. Remember?"

"Yeah well, you ain't my daughter!" Pops shouted.

"Hey! You sent my sister over to some guys apartment?"

George spun Romeo around and got in his face instead. He looked a little scared as George was the only one in the world that could scare Romeo Romello. I loved George.

"At eight o'clock at night," I added.

"You sent my sister over to some guys apartment at eight o'clock at night?"

Dad looked more worried.

"Yeah, but it was that Caville kid's apartment. I'd already checked him out George. He's just a kid, ya know? Nineteen or something. He wasn't gonna do nothin'. I thought they were just gonna have a nice sit and talk."

"I weren't no kid at nineteen," George growled, "I didn't have no kid thoughts neither, especially with no eighteen year-old girl."

"Neither did I," William spoke up.

"You stay outta this!" George warned him.

"Yeah well – well –" dad stuttered.

George was all getting in pops face and his eyes were bugging out of his head like they did sometimes. Pops was trying to figure out what to say.

"Yeah well what?" George asked.

"Well, this kid, he ain't you George. You were handsome."

"Were?"

"You are, you were then, you are now. You've got broads knocking your door down like I do, ya know, chip off the old block, you should be in pictures you know? You shouldn't be getting your face knocked in night after night, I told ya you'll ruin your looks Georgie!"

"This ain't about me, this is about Cece!"

George is grittin' his teeth like he was gonna turn his sitting room into some ring and start sparring with our dad.

"Yeah well just calm down Georgie. Henry Caville ain't no lady-killer, he's probably lucky to have any woman, especially a nice lookin' girl like Cece coming over to his apartment at eight o'clock at night. I mean, he was probably just sitting doing his reading or something. I think he's in school ya know, like a scholar. He ain't you. They were just to have a nice sit and talk."

"School or no school, ain't no eighteen year-old woman and nineteen year-old man having' no nice sit and talk in an empty apartment at eight o'clock at night," George grumbled.

George was all close talkin' and spittin' on pops face and it was funny.

"I don't wanna hear it! Not when that eighteen year-old woman is Romeo Romello's daughter!" Dad yelled, "Ain't no man no age gonna have nothin' other than a nice sit and talk in an empty apartment at eight o'clock at night with Cece Romello. That's if he knows what's good for him!"

George looked at me then shook his head.

"Not if he don't know she's your daughter."

"What you mean, Georgie?"

"*I mean*...maybe Cece didn't tell him that she's Romeo Romello's daughter. Maybe that's why he felt so free to do anything other than have a nice sit and talk with her."

"You think?" Pop's asked. He's throwin' the idea around in his head. We could see the wheels turnin'.

George was wise to my con. He scowled, "I don't want to hear it. School or no school—a man's a man!"

"If she didn't tell him she were Romeo Romello's daughter," Pop's continued, "what'd she tell him then?"

They're both lookin' at me now. I'm slumpin' down in my chair.

"Well—" I started.

"—And what you doin' eatin' that apple?" Dad lost it, interruptin' me.

"What?" William looked confused, chompin' on his apple with his three teeth.

"Have you been eatin' an apple while my daughter was missing?" Dad asked.

Then George lost it. He really lost it.

"Hey! How long you been eatin' that apple?" George asked.

"I didn't start eatin' this apple till I heard her walking through the front door! I swear!"

"So...you can hear me coming' a mile away, huh?" I added.

George and dad both turned attentions back to me for some sorta answer. All I could remember was sharin' a cold roast beef sandwich with Henry and it was all worth it, I swear.

"Dad...daddy..."

"What?"

"I love him."

"Here we go," George waved me off, "Silly girl—she got some little crush."

"I mean it!" I yelled, "Henry's great! I love him and he wasn't gonna give me no chance no other way, cause of *you*!"

"Me?" Dad looked shocked.

"Yeah, cause he blames you for gettin' his pops killed so he don't want nothing to do with mugs!"

"I ain't no mug!"

"Yeah well, says you."

Pops got all upset like he did sometimes when he started gettin' all sentimental on me.

"Hey—you ain't never called me nothin' like that before," he pouted, "I shoulda known when they come to me about you dancin' in that juice joint. I shoulda known you ain't no little girl no more and if you ain't no little girl no more, than that means you had more than a nice sit and talk with that boy! That means that you two was makin'...ah well I'm not gonna say it."

"*You better not say it*," George warned.

"Well hell, I wasn't gonna say it," dad said, "I wasn't even thinkin' it."

"*You better not think it neither.*"

"Well maybe I was thinkin' it...but I weren't gonna say it!"

"Better *nobody* say it," George was fumin'.

It was silence, then that two toothed son-of-a-bitch William sticks his head 'round the corner to ask...

"Cece...was you and him...*makin' whoopee?*"

We heard a smack. William hit the ground hard. Pops and George was on top of him like they was street fightin'. I didn't do nothin' to stop nothin', cause I didn't much like William sayin' what he was thinkin' all the time. He got what he got.

"You stop thinkin' and sayin' that!"

I heard George say as he's punching William. There was blood everywhere and I wasn't sure if William was dead or not until I saw him sit up and realized that the blood was from his mouth. There was a tooth layin' on the ground next to them.

"Now—you're gonna clean this mess up, William!" Pops yelled.

George was mad cause he got blood on his silk bathrobe. He's over there tryna find a wet rag.

"Dad," I finally spoke, "daddy?"

"What?!"

"I'm still your little girl," I spilled, "Henry only took me dancing, I promise. Then I came back here. Got a little carried away drinkin' and dancin'. That's all. We weren't doin' nothin', I swear it."

"Really?" He asked, he face was changin' into some sort of happy.

"I told you my little sister weren't no chippy!" George nodded.

"Well, I knew that! You're telling me somethin' I already knew!"

Pops smiled, he put his arms around me to hug me, but I waved him off.

"Just cause I'm still your little girl don't mean I don't love him."

"Here we go again," George sighed.

"Listen, you can't love him cause that's not why I sent you there," Pops claimed.

"Yeah, but I do love him and that's that."

"Well you can love him, but I damn sure don't gotta love him."

"You don't gotta love him, but when I tells you I'm goin' out to California with him, you just gotta let me, is all."

"California?"

All three of them lit up, even William who was still on the floor wipin' his own blood in a circle with a rag.

"He's gonna be a picture star and pops is gonna let me go cause I gotta help Henry. You's owe it to him for gettin' his pops killed."

"You talk too fast," William said.

"I don't owe him nothin," pops said.

"You do!"

"Don't matter if pops is lettin' ya, cause I ain't lettin' ya. We got plans remember? Tomorrow we gots to go to the Alford school interview!" George chimed in.

"Yeah, yeah, Alford,"

Pops smiled like he just remembered their plans to keep me locked away for yet another four years. George is all in my face gettin' real preachy.

"I swear if my little sister gets her heart broken by a hoofer with a father who was a boozehound...I'll break his goddamned neck and sit in the big house for life cause of it! Don't care! And you know I'll do it!"

Ain't never was no point in arguing with no man in my family, so I got up and started walking to my bedroom. George and dad were all following me around like they weren't done talkin', but I was done listenin', see? And when Romeo Romello's daughter is done listenin', she walks!

7

Being a Lady and a Scholar

Growin' up, my brothers taught me the difference between bein' a lady and a tramp. When it came to females, they was listed in categories: *the easy's, the hard's, the make hard's, the too old's and the unwanted's.* A lot of those easy, loose women would be walkin' in and out of our pop's house at night. I'd watch em' as they drunkenly crawled across the street, barely dressed, gettin' skinned knees. I knew for sure I didn't want to grow up to be them types of women and maybe that's where all that dancing did lead, eventually. Sure—I liked a lot of attention and wanted to be seen, but not at the expense of bein' thought of as a comin' and goin' girl. In time, I saw George was right. Their type didn't get no respect in no way!

Thinking back on what it meant to be a lady...I guess the only true lady I ever known was Miss Ervine. She was Regina's best friend and closest confidant. She taught Regina class and grace when they moved to Park Avenue. She introduced her to the best places in New York, helped her plan dinner parties at the house, got her involved in charity functions and had her networkin' with the who's who of NYC. But Regina was notorious for ruinin' things and sabotagin' her own self. It was her loud mouth and tough talk —gettin' too drunk and slurrin' dirty words. Miss Ervine would surely laugh it off, make some excuse for her and clean things up in front of a crowd. With such a positive outlook and a *'try it again tomorrow'* type of attitude, Miss Ervine was a real lady.

She came from money, but didn't flaunt it like the others. Her father was wealthier than Romeo Romello could ever dream of— they was old money. Miss Ervine grew up traveling the world and having the best of everything. She'd tell me stories when I was young —stories of Arabs in the desert taking her on camel rides, eatin' *'decadent French cuisine'* in cafes, and sailing away on yachts visitin' far away islands. She told me about explorin' tombs in Egypt and buyin' expensive renaissance art in Italy. Miss Ervine was young and pretty and full of energy, but she didn't flaunt that neither. She was considered a socialite. She had never been married, simply living a bachelorette lifestyle and bein' courted by some of the *'cream of the crop'* around the country. She'd have senators, governors, company men, and oil men all come callin'. It was considered a potential scandal for Miss Ervine to be seen with someone as crude and unrefined as Regina. Not to mention the fact she was married to Romeo Romello, a man who all of New York knew only for his shady business dealings and multiple run-in's with the law. They chastised Miss Ervine for it, but didn't dare more than whisper their judgements around Regina and Romeo. Through all the gossip and bad publicity, Miss Ervine and Regina stayed friends. The relationship never really hurt Miss Ervine's image or prospects no how. Nothing could, since she was a real lady.

I were doted upon by Miss Ervine. She dressed me up and bleached my hair and taught me how to be respectable. My pops said she'd asked to be my godmother, but Regina refused her. She had plans for me I know, cause she said it. There was tea parties, debutante balls, and elocution lessons. She bought me a dollhouse so big and magnificent lookin' that I could have probably lived in it. She taught me to make little tea sandwiches and wanted me learnin' languages for when I traveled...*'and you will travel,'* she'd promise. Miss Ervine would have hated to see me runnin' around wearin' boys clothes with dirt on my face, followin' Pops and gettin' into the life the way I did. She taught me the difference between a woman who goes looking for attention and one who gets it. *'Let the them come to you'* she said *'and don't let that Romello name change you. Don't let it claim your reputation. You're more than the family business, my love...you are your own individual. You are Cece.'* She ain't never called me Cecelia neither. She always called me Cece and that's when all the rest started callin' me Cece too.

"Yeah, I had a crush on Miss Ervine that wouldn't quit," George said, "yup Miss Ervine would have wanted ya to go to Alford."

He and I had boarded the train and we'd be upstate in two hours. We had a car to ourselves, with all the blinds pulled down —no natural light cause of George's issues. He had one of them blindfolds on too and he's resting his head on my shoulder. He knew best to bring up Miss Ervine. It had been years since I thought of her and I upset myself for even forgetting. One day she just vanished. I was around five, yes, but we couldn't mention her name in the house. Regina wouldn't speak of her, never again. I was upset, mad at Regina for not telling me, confused why nobody would talk about it... why nobody would say.

"What happened to her?" I asked.

"Huh?"

"Miss Ervine...where'd she go?"

George grumbled, adjusting his position in the seat.

"Well, you didn't hear it from me," he started, "but Regina found her and our old man doin' more than neckin' in some hotel room."

"Miss Ervine?!"

He laughed, "don't sound so shocked. Them high society dames are the biggest sluts,"

I ain't want to believe it. George was makin' me real mad, he was, but he continued.

"but she found out the hard way that Regina was packin' heat back in those days. Whole time she thought she was special, like cause they was friends she couldn't get an ass full of lead."

"What did Regina do?"

George shook his head like he was sorry he even told me.

"It's old business, forget I brought it up," George said, "and don't spill nothin' on that dress, it's on loan."

He peeked over his blindfold as I was shaking orange juice round in my glass. Truth was I ain't never been on a train before and this talk of Miss Ervine and Regina weren't doin' nothin' for my nerves.

"What I gotta say to her again? To the lady at the school?" I asked.

"*You are most interested in higher education, and you're looking forward to attending such a prestigious school such as Alford,*"

That was Dellafield walkin' into our train car in her most proper voice.

"and that dress is from my personal collection, please don't wrinkle it."

"I told her, I told her it's on loan," George assured.

"No George, it's a gift. But please don't wrinkle it. Headmistress Fink doesn't like wrinkles."

"Her face sure got enough of em'," he laughed.

Dellafield smiled and sat across from us, tucking one leg behind the other and smoothing her own dress. I looked at mine, lavender hanky hem with all floral lace on top. She'd done my makeup and hair at George's, nothing real swanky but she kept saying '*it'll have to do – you'll have to do – she'll have to do George, it's all we've got at the moment*'.

"Are you excited?" Dellafield asked.

"I guess."

"Get that puss off your face cause you're goin'," George said.

"If she doesn't want to go George—"

"—she's goin'!"

"What about –" I started.

"What about what?"

George was lookin' real upset and I was almost scared to end the sentence cause we'd be arguin' over this nearly the whole way to Alford.

"What about Henry?"

There was the fight, blindfold off, and I moved away from his fumin'. He's lightin' his cigarette and lookin' all smug like he forgot, but he ain't forget nothing. Dellafield looked down, chosin' this time to clam up, just when I mighta needed her to be on my side. Just when I thought I was likin' Dellafield and all, she turned yella on me.

"I know a lot," George said, "only cause I do my research, see? You think I'd let my baby sister run around with some Henry Caville without as much as givin' him the once over?"

Now I knew what people meant by the once over, but then I also knew what George meant by it and that scared me cause George's 'once overs' never did end well.

"What'd you do?"

"Don't ask me what I did, ask me what he did! He ain't what ya think."

"So, didn't ya think I was smart enough to figure that out for myself if there was somethin' to figure out?"

"Nope. You ain't too smart when it comes to him."

"What'd you do?"

"He's a punk. Henry gives dancin' lessons to them old skirts down Moxie's and sometimes they ain't only dancin' and if it wasn't on account of them cheaters he wore, you'd be able to see right through him."

"He ain't no punk! He told me he was workin' Moxies and I don't believe they ain't really dancin'. I believe Henry. There weren't no secrets last night."

"Did he also tell ya, did he also say he's going out with some blonde dame? Some Bonnie?"

"He ain't going out with her. They was goin' to California together, but they ain't no more, cause he's goin' with me soon as I give him the say so. They was just goin' cause she dances too. They was just goin' cause its easier two goin' than one."

"Yeah she dances alright...Cece why you talkin' all this grown up stuff, you're still a baby. So naïve."

"I ain't naïve."

"Then tell me how I know they're engaged? Him and that Bonnie. Tell me how I know."

I felt my heart drop to my stomach.

"Engaged?"

George started lookin' guilty.

"I wouldn't be tellin' ya all this if ya hadn't pulled it outta me."

"He ain't engaged. It can't be true. I gotta ask him, ask him myself. He wouldn't have lied, he just wouldn't!"

George is shakin' his head, puttin' his blindfold back on.

"You ain't tell Pops, did ya? You couldn't! Please tell me ya didn't," I begged.

"Had to, cause I had to let him know how wrong he was sendin' you over to that no good's house. Had to rub it in his face a little."

"What'd he say?"

"He ain't say nothin' cause you put him in a bad way. He knows you got Henry believin' some sap stuff 'bout you not being a Romello and he don't wanna spoil your con, so he told me he ain't gonna rough him up."

"Oh."

"But remember I told ya what would happen if your heart got broke by some hoofer whose father were on the sauce?"

"Oh no you couldn't—"

I could picture what happened before the words ever come out his mouth. I could picture goons surroundin' Henry outside his apartment, maybe draggin' him down to the stairwell and beatin' on him pretty serious, all at George's request. Poor Henry's face musta been bloody and cut up all to hell, so how was he gonna go out for the pictures now? George were smiling this smile like he already thoughts of it and it were almost evil.

"Oh, I could and I did and they let him know it was comin' from me. They let him know that Cece Romello ain't no good time girl, and she ain't gonna be fooled around with!"

I knew George weren't lyin'. He was a prizefighter, yes, and he were out the life for years, sure. All that said, I seen him order hits and carry em' out hisself and I knew he had no regrets about none of it. When he got like that it was somethin' in his eyes that I hated, somethin' none of my brothers or my pops or any of them other goons had. It was somethin' like the spirit of the devil hisself.

"Now, dry them tears. Can't be lookin' all red and puffy for Alford," he ordered.

Dellafield handed me her cloth napkin, eyes still lowered like nothin' was none of her business. After twenty minutes of silence and my snifflin', she finally broke.

"Alford's a good school, Cece, it's a very good school. You'll like Alford. You'll do fine in Alford."

Hidden away behind more trees and grass and fields than I'd seen my whole life, there was Alford Preparatory School for Girls. Even if they hadn't told me I was still in New York, I'd have been surprised all the same. The school looked old, but it smelled new, the paint and the wood when you walked through the halls, the shiny tile clacking underneath my heels, all had some type of chemical stench. Outside was cobblestone, flowers on vines around tall columns where I was sure I'd be smoking cigarettes and hatin' my life.

Girls walked by us, students, and they was looking at George all googley-eyed even with his bruises on his face. He had his three-piece suit on, gold jewelry everywhere and tippin' his hat to the plaid, long pleated skirts and argyle sweaters that passed him by. I'm sure he wasn't even paying attention to faces just the button-down shirts and imaginin' those buttons poppin' everywhere and school books droppin' by the way side in the back of his Rolls.

"Hello Sir," they giggled the way schoolgirls do, almost fallin' over each other tryin' to get his attention. George loved it, takin' his hat off and wavin' it towards em', staring em' up and down without a care.

"Yeah, I'm gonna like you in this place," he smiled, "I'm gonna have a good time comin' to visit."

"Oh George, they ain't even nineteen and aren't ya engaged to what's her name?"

"Yeah I ain't say nothing, just talkin' about visiting my sister that's all. Save all that deep thinkin' for school, okay?"

The Headmistress of Alford College were this rat faced woman named Mrs. Petula Fink whose glasses sat on the bridge of her sharp nose, attached by a pearl string around her narrow head. Dellafield of the Philadelphia Dellafield's couldn't say more nice things about her on the way, but don't think I didn't hear her whispering to

Georgie when we got off the train. *I'm gonna go catch up with some school friends, and get some lunch. You go with your sister, but please don't mention me, okay?'* George looked confused, but Dellafield just kept shaking her head, *'just don't mention me, there's no need for you to. Please George'.*

So, Fink kept looking at me with these glasses and at first I ain't take it as no slight cause I thought she just had some type of nervous tick and all, that was until her tone started bein' awkward. She started coughin' and shufflin' papers around and actin' like somebody who didn't want us there. Normally the Romello name came with respect, ya know? But this woman with her wool frock and her manicured nails and her flat shoes with the tassles, she weren't tryin' to hide the fact she didn't care much for the Romellos so it showed. She started out the interview sayin' just that, but in a way too condescending.

"Thank you for sending all of her documents ahead of time and using your mother's maiden name on the forms."

"Course, that's what you thought was best," George replied.

He looked at her real calm like, chewin' on his toothpick, spreadin' his legs out real long and relaxing in the chair. I was sittin' straight up next to him, with one leg crossed under the other like Miss Ervine taught me. My hair stayed pinned back and my makeup was still real nice and my frilly dress was all sittin' neat on my body. I was smiling so hard my face was hurtin'. I just wanted to scream.

"She has a birth return from the state of New York. Was Cecelia born with a midwife, do you know?'

George continued chewin'.

"Who knows? I was nine. Too busy playing in the dirt and kissin' girls when Cece was bein' born."

Fink coughed again then ignored him, spreading the papers out on the table. It was the first time I'd ever seen em'. They was my fingerprints, birth return, a picture of me as a baby and the application for Alford. My name read Cecelia Marie McAllister. I saw my parents listed as Romeo Romello father and Regina McAllister Romello mother. I saw my sex as female. I saw my race as white. The picture showed me as nearly a year old, but my hair was dark and I had much darker features than I did now, years later.

"We spoke earlier," Fink said, "about how the Romello name may cause bad publicity for Alford if news were to get out of Cecelia's true identity."

"Yeah, I know and again, it's changed. Cece don't have a problem with it, do ya Cece?"

I looked at George and then back at Fink and nodded as his eyes told to me to do.

"I hope you understand and don't take offense, it's just that your father, being what he is and...those tax evasion charges."

"He was found not guilty of thems."

"Yes, but–"

"–like I said, we changed it. She's still a Romello at heart, but if you think McAllister is any different than we can just use that."

"It's the reputation that the Romello name brings with it. I'm sure even you can understand this."

"Oh, even me?" George is tappin' his foot like he did when he was pissed off.

"Alford college is still fairly new. A name like Romello attending class here might give the wrong impression. It could ruin us, potentially."

"Yeah I get it. I ain't as stupid as I look," George said, "but just so you know the McAllister's were travelers – *gypsys* – and our pops had to put up a big fight to marry one, a big fight and a horse, but you know what's best. Whatever gets Cece in here and learnin' fast as we can, that's all that counts."

"Mr. Romello I understand, but we're some time away from deciding. This is just the preliminary interview. Not only is her surname a potential problem if someone wants to start digging into it, but maybe also other factors about Cecelia may be appear as well."

"Like what?"

Fink took a real deep breath and closed her eyes like some sorta meditating. George kept chewin' and tappin'.

"I read a publication very recently. It was about a woman...passing as white," she said.

I looked up suddenly and our eyes met, mine with guilt and hers with judgment. George didn't break his poker face.

"Oh yeah? Get a lotta that around here?"

"No, of course we don't. It's just something that came to mind while taking a look at this case."

"So now we're a case? Why?" George asked, sittin' up.

Maybe she were gonna say somethin'. Maybe she were wise to the con, but somethin' in George's face and the way he had this sorta determined look made her stop what she was gonna say. She caught her breath mid thought kinda like she'd regret her next words. Georgie had that way about him—that way of makin' people do as he wanted.

"Why's that Fink?" He asked again.

"I just think having her start in the fall semester may be a tad overreaching. I'd think maybe the chance may come next year or the following, if Cecelia is still so inclined to join our fine school."

"She's inclined to join your fine school right now. What's the hold up?"

"There's just a few wrinkles to iron out that's all. Just a few things to get straight."

"So, let's get em' straight right now."

"Mr. Romello, we may need a few years to get them straight. I apologize."

George screwed his face real confused and sat up in his chair, looking towards Fink like she was his opponent in the ring. He looked like if he could have he'd knock her square in the mouth.

"I don't understand. I get that my big fat checkbook won't get her in cause you people here have to see lineage and class. I understand that well enough, cause you don't want just anybody comin' in here and gummin' up the works. So, we decided that's why I had to bring her in person, so you can see what a good girl she is. Cece was brought up fine, brought up in a big house she was, not like me and my brothers. She was brought up in the days when my pops startin' gettin' class, she was. Some of these broads comin' in here ain't never even been on Park Avenue before, ain't never had the best food, the best clothes, and butlers and tutors and maids like Cece had waitin' on em' hand and foot,"

Fink blinked hard, tryin' to process what George was sayin' and how close he was gettin' to the other side of her desk.

"but that ain't nothin' special to us. I just don't understand what you're tryin' to say right now, Mrs. Fink, and with all due respect–I don't like your con. The Romello's were brought up on the backbone of con yeah, but at least we're civilized about it. There's a time and place for con and there's a time and a place for business. With all due respect, Mrs. Fink, we took a train ride all the way out here, but I don't like your tone and I don't like you being no sneak neither, layin' out my sister's paperwork on your desk like it's trash."

"Mr. Romello,"

She stood up calmly, but she were forcing her hands on the desk like they was gonna ball up into fists and she was stoppin' it,

"Alford College was built on the foundation of giving opportunity to those who have earned it. The women that attend our school,

Mr. Romello, are a cut above the rest. They have resumes and paper-work showing they are capable, they have a blood line to be proud of. They learned languages. They know how to play multiple instruments. They come in with this knowledge— and they don't have to walk into my office all made up to look like something they aren't–"

Now this time George stood up, less calmly than Fink, and he was forcin' his hands on the desk too, so she backed up scared.

"—no I don't wanna hear that! You called us up here makin' us think like we had a chance. You ain't even talk to Cece this whole time. You ain't ask her not one question 'bout herself or what she's done. This ain't no interview. You wanted to bring us in here to be polite, but that's what you people do isn't it? That's what you people who think you're better than everybody else, you want to show us your big fancy school and all what ya have to offer and wave it under our noses like a shiny diamond what we ain't never gonna have!"

"That's enough Mr. Romello!"

"No, it ain't enough! You ain't never thought of given Cece no opportunity to come here, have you? You just wanted to be able to say ya turned the Romello's down after everything, after every possible thing you said or every angle you tried or every scenario you worked out about her being here. You ain't never wanted her here no way and that pisses me off cause that coulda been a telegraph or a phone call, not a damn train ride up here. It's somethin' we call dis-respect in our family, Mrs. Fink. It's disrespect in the worst way and a complete waste of both our times. I don't care for it and frankly, neither will our pops when he finds out which he'll find out sooner than ya can spit!"

"I don't appreciate the threat!"

"You ain't never even heard a threat!"

George grabbed my papers right off her desk and me by the arm. Quicker than we arrived, we were gone, out of Alford College and away from the cobblestones I'd never tire of and the columns I'd never smoke near. Away from the students, all lookin' for excitement themselves, lookin' on at Georgie like he were the tops as he's yellin', carryin' on. He's rushin' down staircases like he wanted to get that school's smell off his clothes in double time.

"Not good enough for Alford huh?" George yelled crazy, "Yeah, not good enough for Alford! Not good enough for those snobs at Alford!"

I felt bad for Dellafield on the train ride back cause he's all spouting off at the mouth talkin' *Alford this and Alford that* and how could she suggest such a horrible school–what they did to little Cece and our family, they was gonna pay for. I was gonna say somethin', maybe to help her out a little, but I just looked down cause *it weren't none of my busines*s.

8

Being a Taxi Dancer

Moxie's Tea Room was a real ritzy joint, with lots of old money walkin' in and out. It was nestled in the nice part of town where people could afford to keep their mouths shut about their extra-curriculars, especially during prohibition. Regina went to Moxie's a few times that I know of, but there was this one night in particular that Pops and I had to go get her. That was the last time I set foot in the place.

That night I was out far too late for my age, but Pops and I was on a mission to find his beloved. He'd heard Regina was at Moxie's and eyes was on her everywhere. She was a drunken disorderly causin' trouble and swingin' her arms at those old women—makin' quite a scene. Pops finally caught her and forced her into his long stretch Rolls. It was the first time I'd seen Regina get that plastered in public.

"*The infamous Romeo Romello!* Took ya long enough to find me, didn't it? Took ya long enough to care!"

Regina's voice was like a high pitched siren goin' off and Romeo was just tryin' to settle her.

"Gina..."

He repeated over and over, trying to calm her down, but she was swingin' her arms at him too. He kept shushin' her and lookin' around, plenty embarrassed.

"I'm fatter than when you met me," she said.

"Gina, that don't mean nothin.'"

"Is that why ya don't come home nights? Cause I got fat?"

Now he's is lookin' at me.

"Hey! Not in front of the kid."

"Well, I bet *she* knows why you don't come home nights," Regina said, "and why you take her with ya always..."

"Regina, my lovely," he begged.

She kept staring at me with her beady little eyes.

"*Does he touch you?*"

"Stop!"

"Cece, *does he touch you?*"

I could see my pops was gettin' mad and seein' red. The veins in his neck was pulsating.

"Stop talkin' at her like that!" He warned.

"Nah, cause it's true," she said, "he touches you just like he touched your dirty whore of a mother!"

And that's when he hit her. Romeo hit Regina across the face, one quick flick of his wrist and the flesh connected. A big red welt started to form and he was doomed. Everybody, especially my pops knew that was a big no, no! No Romello man never hit no Romello woman–it was sacred rules. If either of us had squealed to one of my brothers, or any of my brothers for that matter, Romeo Romello would have been deader than dead.

"*I'm sorry,*"

Is all he said, with his eyes wide, soundin' like he meant every word of it. Regina laughed in his face. I knew from the tone of her cackle and the darkness of her eyes that she hated him. She'd hated him for years.

"There's a new song I heard," she said, "they're little kids around Cece's age, but they still sing it."

"Then let em' sing it,"

Pops shrugged it off like he wasn't bothered.

"Don't ya wanna know what's it called, Cece?"

"She don't," Pops said.

"Quit speakin' for us women," she barked, "Cece, how's about it?"

"Sure," I nodded, not really feelin' like I had much of a choice.

Regina smiled this big grin, this big scary grin, the kind that's scary to a ten year-old.

"It's called, *the Romello family deserve to die...*"

"Cover your ears Cece!" Romeo ordered, but I didn't.

I was intrigued by her maddening expression, the way Regina moved her hands around in circles as she talked and dramatized every word of her story like a campfire tale.

"*...they don't care about you or I...*"

"Quit singin'!" Pops begged.

"*...they steal our money and live so well...*"

She moved closer. Her laugh was so loud, it had my ear's ringin'.

"*...they should die in prison and rot in hell!*"

My plan that night were to go see Henry, cause I ain't know what else to do and he weren't at his place. I didn't even care about him bein' engaged to no Bonnie at that point, not even about him goin' to California with her either, cause who was I to hold him from it? I just didn't want him to think those were Cece Romello's orders that got him beat up. I didn't want him thinkin' they was comin' from someone who loved him so much, savvy?

Moxie's hadn't changed much over the years. Still big potted plants everywhere and piano music. Real hoity-toity with a dress code and all gold trimming around.

"'Scuse me, do ya got a – I mean," I started, "do you have a table?"

The host was goin' through some big book of his and then looked me up and down real hinky. For all his lookin' and deciding if I was riff raff or not, I just didn't have that type time. Henry coulda been in the hospital as far as I knew, but I didn't think he could afford the insurance. So maybe, just maybe, I thought he'd show up for work after nursing his wounds with some raw meat. It was still a swanky place, maybe too ritzy for the Romellos, but I was wearing Dellafield's dress and my hair was still neat, makeup not smudged cause I'd made sure of that. He'd have to look at me as real proper just as long as I kept the con.

"Reservation?" He asked.

"No – I,"

"—then I can't possibly let *you* in without a reservation."

He snapped the book shut, rat faced like that Fink woman. There are more rat faced people in this world than I'd care to believe, lookin' down their nose at other people. It ain't right.

"Reservation?"

"Reservation only these days."

"Any exceptions?"

"Afraid not."

He busied hisself with other things so as to not look me in the eye or in my general direction. He started fixing the curtains, the tablecloth, his suit jacket, and scribbling on blank pieces of paper, but for all that stallin' he quickly realized I weren't leavin'.

"Is there something else I can help you with Miss?" He asked, annoyed.

"Yes, I'm here to see somebody."

"I'm sure."

"Henry Caville,"

"Henry who?"

"Henry Caville I said, he works here doesn't he?"

"Hmm, let me check,"

Now he's really busy, pickin' up invisible trash off the floor, sweepin' a clean table off, whatever. Then he starts kneelin' down on the ground tyin' his shoe with no laces so I got wise and maybe a wad of bills came out of my pocketbook. Maybe those same few bills flew to the ground, his way. Maybe I kicked the rest of em over with my foot. He looked up.

"You dropped something."

"No, I didn't."

He picked up the bills and he handed them back to me.

"I can't possibly," he shook his head no.

"Maybe I am in your book."

"I doubt it."

"Ms. Cecelia."

"Nope. No Cecelia's."

I got up close to him and leaned in with a whisper.

"Ms. Cecelia Romello."

"No Cecelia Rom—"

It was the eyes, the way the eyes looked at us when they heard the name Romello. That was my addiction, the change in them, the ability to take a person however hoity toity or better than anyone they thought they were and they weren't *letting you in here or letting you do that or talking to this one and that one* and then I said Romello and they'd be frozen in time.

It was eyes rattling around in heads and double talkin' and back peddlin'. This host weren't no different with his brain turnin' thoughts in his head I'm sure like, *'well I can't refuse her, if I let her in I could lose my job, but if I don't let her in I could lose my legs and I can talk to my boss, I can make my boss understand, but I can't make them Romellos understand. They aren't as understanding, yes okay let's...'*

"...Right this way, Ms. Cecelia. Anywhere in particular? Maybe next to the window? Maybe in Henry Caville's section?"

And just like that I was gettin' seated. Just like that Henry Caville worked there.

"Would you please?"

It was a nice table with a nice view and the host slunk away waiting in the wings keepin' a close eye, just watchin' til' I needed him. I had a front row seat for Henry dancin' with some heavy set old lady and he's twirlin' her around the room with a bored expression on his face, fake smilin' at her every so often. She's all gushin' and lookin' like he's makin' her feel sixteen again and I see her friends all gigglin' like little school girls.

"Oh, I'm so glad we had this dance," she swooned.

Henry's jerkin' a nod and leading her to and fro', playin' into the con. The music's fast and he's sweeping her around the floor quick like he's just trying to get it over with. When the music stopped, he looked relieved.

"May I escort you back to your table?" He asked.

"Oh, just one more song."

"We've been dancing quite a while Madame."

"*Please?*"

She slipped him some kale.

"Okay. One more song," he agreed.

This next number was slow, the band was playin' real soft piano and drums, with a little sax in the background. He were holding her close now and she laid her head on his chest. It was the same way he had danced with me the night before, doin' a slow waltz, leadin' as she stumbled her feet on top of his. Anyone could see he was the professional as she barely knew the steps. It felt as though he were draggin' her along. I paid close attention to his feet, as I had been doin' ever since I started wantin' to be a hoofer.

It wasn't til' I stopped givin' attention to the dance that I realized his face had bruises and cuts and scrapes like he'd been into the worst fight of his life. His bottom lip were all swole. He looked like somebody maybe tried to put some powder on it all to cover it up, but it ended up just lookin' worse, all blotchy and discolored. I knew it was all George's fault.

"Oh, I need to sit down, please, help me to my chair," the old broad said halfway through the song, all tuckered out and sore.

"Are you alright?" He looked mildly concerned.

"Just a bit lightheaded is all, I gotta take a rest," she whined.

I saw him walk her over and he's not wearing his glasses or nothin'. His hairs combed and slicked back real nice. His face looked even more handsome than it did the other night, besides the bruising. I seen more men with bruises and cuts and swelling in their face in my life than I care to remember, but it never bothered me none. I could still spot a handsome man under all that mess. Henry's in a tux, like real nice threads, and he's shoving bills in his pockets some kinda smooth after her and her friends fork up the rest of their dough. He couldn't be more of a gentleman with em as he bowed and backed away from their table, with them still gushin' over him.

I'm trying my best to be attractive with my leg all curled up under the other one and dabbing my lips with my napkin. I sip my tea, pinky out, and pretend like I don't see him, flutterin' my eyelashes all coy. He saw me, I know he did, cause we locked eyes and I smiled, but he just turned and started to walk past my table.

"Um, sir, Mr. Caville,"

I called, wavin' my linen napkin towards him. He stopped.

"I'd like to dance."

"You got two feet don't ya?"

He were real rude, then started walkin' away again.

"I'd like to dance with you."

"Nothin' doin'."

I slapped a bill on the table just like that old lady.

"Please?"

It was like when I put the money down, a little bell signaled to that host. He rushed to my table and refilled my water.

"Is everything alright Ms.?"

"No, everything is not alright," I started, "I wish to dance with Mr. Caville. I came here for Mr. Caville. I was seated in front of Mr. Caville and I want Mr. Caville!"

"Caville!"

Henry had gotten halfway across the room 'fore his boss's angry call brought him slinkin' back to me.

"Yes Mr. Townsend?"

"Ms. Cecelia is requesting a dance."

"I'm not dancin' with her."

Townsend looked confused, then turned back to me like everything was fine. He was clearing this matter up for me asap. I smiled sweetly as I could.

"Ms. Cecelia is requesting a dance."

He repeated hisself, taking the bill from the table and handing it to Henry. Henry shook his head and pushed it back at him.

"No amount of money in the world would make me dance with that dame," he said, "not happenin'."

The host got real mad this time, he looked over at me and smiled to make sure I wasn't seein' but I knew how mad he was at Henry.

"Mr. Caville," he started, grittin' his teeths, "Ms. Cecelia is requesting a dance. Ms. Cecelia, that's R – O – M—"

"—I know who she is."

That host looked around quickly, then hushed him.

"Well then, Mr. Caville, you know what would happen to you if you denied the dance of Romeo Romello's daughter. Same thing that happened to your father, if I'm not mistaken."

"I ain't scared of no mugs."

"Well then, do you know what would happen to you here if you denied her a dance?"

"What?"

"You'd be fired."

"Why? I got rights, ain't I?"

"Not at Moxies you don't."

Henry looked at me real angry.

"Am I gettin' my dance?" I asked, smug.

"Yeah, you'll get it alright," Henry answered, "spoiled brat."

"Good," the host applauded, "see to it that Ms. Cecelia has a nice long dance, as long as she wants."

"Yeah, sure I will."

But Henry's expression looked devious, like he had somethin' up his sleeve.

"And Ms. Cecelia, I'm sure you'll tell your family what a nice time you've had at Moxie's."

When the host left, Henry grabbed me up outta my chair and swung me around faster than I could get my bearings. He started dancin' real fast with me, carryin' me from one side of the room to the other in quicker step than the music were playin'. I couldn't figure my feet out and was just being dragged along with him, his rough hands pinchin' under my arms. Other people were noticin' how rough he was bein' with me and then the host came back to call.

"Caville!"

Henry slowed down and let me put my feet back on the ground to steady myself.

"I can see why you want to be in pictures," I said.

"Oh yeah? Why?"

"Cause you're so dramatic."

"This ain't dramatic. Dramatic is waking up at half past seven in the mornin' with three men hovering over your bed holdin' baseball bats. So, you made a call, huh? So, you tried to have me tossed around and taught a lesson? This is why I didn't wanna get involved with no moll."

"I lied and I'm sorry, but you weren't gonna take me out no way if I told you who I really was. We woulda never gotten to know each other if I had told you the truth."

"I don't know you. The girl I met last night wasn't Cece Romello. She was just Cece. That's the girl I drank with and danced with. That's the girl I thought was pretty swell. Cece Romello calls hits and throws jack around. Cece Romello makes people dance with her even though they don't wanna or she'll start havin' legs broken and jobs taken away."

"That ain't true! I don't know nothin' from nothin' about them goons comin' round to see you. It wasn't my orders. I didn't make em."

"That's a lie! When they was roughin' me up they was sayin' *this is comin' from Cece Romello*, that you knew I was engaged to some other dame and you was gonna *beat my face in so I couldn't be no picture star*. That's what they said!"

"But—"

"—and then I thought, well at least they didn't break my legs so I can still dance, but I ain't never dancin' with Cece Romello, never again!"

"But—"

"—and then here I am breakin' that promise to myself, but that's okay cause in my heart I know the truth. Before I used to look at ya like with something, ya know? Like some sorta something and now when I can't even stand ya!"

"What'd ya look at me like?"

"Forget it. That's just the way I sees it now."

"Yeah, well, start seein' it different."

"Never."

The music stopped and so did Henry.

"That's the last dance I dance with you, Cecelia Romello," he promised, "to hell with this job if it's not."

The look on his face was somethin' serious, but it weren't anger no more, it were just hurt...disappointment. I couldn't bear it. I grabbed him and looked up at him, looked deep into those big blue eyes of his and I kissed him. Oh yes, I laid a kiss on him like better than I'd done that night and I didn't care if we was standing on the middle of the dance floor or not, cause I was gonna do it. And Henry didn't push me away neither. He put his arms around me and kissed me back. Even with the host rushin' over and tappin' Henry on the shoulder, he didn't budge an inch. We was gonna kiss anyways, so we was kissin' til' the kissin' was through!

"Mr. Caville!"

The host got excitable, lookin' around to the other guests who was just as shocked. The old broad he'd been dancin' with earlier was lookin' at us all dreamy, while her friends was bein' offended.

"Didn't he just dance with you?" They asked in a huff.

"Mr. Caville!" The host is calling.

I pulled away from Henry and looked towards the host with my finger waggin' in his face.

"Hey! When Cecelia Romello is kissin', nobody interrupts, see?"

Fella backed away real slow and Henry pulled my face back up to his to start kissin' on me again.

So, there was a funny thing about people and I'm gonna tell ya somethin' about em now. People didn't mess with me. They didn't mess with no Romello neither. My problem weren't people, no way. My problem always been other Romellos. The only reason why I pulled myself from Henry finally, even though he'd forgotten where we even were mid-kiss, was cause I didn't really want it gettin' back to my pops or George or any of em that I was standin' in the middle of Moxie's Tea Room in late afternoon kissin' a hoofer that the Romello clan just had roughed up. I didn't want that for Henry. He didn't deserve more torture from my family.

So, with that, I pulled away and we sat down at my table. I didn't care that all eyes were on us, it was just like the night we'd spent together all over again. He was havin' that gleam in his eye and he was leanin' his hand on his chin, just starin' at me and talkin' real close like he'd forgotten all about the chip on his shoulder.

"I like that dress," he smiled, "looks real pretty on ya."

"Awe, thanks," I answered, all shy like he made me when he was lookin' at me real focused-like.

"Did ya dress up like that just for me?" He asked.

I nodded.

"Real pretty," he said again, his eyes wide, lookin' me up and down.

"Henry, I gotta tell ya before, before you go—I didn't mean ya no harm. I really just went over to your house last night cause my pops wanted me to. He wanted us to have a nice time that's all. And I was so grateful to him, cause we did have a nice time, we had a great time actually. I wanted you to know that. If you're mad at me then don't be, cause I didn't know nothin' about what George was gonna do and that ain't me. I don't call no hits out on people. I don't start no fights or go out on no jobs. I do paperwork, Henry, that's all I've ever done for the mob is paperwork."

"Yeah, yeah alright...I believe you."

"Okay good now tell me about you bein' in pictures. You're still goin' ain't ya?"

Now this time I was all focused on him, leanin' my elbow on the table and grinnin'.

"It's nothin', I'm just gonna go try and get myself a bit part somewhere. It's some walk on role, like they call it. That's why I've been readin' those books. I'm tryin' to educate myself."

"That's swell Henry!"

"Nah, it's nothin' really," now he's gettin' shy, "I figure I'll be sweeping the floors in the studios in the beginning and sleepin' on park benches."

"Don't say that! You need mazuma? I can take care of that."

"No, I don't want nothin' from you or anybody. I pay my own way or I go without. Always have."

"No Henry, I wanna help ya. You can pay me back after—when you're a star!"

"I can't, it'd be too much pressure."

"It's no pressure at all. Just remember Henry, you gotta believe in yourself."

"That's what Bonnie keeps sayin'."

I caught my breath. He had the *nerve* to say that broads name at my table.

"Isn't that the one you're, uh, goin' out to California with?"

"Yep."

"Ah, that's fine then," I was lyin' through my teeth, "how long you known her?"

"Not long. A month maybe."

"And you're going all the way to California with her?"

My voice sounded a little more concerned than I wanted to let on, but my poker face were slippin' and I couldn't catch it for the life of me. Henry realized this and the dreamy look in his eyes changed. Mugs want ya to pretend not to care. Once ya don't, it's all you can do not to try and take it back as soon as possible. I couldn't take it back.

"What are you, my old lady or somethin'?"

"I'm just sayin'."

"Don't be sayin', when it comes to my life. It's my life, alright?"

"Yeah, okay, but are you *really* engaged to her?"

"What'd I just say?"

"Okay, okay, forget it."

Henry sat back in his chair and was playing with his napkin.

"So, where'd ya meet her?"

"Really? Twenty questions, huh?"

"I didn't mean to."

"You must think this is more than it is."

"What?"

"Listen—I gotta confession to make," he started, "and once I make it then we can stop this foolin' around."

"Foolin' around?"

"Yeah, you see, I gotta let you know because I don't really want you to be stuck on me."

"I ain't stuck on ya," I lied.

"Yes, you are," he rolled his eyes, "I see it and I'm stoppin' it right now."

"Why?" I asked, nearly crying, "why do you want to stop it?"

"Because you're a good kid, but that's all you are...just a kid. You don't understand the world and how things work for guys like me."

"How?"

"I don't have your daddy and your brothers, all the money on hand and everybody at my beckon call like you do."

"Says you."

"The real world ain't as easy as you think."

"The real world?"

"I give dancin' lessons to Bonnie. I met her in some juice joint."

"Dancin' lessons?"

"Yea, dancin' lessons."

"Oh."

I looked down.

"Yeah every Monday, Wednesday and Friday on account of she's got a Henson Brothers studio contract to be a hoofer and she couldn't dance a lick when I first met her, so we been practicing. I'm goin' with her to California to try and get me a contract too and that's that. We ain't engaged, but that's none of your business anyway."

"So, you're both gonna be sleepin' on park benches?"

"No park bench. We're gonna get an apartment."

"Wait, so, you're gonna be – together?"

"Yeah."

"Livin' together?"

"Yeah."

"But you ain't married!"

Henry smiled.

"I guess I'll have to sleep in the bathtub."

I slapped him.

"What was that for?" He asked, angry.

"Cause you're no good Henry Caville. In here kissing me—leadin' me on!"

"I never lead you on!"

"You did and you're no good for it!"

"Don't call me no good, you're no good. Don't be slappin' people! Oh, I forgot, that's the Romello way. When we say somethin' you don't like, you start hittin'."

"What?"

"Yeah, and come to think of it, you most certainly did have all to do with me gettin' my face smashed in. I didn't really know it then, but I know it now…"

"I told you I didn't. I was at my Alford College interview."

He laughed like he was better than me.

"Yeah, sure, like some college would ever let you in. What qualifications do you even have other than doin' paperwork for the mob?"

"You know what," I looked down, tears formin', "I would be alright if I never saw your face again, Henry Caville."

"And it would be just okay if I never laid eyes or lips on another Romello for as long as I live on this big round earth! You got me shook up ya know? But I gotta remember you ain't just a woman, you're Romeo Romello's daughter and cause of that ain't no real man can never have no thoughts of being with ya. I pity the next sad sap who tries to have any type of feelin's for ya. I might just warn the poor fool myself!"

Romeo Romello's daughter don't cry over no man, 'specially in the middle of the afternoon somewhere as gaudy and phony as Moxie's Tea Room, but it was what he said next that made the tears flow harder. Even then it was the way he said it, comin' from the man I'd danced with and drank with and made plans with. It was comin' from the man that I really thought I loved, but truth be told, I knew right then and there that I didn't. Maybe I was really better off without the guy. And how he knew that dumb damn song anyway, and how he had some right to sing it in the middle of Moxie's at me, I'll never know. It was the look in his eyes when he sang it, like he meant it every word and maybe like he even wrote the dumb thing hisself...

"*The Romello family deserve to die! They don't care about you or I! They steal our money and live so well! They should die in prison and rot in hell!*"

9

Being a One-Eyed Bastard

Romeo Romello was smart back in the day. He didn't believe in no banks or no stocks, which helped when the economy started crumblin'. He wanted his money in the speaks. Prohibition had done him well and he was makin' a fortune. Men like Sal Santini hired *real* accountants and men who ran his businesses for him, but pops didn't trust all that. He had me, he had his sons, and he had Jewels. He had his men who wouldn't dare put a foot wrong. All of em' were just trying to please him and feed their families. He ain't never raised em up out of poverty neither. He found mugs who didn't want no Park Avenue lifestyles, they didn't want to lead nothin'—didn't want to take his chair from him. These men just wanted enough money to eat and drink and spend on women. *Them types of men would always be loyal*, pops said, *cause they ain't ask for too much*. Yeah, Romeo was smart back in them days, but he weren't none too wise.

When it came to loansharkin' and horse bettin' and sellin' booze, he knew what he was doin' for sure...but when it came to family, *his own flesh and blood*, he was just plain stupid. Maybe it had come from the fact that he ain't never had a family before us. Maybe he shouldn't have had so many kids, maybe he couldn't handle us all. He told us he ain't never do nothing little, or small time, and that was his cross to bear. He was an orphan havin' a mess of kids to take care of when he was nothin' but a teenager hisself and a wife that didn't know nothin' about takin' care of babies. But I'll tell ya, my pops and I never had no problems when I was a girl, but we did have many when I became a woman. That's why I said that me turnin' eighteen started my real life, cause I was seein' things different and everybody around started seein' things different too.

When Romeo got off on those tax evasion charges, he ain't get all his stuff back, but didn't matter no way cause the house was transformed. It was headquarters now, with more mugs walkin' in and outta that place than I'd ever seen before. I had to lock my bedroom door on my own cause I didn't know what new goon were trampling up the steps. There'd be some big muscle stooge that Joey found sleepin' on a street corner, them *'just got outta jail'* types. It was always my job to make sure the men got paid and to keep track of who pops had workin' for him, but things changed kinda sudden. It was also my job to keep the books and make sure I let pops know when he was spending too much and on what, but that all changed too. Pretty soon there was no more books and no more lettin' Cece in on things.

'Don't worry about that Cece, we got this Cece', he'd wave me off so much that I'd have nothin' to do most days. I had nothin' to do but think of Henry out there in California somewhere. A couple of weeks gone and I hadn't heard no peep from him. Maybe he was out gettin' small bit parts where he was walkin' on and off the stage. I used all that free time to go to the pictures, spend my money in the theater, spend all my times watchin' close—eyes glued to the screen seein' if I could spot him and sometimes I did. Sometimes I seen him in the corner of the frame, I swear I seen him!

"You ain't seen him," Tony said.

"What do you know?!"

Tony'd be lookin' all smug and then he'd disappear into the Everything Room. That's when I started gettin' wise to my real place in this family. It was startin' with that Everything Room. The *everything* room, the *keep out unless you're one of us* room. It was sort of like a bunker, set deep below the house and it'd been there since I was small enough to sneak in front of the door and put my ear to it. It weren't no place for a little girl, I understood that, but I weren't no little girl no more and yet, it still weren't no place for me.

It was reserved for the big players, my pops said, the big boys, the important guys. The Everything Room was what I named it, cause it meant everything to me in them days just to be invited in. I'd waited for the day—prayed for it. *You'll be one of us one day,* pops said, *you'll be in the big meetings, don't worry.* Regina didn't like that room. She'd put a pad lock on it and make the guys warn her when they was comin'. She told me when they was all gathered in that room that they was a *little further from God.* What happened in there anyway...I was dyin' to know. I imagined a bunch of big, burly men in three-piece suits smokin' cigars and drinkin' expensive whiskey. There was this one and that one decidin' where hits were gonna go and who owed money to what cause. There had to be pictures of FBI agents on the walls with big red x's drawn on em, bulletin boards with pins creatin' pathways under banks and hidden tunnels for vaults underneath federal reserve buildings. Tables in the back with guns all pulled apart and handmade bombs and ransom notes...

My brothers, at early ages even, had been invited in. Even Tony, who I didn't think had any less of a right than I, would just brush right past me all smug. I used to ask em what was happening, who was going in and out of that place and they'd just put a finger to their

mouths sayin' *'that's confidentials Cece, that's not for us to tell'.* All
the while they'd be whisperin' and talkin' amongst themselves about
what politician *'need not be named'* kept bangin' the table tellin' our
pops he needed this hit to happen today, before the election. Don't
ask me what election, I was little. And so, they'd be negotiatin'
prices and the higher the profile—the higher the ask—the higher the
cheese. What made me angry on that day in particular weren't the
fact that Tony had walked in, but that the door hadn't been locked
yet and there was one more chair empty, I could see it from the top
of the stairs and my pops was lookin' up at me wavin' like maybe I
was getting the invite.

"Hey doll,"

Nah, *nuts*, who was taking my chair but that one eyed bastard,
that Mackie Jones.

"you look beautiful today Cece, I gotta take ya on that date I
promised ya."

"How ya holdin' up, son?" pops asked him.

"I'm fine sir, just fine,"

And with one swift slam of the door, that forbidden lock clicked
and I might as well have been on the other side of the world. How
could I be shut out for that slimy, no good son-of-a-bitch? And to
have him take my chair—the chair that was supposed to be mine
when I turned eighteen! I told ya, Romeo was smart, but none
too wise and he started gettin' dumber as soon as he started lettin'
Mackie in. And why would he let Mackie Jones in, you ask? Well
it did start with Joey's homecomin' party, the day of my eighteenth
birthday, which was when things started gettin' real rough between
me and my pops—real rough indeed.

Romeo Romello, in his infinite wisdom, had some type of impression that Mackie Jones took a bullet for Romeo Romello Jr. Sal
Santini weren't as great a shot as he claimed, so when he tried to off

my brother that day, the bullet flew the other way and it was Mackie Jones who got hit —just enough to be all messy and end up in the hospital. But the way my pops saw it was different. He ain't seen the fact that Mackie *just happened* to fly in front of the bullet, no way! He saw it as Mackie savin' the life of a true war hero and there was his special mission completed. Mackie Jones was in...all the way in.

My pops made sure Mackie was put in the best hospital room with the best doctors and nurses our money could buy. He went to visit him daily, with flowers and gifts and food. He dragged me along each time—I was surprised he didn't put a big fat bow on me the way he was passin' me off like some sorta gift! Meanwhile I'm tellin' my pops the truth, that Mackie didn't take no bullet willingly. I saw him duckin' and dodgin', but he couldn't get out the way fast enough. Mackie was as yellow as his rotten teeth, I told him, but all the talkin' in the world couldn't sway him.

'I saw him with my own eyes,' I'd say, *'and when's last time I lied to you pop? When's the last time ya couldn't believe what I was sayin' was true? That damn Mackie Jones woulda thrown me in front of the bullet if I'd have been within arms reach. It was just a wrong place wrong time sorta case. Don't do no good givin' him no heroes metal, cause he ain't no hero!'*

'He's part of the family now,' he'd answer in some sort of trance, *'it's the ultimate sign of respect that is. You come with me to see him and you be nice, okay Cecelia Marie?'*

Cecelia Marie—Cecelia Marie—that's all he called me in them days, so when the meeting was over and I heard him in the Everything Room talkin' some "Cecelia Marie," I jumped.

"Yeah pops?"

"Come in here, let me talk to ya."

There was the invite into the Everything Room, but I couldn't even enjoy it cause I was steamin' mad. It was dark inside, dark and empty, with no boards, no cigars, no naked women sittin' on the tables. It was just Pops and me and the dim of an oil lamp light. The door locked behind us, soundin' like a vault.

"You got your mother's stubborn streak," he said.

"Which mother?" I'm askin', sarcastically.

"Your real one," he replied, "Cookie."

That was the first time I'd even known what her name was. It was enough to make me sit down, all nosy.

"What was she like?"

Pops smiled and finished rollin' his cigarettes. He handed one to me.

"She had an attitude on her—tough as nails. She was a woman who didn't know no better than to mix up with a guy like me and she didn't care neither."

I hesitated to light it. Pops usually didn't like me smokin', but in this room he seemed fine with it. I took a drag and coughed my lungs out. He laughed.

"There ain't no bad feelin's no more, Cece."

"Bad feelin's?"

"Sal Santini...it was a misunderstanding...that's all."

"What? He tried to kill Junior!"

"Yeah, but he didn't kill him, did he? The fat bastard didn't even aim straight."

"That's a lie! Aim or no aim, he had every intention of comin' over and shootin' Junior. That was—what did Tony call it? Oh— premeditated, attempted murder!"

"It's a partnership between the Romellos and the Santini's. A real Romello would know that."

Pops was lookin' bold, starin' me straight in the eyes. We'd had *real* Romello talks before, but not like this.

"So, he just gets to burst through the front door of our home, try to shoot your son, and there's no bad blood?"

He shook his head.

"No bad blood."

"So, you chose Sal over Junior that's all. You chose that big fat slob over your first born— your eldest son?"

"Didn't say that."

"You don't love Junior?"

"I love him very much. I love all my kids."

"You love him so much, but you wanna see him in the ground?!"

"Listen little girl, you ain't talkin' right!"

Sometimes Pops scared me yes, and this were one of them times. His body stiffened, his eyes got all black and I trembled under his steely gaze.

"You gotta understand the position that Sal was in. We ain't talkin' sons, we're talkin' daughters. And if the roles were reversed, my daughter and his son, well I would've done the same for you," he said, "emotions that's all— it's just emotions when you got a daughter dealin' with mugs. You start fightin' different."

"You ain't like Sal. You're better than him. You're Romeo Romello. You don't settle deals like him. You don't kill no innocent. You don't go into nobody's house, you don't pull no gun on somebody's kid—"

"—*you don't know what I've done!*"

Sometimes when I was talkin' to my pops and I knew I couldn't get through no more I just stopped tryin'. Nothin' I said meant nothin' at that point. He knew I never held no gun. He knew I'd never been on no job with him. That's where I was different than my brothers and even them goons that worked for him. I couldn't relate to him like they could cause he kept me away from that side of the life so I didn't know no better. This way, I guess, I could stay innocent. I was in the mob, but I was out cause I ain't never been no trigger man. I could be his little girl and still run with the boys like he said. But none of it ain't mean nothin' to me if I weren't gettin' no respect. There weren't no point in our conversations no more, cause I couldn't add much value to him. When it came down to it, we just couldn't relate and I really wished I had fired a gun one day. Maybe then my opinion mighta meaned somethin' to him.

"I'm settin' Mackie up for a spot," pops said after a long while of keepin' our mouths shut.

"What spot? My spot?"

He ain't say nothing else, just stayed smokin' his cigarette and sippin' his drink.

"You want to give Mackie Jones my spot?" I repeated.

"I want to give Mackie Jones my daughter."

This time I'm the one shakin' my head.

"I ain't marrying him," I snapped, "and that's final."

My pop's let out this short kinda chuckle and I'd have thought he was laughin' if his expression wasn't so grim. Anger poured over him, skin turnin' beet red and fists clenching.

"You know—I put more time into you than any of them dumb cluck brothers of yours. If anybody should know where this business is headed, it's you. If anybody should know what their place in this family is, it's you!"

I couldn't believe my ears, my father, talkin' to me like some little chippy—like I really was some pro skirt he used to do business for him. Maybe that'd been his con all my life...*send a little girl in, they won't do no fightin' and carryin' on with a little girl in the room!* That's when I realized, for sure, my own pop's have been usin' me!

"Strong leader, strong team – a partnership, remember?" he'd be dronin' on, "that's what this is about. You're goin' to get married. You're goin' to have babies. You're goin' to have your duties to your family. I need to know someone I can trust put a ring on your finger and I need to know that Mackie won't fall out of line so help him God, because if so he'll have you to corral him! This is your special mission Cecelia. Do this and you'll be set for life."

"But...I don't love him."

"You *will* love him. And you're love will be for bigger and better reasons than for any silly romantic fantasies. It will be for the family —for the legacy. You will love him, and he will be good to you. I'll make sure of that."

"I thought you trusted me, thought I could handle things for you. I thought you wanted me to lead this family, maybe take over the business one day."

"Take over?" He laughed.

"Or maybe not, maybe I ain't want no top spot, but at least I could be happy that you thought of me first before any of your sons. Remember our plans for me to be high up in the organization? Me—your daughter? I was always honored that you thought I was strong enough to handle it."

"Cecelia, it ain't like I don't think you—it's not that I—listen, it's them other things you're gonna want."

"What other things?"

"Them dinner parties and fancy dresses and butlers and maids and keepin' after the house and the kids like Regina did. You're gonna want all that, a real family life, and I want a man who'll give it to you willingly."

"You've never asked me what I wanted my entire life," I said, "you just said you were groomin' me for a spot at the top of the mob, that I could have my pick at eighteen and I could be runnin' this whole place. You remember that?"

"I'm surprised you remember it."

"Surprised? It just must have meant more to me than to you, I guess.

"Cece..."

"So everything you said didn't mean a damn? They was just empty promises made to a child? A child you was hoping would get older and just forget?"

Pops looked across the room and took a drink. This time he ain't look at me.

"You think you're tough so you wanna be in it, huh? In the thick of this?"

"I am in the thick of it."

"YOU'RE NOT!"

He slammed his empty glass on the table, nearly chippin' the side, and stood up. He was grabbin' for one of the guns that Joey kept on the back table. He slid it towards me and I stopped it from fallin' clumsily with my left hand while my right was shakin' in fear.

"*Hold it!*" he ordered like I was one of them men he hired off the street.

I looked at that hunk of metal like I didn't know what it was, but I knew what it meant.

"Go ahead and hold it proper," he called out, "if you hold it wrong it might fire on accident...there you go that's it. Now—point it at me!"

"What?"

I was holding the gun, feelin' the cool body of it in my hand, still shakin' like a leaf.

"I told you to point the gun at me," he said, "you think you earned a seat at this table? You think you're in the thick of it? Go ahead, if you're so tough you shouldn't have no problems pointin' it at your father!"

I looked down at the gun and didn't even know if it was loaded or not, to be honest. My eyes met his and they were wild like flames in em or some sort of animal comin' towards me. He grabbed the chair nearest to me and sat down, inchin' his way closer til' he was so close the air tightened around us and I could feel his sweat drippin' on my arm.

"You think you want this chair, top spot?"

He took my hand in his and made me point the gun to his head, movin' closer until the barrel was up against his skin. There was an emptiness in his eyes, like emptiness washin' over somebody's soul.

"If you want a spot, at the top of the mob, then go ahead and pull that trigger right now cause that's the only way it's gonna happen. If you pull that trigger right now, I'll know you're ready and you deserve it. Even if I'm in Hell, I'll know, and you can have my blessing."

Tears were welling in my eyes and I shook my head angrily, no. I tried to wrench my hand away from his, but he held on tight and kept the gun to his forehead. He was much stronger than I was, and I know he could feel my weak, frail arm shakin' underneath his fingers still wrapped 'round my nervous wrist.

"What are you doin' this for?" I cried.

"Cause you think you're so smart and so tough. You think you know it all, huh? You know all about me and what I done and what I'm capable of doin'? You wanna talk over people and act like you don't wanna hear somebody out cause you're too damned spoiled, so well get it over with—just fuckin' pull it!"

I shook my head like I didn't know.

"Every single one of your brothers put this gun to my head and they weren't afraid, so you want to be tough as the men, then you go right ahead!"

He grabbed my drink and downed the rest in one shot, still holdin' my hand and his gun to his own head with the other hand.

"No I—"

"—no you ain't it. Until you're ready to see me die at your own hand, you won't know a damn thing about what happens, cause I won't allow it."

"But that's what this is," I cried, "this is a family and you don't do that to family. The Romello clan—we don't act like this."

"How the hell would you know? But by all means, if you really think you can do this job, stop stallin' and pull the damn trigger!"

"I won't."

"Pull it you wimp!"

Our hands fought and fought and fought until finally—the trigger went off.

Romeo's eyes bugged out of their sockets. I think I screamed louder than I'd ever screamed before, jumpin' straight outta my seat. I backed away into the corner, cryin' like a baby. We ain't heard no big bang, and nobody's ears popped. It was just one single *click*. I forced my hand away and the gun dropped onto the table. Pops smiled.

"I taught you a lesson, girlie," he said, "every single one of your brothers had the damn nerve to pull that trigger on their father's head, even Tony...and every time that gun cocked back and never fired cause it ain't never have any bullets."

"That's a dirty trick!"

"Yeah, well that's the con. At least those sons of mine had the guts to try, to call the old man's bluff. That's the difference between men and women, you're too damn emotional—sentimental. A woman at the top? It just can't be done,"

Pops wiped the sweat from his brow, and I saw a glimmer of relief in his eyes, although he tried to play it off. He held the gun in his hand with a comfortable strength, showin' off.

"Regina wanted to send you to boarding school," he continued, "she wanted to dress you in little pink frocks and make you curtsey and do ballet. She had plans with her high society friends. It was gonna be all country clubs, tea parties, beauty pagents and debutante balls. She always fit in with that group better than I,"

Pops started gettin' emotional talkin' about it.

"she wanted to have you makin' little tea sandwiches and learnin' languages—hell you'd probably know five languages by now if I'd have let her have her way. If she'd finished what she started, you'd most definitely be gettin' engaged to some Harvard grad, some governor in training. You'd be one of those women who never got their hands dirty, with her husband always takin' care of things. You'd be havin' the best of everything. You'd be one of those people that didn't give a care about people like us, never cared about the kind of trash what grow up in the slums. That's what you'd think of me as...you'd think of me as trash...as beneath you."

I stood stayed put in the corner, wipin' my eyes.

"Maybe I ain't done plenty right by you," he said, more to hisself than to me, "yeah maybe I ain't done any right by nobody."

Pops pointed his gun back towards his head and pulled the trigger. I jumped, forgettin' it was gonna click again. Then he pointed it towards the wall and pulled the trigger again. This time the barrel blew a bullet into that strong brick with a loud, unbearable ringin' sound that followed, makin' me shudder. I saw the hole it made and I turned, my eyes wide with shock. He looked down, confused at the smoking gun, and then he let out this maniacal sort of laugh that I ain't never heard from my pops and ain't never wanted to hear again. I decided right then and there that if this is what happened in the *Everything Room,* then I was better off keepin' my ass out!

10

Being Cece Romello's Defense
Attorneys

'Go West, young man!' they said and Henry had—yes he'd been changed from it. When he returned, tail between his legs, he'd landed in the worst place imaginable to lick his wounds. I couldn't believe to see my Henry after all this time in George's livin' room with the rest of my brother's swarmin' him. He'd been chewed up and spit out by that mean old California and now they'd start roastin' him every which way. They circled him like prey, they did, all while Dellafield served her infamous tea and light refreshments. The whole bachelor penthouse had been transformed by her hand, her own feminine touch, and she was just smirkin' lookin' proud comin' towards me carryin' her tray.

"He's come to ask for a job."

She winked, a smug face as if she hadn't seen his sufferin'. All she cared 'bout was her new wallpaper, the smell of fresh linens and tellin' stories of the two maids she'd fired in one day. She ordered Tony, Joey and William to wipe their feet at the door, to take their shoes off on the fur rugs and wash their hands before eating. It was some sort of success for her to be orderin' mugs around, so she'd been smilin' all afternoon.

"What job?" I asked.

She laughed, "a job with the Romellos, silly."

"Why's he want that?"

"Beats me. The man can't even hold a gun."

"What do you know about holdin' no gun?"

She raised them drawn on eyebrows and put one of them boney little arms on her hip, her bracelets clangin' from this side to the next.

"About as much as you do...dearie."

True story was that blonde bimbo, Bonnie, got engaged to some big wig in Hollywood. She left Henry to sleep in the bathtub of a motel room he couldn't afford. He grew tired of not gettin' no real acting gigs, not even little bit parts. As close as he could get to the big time was sweepin' sets that's all, just cleanin' jobs and waiterin' and them sorts of things. He had too much pride to call on me, especially knowin' the terms we'd left on. But, the poor soul had nowhere else to turn to. He'd saved enough money to get hisself back to New York. He tried to crawl over to Moxie's, but they wouldn't take him. The old apartment had new tenants. He figured the Romello's owed him that favor, for the time he didn't squeal on William. He figured we owed him that much and he mighta been right. Just a couple more nights of goin' hungry and he thought maybe the mob was the way to go.

Thing about New York in them days was if ya asked around too much about wantin' to see the Romello's, then pretty soon you'd be escorted by a couple of big goons with a knapsack over your head ready to introduce ya to em quicker than can say. George found out it were *that Caville kid*' and wanted to have real fun with him, was all. By the time I seen my poor Henry, he was beat up pretty bad and for all that I weren't gonna let him have no parts of our gang. He weren't gonna be George Romello's pinata if I had anything to do with it. That's when I rushed into the room and laid down my law!

"He ain't gettin' no job with the Romellos."

"Who says?"

"I say—"

Henry were too sweet, too innocent. He weren't gonna cut it with them mugs. He had that face, that smile, that belonged in pictures—I weren't gonna let him ruin his life.

"—and I love him, so don't argue!"

I picked up them nearly broken glasses of his and dragged him into the washroom to start cleanin' him up real good. All my brother's looked on from the other room, but weren't none of em gonna say a word about it.

"Cece, don't fall for me," Henry said lookin' all pitiful as I'm wipin' the blood off his face.

"Yeah, well, I already did so that's that."

Once I'd cleared all that mess off him, he'd been good ol' Henry again, 'cept all that was left was this look in his eyes like he'd been defeated. That dreaminess about him I always admired were gone and his skin were all sunken in like he'd lost so much weight. I'd stolen the cheese sandwich right outta William's hand and fed it to Henry. He'd eaten it so fast like it were some gourmet meal and I ordered William to make him three more.

"I'm not good enough for you," he started, mouth full of bread, "you got all those fancy clothes, that jewelry, the big house—what do I have?"

"Quit talkin' and eat," I ordered.

"No Cece, I want you to know I want those things too, see? Your pops and them, they ain't so bad. Your brothers said they'd fix me up nice, start me takin' bets all down the speaks. I can go and collect for em. They said I can start there, easy work. I'll climb up the ranks, Cece. I'll make a million and make ya plenty proud of me!"

"I'm already proud of ya. I was proud of ya when you was goin' into pictures."

"You were?"

"I looked for ya in the movies didn't I? I waited for your letters. I wanted to see you in lights cause ya wanted it so bad. I believes in ya, I always did. I was proud of ya for wantin' something more than being Romeo Romello's hood."

"Well I tried to write you a few times but, I never had nothin' good to tell you so I just – didn't. I figured no news was better than bad."

That's when Henry started tellin' me about this road, long and winding. It were dirt, wth no pavement, just hills and valleys and rock. If ya had money for a ride, ya could drive up it. But with no spinach ya had to walk, and he did walk miles from the train station, with dirt on his shoes and dust blowin' up from the ground through his hair, smackin' his face. Up that hill he swore it were worth it, cause when he made it, he saw it and he knew he belonged. At the top that hill were big white letters starin' him down, this big sign that said, *Hollywoodland*, and they was greetin' him like he was home.

"So, what if we go back? You and me? What if you try it again?"

"I ain't doing it, no I ain't doing it and I damn sure ain't luggin' you with me!"

"Don't ya love me?"

He thought for a minute then looked at the holes in his socks.

"I like you fine."

"Yeah but, do ya love me?"

"I said I like you fine."

"Oh..."

Now I start lookin' down at my own feet, but he caught my chin with his hand all gentle.

"I like you enough to come back for you, come runnin' to you. Only —I was trying to come back to you with a little somethin' to offer. A guy just doesn't start talking about love to a woman until he makes sure he's got something to offer her. Your pops wouldn't bless a marriage on the last two dollars and fifty cents it took me to get here, would he?"

"Maybe he would, maybe he wouldn't," I said, "but I don't need his or anybody's blessin' to know I love you Henry Caville. I don't need nobody's sayin' so."

That's when he kissed me and I weren't expectin' it, but his lips were nice and warm, somethin' I'd waited for since that fated day at Moxie's.

So, maybe Henry wouldn't carry no guns or make no deals. Maybe he wouldn't make other men cower in their footsteps when he walked by. But, why did he need to? Why couldn't he just stay sweet? Kind? Gentle? Why couldn't people say his name without some type of fear behind it? Maybe I wouldn't know no more power as *Cecelia Caville*. Even if he didn't make nothin' of hisself, I loved Henry and I didn't need no fancy dresses or parties or butlers or maids to keep lovin' him.

We walked back, together, hand in hand in front of the firin' squad of my brothers, pacin' round the room, just waitin' and hoverin' like vultures. They was still grinnin' til' they heard Henry were leavin' again and wouldn't stay to be their punchin' bag. They was still smart alleckin' til' they heard I was goin' with him this time too.

"Exactly how much money are you bringin' in from this little acting gig?"

That was George. He was blowin' his cigarette in Henry's face, real angry, huffin' and puffin'.

"Well—" Henry's stutterin', "well..."

"Well? How much? Go on boy spit it out!" George ordered.

"I don't quite know yet," Henry said.

"Oh he don't quite know yet boys," George laughed, "he don't quite know yet."

"He's gonna be famous," I told em, "just look him up and you'll know how well he's doin'!"

My brothers aren't payin' not a one bit of attention to me. They're jumping over themselves and interruptin' themselves, just makin' fools of themselves to get a word in.

"You gonna make my sister do some typin' or waitressin' or housekeepin' jobs?" - William

"No, of course not." - Henry

"My sister don't do no typin' or waitressin' or housekeepin'!" – Joey

"If I have to do it, I'll do it!" – Me

"Over my dead body you're doin' it!" – George

"She won't need to do it." – Henry

"She ain't gonna be out makin' your clams cause you ain't got no real payin' job." – Joey

"Henry ain't no dewdropper!" – Me

"I can get my own job back at the diner." – Henry

"Oh, now he's waitressin', I thought he was supposed to be actin'?" – William

"He had three jobs, plus his actin' out West! He ain't no slouch!" – Me

"She ain't no cook neither, don't be making her cook ya nothin'!" – George

"She ain't goin' out there to do your dirty laundry neither!" - Joey

"Pops ain't gonna stand for it." – William

"You tell pops and I'll end ya!" - Me

"Don't worry about pops, it's me ya gotta worry about!" – George

And then Tony stands up, takin' off his cheaters and pullin' at his suspenders like he's ready to talk. That was one thing about Tony that I wish I carried from him, was that he sat and he thought before he came out his mouth about somethin'. That's the only part of Tony I admired. The rest was ruined when he looked at all of us real hoity toity, with his knowin' and speakin'.

"How about the law?"

I'm rollin' my eyes and groanin.

"I ain't talking 'bout no law with you," I said.

"You let him talk!" George ordered.

And there goes Tony with still clutchin' his suspenders and pacin' in circles around us.

"First things first your eighteen. Nobody can stop love if you love what's his name–"

"–Henry," I corrected, "and I do love him."

"Yeah so ya love him, that's fine," George took a drink.

Tony continued, "yeah so, the law says you're eighteen and you have every right to leave father's house and go across state lines with him, but this is what the law also says. It says that you go out there and not be married to him, but that he doesn't have to pay a dime of that big paycheck he's...well he thinks he's going to make, *no offense*."

"You hearin' him?" George yelled.

"Yeah so? I don't need his money."

"*I would take care of you*," Henry mumbled, I could barely here.

"Yeah so this," Tony continued, "if he leaves you high and dry out there on the other side of the states, what are you going to do? What's Cece Romello's master plan for that?"

Now all their eyes were on me, lookin'.

"Henry wouldn't do that? Would ya Henry?" I asked.

Now all the eyes were on him, lookin' even harder.

"Course not," he trembled.

George took another drink and left the room.

"Look, think of things logically little sister," Tony said, "no offense included Henry, there's no hard feelings when it comes to the law. But logically speaking, you should really be looking out for number one. That means you, *Ceceliaaa*."

"Me?" I asked.

"Yeah you. We got pops now, but one false move with the police, and he's finished. You do know they're trailing him big time right now, yes? One more stint and what would you do, huh? Without his money he couldn't save you cause he couldn't even save himself. He wouldn't have not one red cent to bring you back,"

Then Tony started trailin' off into his own thoughts.

"what would we all do actually? Has anyone else thought about this?"

"Oh, now you're gettin' spooky," Joey said.

"I'm saying," Tony said.

"I don't know about your pops," Henry piped up, "but I never said I *wouldn't* marry Cece."

A glass broke and shattered from the kitchen. George ran out, makin' a beeline for Henry and grabbed his shoulders, rippin' towards him so they was inches from each other.

"You gonna marry my sister?" George was yellin' crazy.

"I – I never said I wouldn't—"

"—then you do it now!"

"George, just sit down, gonna give yourself a coronary," Tony said, "there's nothing wise about a shotgun wedding."

"No, no. You do it now, boy! You do it now, right here's as good a place as any,"

George ripped off one of his many gold rings and threw it at him, "you get down on one knee and you *do it*!"

Henry's just looking at him, I never seen him so scared. He bent down to pick the ring then turned to me. It felt like minutes he was just starin'.

"You don't gotta do that Georgie," William started.

"Yeah Georgie. You don't gotta do that," Joey said.

"Shut up!" George yelled, "he's the big man, says he's gonna marry her, I'm just givin' him a little help, that's all."

Then out came the pistol, gun cocked, metal to flesh. Henry was shakin'.

"Ya ready now?" George asked.

Henry started to lower hisself in front of me and looked up. I swear there were tears wellin' up in this man's eyes. Then the rest of my brothers clammed up too. Tony, Joey, and William, was all too lily livered when it came to George. George could put a gun to the love of my life's head without em sayin' boo. If he shot Henry dead in his penthouse that night, you think any of them Romello brother's woulda turned yella? Heck no! They would've turned a blind eye to it and kept mouths shut. I imagined all those mugs, helpin' him bury poor Henry's body upstate somewhere, while Tony paraded on the stand, defendin' George's honor.

"George, stop it!" I yelled, only one seein' sense, "he ain't gonna propose like this! Ain't nobody should be made to do it like this!"

"If he don't do it, you ain't leavin'!"

"I'm leavin' whether you like it or not and none of yous are gonna stop it! I ain't no kid no more Georgie, and I ain't need to listen to you no more like I'm one!"

George is lookin' surprised like I ain't never spoke to him like that before and truth be told, I hadn't.

"Then to hell with you both!"

George threw his gun down on the ground and it went off, the bullet lodged in his armchair. Dellafield shrieked, but only cause she'd spent weeks pickin' it out and havin' it flown from overseas. She'd been used to it all by now, my brother George and his face all bloody after comin' home from a fight. She'd been used all to the noise and chaos, the goons comin' up lookin' for revenge and gettin' more than they'd bargained for. She'd stood in there soakin' it all in, laughin' and lovin' the thrill of laughin' at me and Henry's expense. Well we weren't gonna be no trust-fund baby's thrill, I'll tell ya that much!

I screamed, "then to hell with you and all!"

I was in between Henry and George now as the veins on his neck was poppin' out. He weren't a man—he were an animal, enraged. George was tryin' to get to him while I was playin' defense, but it didn't matter. George was lowerin' his stance and voice, gettin' real calculatin' like George always did in a fight.

"Ya know, I never used to use no gun on a mug," he said, "I used to use my hands and I got to the point where I'd beat a guy so bad, I'd stop recognizin' his face—that he were even human. Pretty soon I'd forget who I was even fightin', he's be so mangled up, but by that time I'd be into it, savvy? I'd keep beatin' him til' the skin stretched off and he weren't barely breathin' no more, just cause I liked watchin' him weeze,"

Now Henry's hidin' behind me and I can feel him shakin' and sweatin'. George is grinnin' somethin' like a maniac.

"yeah, I never needed no gun...*just these hands*."

He was makin' fists and stretchin' his fingers out wide in front of his face gettin' closer. I got up as much courage as I could to stand up to my favorite brother and just cause he was my favorite didn't mean he ain't scare the hell out of me most times.

"Then—then—you'd have to beat me too, George," I stuttered, "you'd have to get through me— to get to Henry."

"Ain't no problems," he's smilin' with his great big shark teeth.

"And—I—I hope all my brothers and— and our pops are standin' round to see it."

George is inchin' closer like he really ain't believin' me. All my brother's are just watchin' and holdin' they breath.

"I ain't afraid – I hope you have to bury me like Regina," I continued, "I'd hope you bury me in all the furs—and—and the jewels it'd take for you to stop feeling guilty – guilty for the rest of your life over it!"

"George, let her go," Joey said.

"Yeah George, let her," William said.

"She'll be fine George, calm down," Tony said.

George's shakin' his head and he's runnin' round his own place lookin' stupid.

"I weren't gonna mess up my own sister, my own flesh and blood!" He yelled, "whatcha damn guys think I'm stupid? Then let her leave! She can leave! But she ain't no sister of mine no more! She can take them curtains too—that bedspread, them pink little flowery bullshit pillows—get it all out of my house!"

And then he's back, waggin' his finger in my face real close.

"When he leaves ya high and dry, don't call George Romello! Don't you even dare!"

Dellafield ran to George, but he wouldn't have none of it. He shut hisself in my room, the room he had made for me and wouldn't let her in. For all the mess it caused, I loved my family and I knew it was outta love we'd be in this type argument. George had been lovin' me all his life. He was the one that stopped Tony from whippin' my hands with a ruler when I was young, recitin' my times tables. He was the one that opened the door when that damn Joey locked me in playin', thinkin' he was funny, scarin' me with rubber spiders. He was the one who beat Mackie Jones within an inch of his life when he caught him looking at me in the bath. George been protectin' me all his life, so at end of the day I couldn't never be real scared of him, cause I knew he loved me more than anybody. He loved me even maybe more than my own Pops did, dare I say it.

I knocked on the door a couple times and it finally opened for me, but only after I promised it were only me that was comin' in and not Henry Caville too.

"I'm sorry Georgie," I said, when he finally let me talk.

"Ah, save it."

He was lookin' real weak, them lines of white powder all over the dresser and his face. It was like them nights after a fight. He sat in the dark, not to be disturbed, when he took his drugs. Who knows what he was thinking, lookin' round my room, the way it was in shambles. He'd ripped the curtains from the window and the paper off the wall. The mattress was all turned sideways and the bedspread were on the floor.

"All of em out there are lookin' at me like I'm crazy! Is it my fault I want ya with a good guy? Is it my fault I want ya with somebody that's got somethin'? What'd I say to ya all them years, huh? What'd I say about the guy I wanted for ya?"

I smiled at him cause he were my big brother, my favorite brother, and he were always gonna be.

"You said you want me to marry a guy so smart –"

"—how smart?"

"—so smart that you can tell him a math problem and he just rattles off the answer."

"Just rattles off the answer, just like that, no writin' it down or lookin' in a book—I said!"

I shrugged.

"Henry can't do that."

"Yeah well," he's huffin' and puffin' again, "ya really love the bastard, don't ya?"

"Yeah, I do," I nodded.

He tried to take hold of me, but I shook my head no and backed away. For all the love I had for Henry, I loved George too, but with George it was like ya couldn't love nobody else but him in his head. It was like lovin' somebody else meant takin' sides.

"You ain't never told nobody right?" he asked.

"No."

He sighed relief.

"It ain't right, ya know. It ain't right what I did."

"It was all kid stuff. Water under the bridge."

"It weren't kid stuff Cece."

This time he grabbed me, threw me on him in haste, and put his arms round me so I couldn't leave.

"Mom wanted us all against ya, you know? She wanted us all against ya, cause she said you weren't blood," he cried.

I was wrigglin' away, but I couldn't move,

"George stop!"

"And ya didn't look like us, you weren't no Romello, you was that colored woman's daughter,"

and he was huggin' me so tight that I was fightin' for each gasp of air,

"and so pops started lockin' your bedroom door when he found out what I'd done, but I just started lovin' ya that's all. And why couldn't I? You ain't blood. You ain't no real Romello. Why couldn't I love ya like a wife?"

"George—get off!"

That was Henry.

That's when I knew I loved Henry, really loved him, cause even when all my brothers were too lily-livered to do it, Henry weren't and he exploded through that door to grab me from George's clutches. I was safe in Henry's arms and George was all lookin' upset and guilty with hisself. I was cryin' cause George started bringin' up all that stuff, all that old business, all that stuff I didn't understand and had tried too hard to forget. All them years ago and all those kid games that weren't really made for kids, so why did I love him so much? Why he couldn't just let hisself be my favorite. Why'd he have to go bringin' up all old stuff, huh? That unlocked bedroom door didn't mean nothin' as long as I'd be trapped in New York with the rest of them mugs in my family. Maybe leavin' meant less for Henry and more for me. Maybe leavin' meant I could finally be free.

11

Being Free

Henry and Bonnie had stayed in an apartment near the famous Henson Brother Studios. Every single day Henry hung onto the gates of the massive complex, waitin' to see if there'd be work for extras. They threw him a bone a few times, a walk on role here and there, but them big wigs just never liked the look of his face. Bonnie passed by the studio, on the same days as Henry, but she was wearin' a frilly dress with her skin out. She caught the eye of the head of the studio, Vincent Henson, who very much liked the look of *her* face. They was engaged quick and Bonnie left Henry, headin' off to Vincent's house in the hills with an engagement ring on her hand. Henry was left to fend for hisself and we all know the rest of that story. This second time around in California was different. It started with the three of us gettin' a place; me, Henry and that old bastard Jewels.

Being Romeo's daughter, I couldn't just up and leave without permission. As much as my big mouth wanted to rattle off reasons why I weren't gonna tell my pops, I knew good and well that I still had to tell him and there'd be a big official meetin' about it in his *Everything Room*. Pops had to give his blessing and know where we was goin', what we was doin' when we go there, and he had to give me some money to do it. Pops wanted to make sure I was taken care of and stayin' in a safe place. He also had to send along somewhat of a chaperone—someone to watch us, hold our hands, and report back to him on the regular. Henry ain't say a word about it cause those were the rules and until he got the courage or the cabbage up to marry me, those rules would stay.

Immediately off the train, we made roots and got the sleepin' in order, *Jewels was insistin'*, and then it was my idea to reach out to Bonnie. Henry, reluctant to the plan, would have made me drag him by his ear to see her and he'd be whinin' and complainin' the whole way, only cause of pride, see? But like my pop's always said, there *'no room for pride on the way up'*, and *'no hard feelings if it's only makin' connections'*. I went solo, but only cause it was easier woman to woman, 'specially so she knew I had no hard feelings for her takin' my mans.

By the looks of her, she sure were livin' the high life on a studio executive's spinach. She had one of those witchy-nosed faces and a high-pitched squeal—I was wonderin' that she must be so good in bed, cause she weren't much of a looker, ya see? Her eyebrows were all drawn on like they do and all but hidden beneath the biggest hat I'd ever seen. It were nothin' we'd wear back in the city. I was still walkin' round in my long-knit threads and sweatin', while she looked real cool in a little number she called some jatzen suit. She had her legs crossed with her red high heels, those sunglasses pointed towards the sky and an attitude to boot. She smiled with her teeth so pearly white, with the sun's rays hittin' em just right and her body nearly glowin', with her glistenin' tan.

"Isn't it gorgeous out?" she sighed, "it's always gorgeous in California."

The café were fancier than I'd imagined and for a speak it was ritzier than what we had in the city. Bonnie had murmured a password to get us in, then ordered fresh squeezed orange juice and vodka with three ice cubes and started suckin' it down like water. Brunch was french toast with strawberries and whipped cream on top and the thickest maple syrup I ever seen. She wanted chocolate drizzle and when they brought it in a fancy silver cup, she poured it all over her plate without care. Bonnie finished her food and a whole cigarette 'fore she gave any more attentions to our conversation. She picked those cherry red manicured nails clean with a cloth napkin, just sittin' there like time moved slower for her than anybody else— like the whole day didn't mean a bean.

"I don't have to do anything anymore," she grinned, "baby takes care of me."

"That's swell, Bonnie," I'm fakin' like I cared.

"A house in the hills and a ranch in Nevada where I can go anytime and pet the horses."

"You ride em?"

"Heaven's no, they're just nice to have."

"Ya always wanted horses?"

"Well no, but I never knew I wanted them til' I could afford to have them. I love to just to look at them. You never know you want something until you have it, ya know?"

She looked at me like I was just supposed to pick up on what she was saying—like we had some sorta telepathy or female's intuition. Truth be told, female or no female, I was lost.

"I'm not sorry for what I've done to Henry. It's just business, that's what it was. He knew our fling was only temporary. He came out here to get a job, sure, but I came out to get a husband," she chuckled, "I just happened to find what I was looking for quicker than he did. By the time I told him I'd gotten him a bit part for his troubles, he was gone. Back to New York, I heard, and down in the dumps, but for what? This town's not for everyone, as Vince says. There's no shame in not being cut out for it."

"Well you ain't make it easy on him, all them jobs he took to pay his way and yours. He was just too damn tired at the end of the day to do any real actin'."

Bonnie had this snooty air about her and I'd have acted that way too, I'm sure, if I had a house in the hills, a rock on my finger the size of Wyoming and some horses just for pettin' and bettin'. She had every right, she did, yes every right to be lookin' all down her nose at me and huffin' and puffin' when I talked of what she did to Henry.

"That's the difference between men and women, I guess," she shrugged.

"What difference?"

"Well *you know*. You *have* to know,"

She was insistin', but when I kept the blank stare glued to my face she rolled her eyes and explained.

"men spoil women like us, they live for it. Yes, it's much easier for women than men."

"How many actin' jobs did you get?"

She laughed, "oh not me, I don't act, I only dance, but I let the others do that type of work now. Like I said, honey, it's much easier for women than men."

"So, what ya do these days?"

"Oh...I relax by the pool. I relax by the beach. Sometimes...I just relax."

"Sounds...relaxin'."

My eyes went all wide and she's sittin' up—gettin' defensive.

"I've earned it. The rest are just jealous."

Bonnie weren't much older than me and truth be told, I mighta been jealous too, but more so tired of goin' round and round with her all mornin', so I just came out with it.

"Will you help Henry or no? Cause he don't want no help from ya, but I'm askin' for the both of us."

She finished a whole nother' cigarette and then exhaled all the smoke, finished her fourth mimosa and ordered an omelet with the little diced ham and onions all on the side, specifically, all before she nodded at my request.

"Yeah, I'll help him."

"Thanks."

"What's in it for you?"

"Nothin'."

"Ah, give it up, you can tell me."

She's smilin' smug and winkin' and maybe it was cause Bonnie was beginnin' to like me that I could now appeal to her woman to woman. She knew I was eyein' her rock all the same.

"You know," she started, "I can set you up."

"Set me up how?"

She rolled her eyes like she couldn't believe, thinkin' I was playing coy, but I wasn't.

"There's plenty of men in this town, hordes of them. Oh yes, New York's got nothin' on this place. You like?"

She shoved her ring finger in my face, the diamond on that band glistenin' like her nail polish. Her body swayed to and fro from too many mimosas.

"Nice."

She laughed, "not just nice, my dear, extra—vagant."

"Yeah, like I said, nice."

She shook her head at me like I just weren't understandin'. She leaned in like she was tellin' me a secret that she wanted everybody else to hear.

"The ring is eighteen-carat and the wedding, oh the wedding was glorious. The honeymoon was even nicer, we were in the French Alps—three whole weeks. Then we went to visit his family, he's from England you know, and they're very *old money*. His family has a big estate near Cambridge, it's a castle! It'll all be his when that old bastard kicks off—seventy-nine I think he is—seventy-nine and he's had too many kids to count. They're all estranged, except my Vincent. The old man sits in a wheelchair with a blanket over him all day long. I met him a couple times when we visited, nice man but he's most obviously seventy-nine. Doesn't get about much, Vince says, and it shows."

"So, you'll be moving there?"

"Heavens no! Vincent loves America, he wouldn't move back to Mother England for all the money in the world, he says, but it's just another place to go, ya know? Real estate, he says, is just the best type of investment and he's so smart with his money, so saavy. I didn't think of it until I had it and now that I have it, I'm beginning to agree with him. Another drink?"

"How about Henry?"

She frowned while I were shakin' my head no to her offer of a drink, but the biggest mistake my pops and brothers made that I didn't was drinkin' while doin' business. Weren't no time for the juice when there's deals to be made, I say.

"What about him?" She asked.

"There's still a part?"

"Gotta talk to Vince baby, but I'll tell him, and set Henry up for sure. I can set you up too, if you want. You're very pretty—very pretty indeed. Why don't you let me talk to Vince? He'd like you. I'd put in a good word."

"I don't do much actin'," I said.

"What about dancing?"

This time her eyes went all wide when she said it and she musta saw some type of gleam in mine too.

"Ah, dancer," she smiled, "a dancer knows a dancer, everytime. Have another drink with me, please?"

Yeah so...I had another. But we was done doin' business.

"So, you have tell me why you want to help Henry so badly. I mean, I can set you up, like I told you, you're real pretty and I can think of five of Vincent's friends right off the bat—five of them that have houses and cars and you'd have a ring like this in a heartbeat!"

"I love Henry," I said, "that's why I'm helpin' him."

She waved me off and finished her drink.

"Love, hah! Love don't have nothing to do with anythin' dearie. I'll get Henry that bit part cause, I feel bad I really do, and I probably wouldn't have had the nerve to come out here on my own. Lots of creeps on the way here—lots of men looking at us women like we were just put on this earth to be looked at by them, ya know? But between me and you, I don't see why you bother. Take my advice— hook yourself a big fish...a *real big fish*."

"I know Henry's gonna be somethin' someday and I want to help him do it."

"Awe," she raised her glass, tipsy, and grinned this wild at me, "I need a friend like you...so sweet and so stupid—sorry, I mean naive."

Two more mimosas and not only did Henry have that bit part, but we also had a meeting with her husband and the promise of a ride on his yacht. Henry was grateful, so grateful we spent two days in bed together and runnin' round West Hollywood seein' sights and grabbin' lunches, hidin' from Jewels the best we could. But the closer and closer it came to him bein' on set, the more he'd get so nervous and stop rememberin' there was a world turnin' round him and others livin' in it.

"That's the script?"

"Yeah."

"Lemme see it."

"No!"

Henry was gettin' real testy and secretive, like all of a sudden he ain't want me to know nothin'. He laid the script upside down on the table and went to the bathroom to change 'fore curtains. I snuck a peek at them words and saw he had a few parts circled, but he didn't have a whole lotta lines and then I saw what his part was— butler three.

"Who's got three butlers?" I asked, "even my pops ain't have three butlers. Three maids maybe, but never three butlers."

He ran out the bathroom, shavin' cream still on his face, wavin' his big finger around like 'how dare I'.

"Don't be reading that," he said.

"Why not?"

"Cause, I ain't proud I'm only playing one of three butlers."

"It's okay, it's just a start," I said, still readin'.

"Well," he's lookin' real worried, "just don't crinkle it, cause I gotta give it back to em, it's on loan. All us three butlers gotta share one script, see?"

"Yeah, yeah,"

I waved him off, reading the line he circled,

"tea or...tea?"

"Don't laugh," he mumbled.

"I ain't laughin', what's it mean?"

He went on shavin'.

"Well —there's three butlers, the first two are real proper and then there's the third butler, *me*, whose not. Right there I'm supposed to be offering them tea or somethin' stronger."

"Oh, so you're the comedy?"

"Yeah I guess."

"That's nifty!"

"Why?"

"Cause everybody likes the comedy person."

"Really?"

"Yeah, you're like um, like Buster Keaton."

"I ain't no Buster Keaton."

"Yeah, well...maybe not..."

He kept shavin' and I'm readin' more, laughin' my head off, and he comes back in the room snatchin' the script from me like a damn wet blanket.

"*What's the deal?*"

"I just didn't want to be the clown, okay? I want to be a serious actor and —well that's all."

"Ah nuts!"

I started puttin' my shoes on and walkin' to the door.

"Where you going?" He asked.

"I'm comin' to the studio with ya."

"No, no—absolutely not."

"Why not?"

Now he's pleadin' he don't want me goin'.

"Listen, I came back for you didn't I? We had a great time, a real good time, these past few days, but right now, a guys gotta be on his own when he goes to work. This ain't fun okay? It's work. Besides, I ain't nobody, they wouldn't let you in for nothin'. I gotta give this script back. I don't even have a chair to sit in like the others. I got some lady that slaps makeup on me in the back room, then tells me to scram."

"Yeah, alright."

"Besides," he looks down, "I don't want you to be—"

"Be what?"

He starts grabbin' the rest of his stuff and makin' his way for the door.

"I don't want you to be disappointed in me," he said, "if I mess up."

"You ain't gonna mess up."

"Yeah, well, we'll see."

With that he was gone to work, and I knew I had to do something, so I started gettin' ready anyway cause Henry needed me. What was the point of me goin' with him out here if he weren't gonna benefit from my wheelin' and dealin'? Oh no, he needed my brains or we was both headed back for New York with our tails between our legs, and I didn't wanna hear no I told ya so's from any of my dumb cluck brothers.

"What are we doin?" Jewels asked.

He was just wakin' up from his tenth nap that day, still wipin' the sleep from his eyes, his clothes all wrinkled without a care. Too many late nights with his drinks and his cigars, just tryna get the fight to run on the radio and gettin' angry hearin' nothin' but static. He started movin' towards it like he was set to try again.

"Oh no, come on ya old coot. We're goin' to the studio."

"He don't want us goin'."

"Yeah, well, I ain't want you goin' with us neither, but I ain't have no choice, did I?"

"He ain't never gonna marry ya, if ya keep naggin' him."

"What do you know about it?"

"I know men and I know we don't like being nagged. And you the biggest nag ever lived."

"Yeah, well, what woman ever wanted to marry you?"

"All of em, but they was too much naggin' me, so I ain't never accepted no proposals!"

"Awe hush up and get your jacket on!"

When we got to them gates, I didn't know what to expect, but when I saw one guy in a guards outfit lookin' like seven kinds of stupid, I figured I could get over on him easy. We get up to this guy and he looks like he was just eatin' a sandwich, but maybe he wasn't supposed to be, so he shoves it in his pocket. The lettuce and mayo are just a drippin' down his pant leg, see I told ya—easy target.

"Can I help you?"

"Yeah we're here to see Henry Caville," I say.

I'm all flutterin' my eyelashes and talkin' real hoity toity and I got my best and most flatterin' dress on, the one that shows my gams off. He's lookin', but he's too stupid to notice, or maybe it's Jewels wrinkled up old face scowlin' behind me, so's he wouldn't dare to notice.

"Um, well, mam I can't just let you in."

"Why not?"

"Well, cause ya see, I don't know who Henry Caville is."

"Ugh, ya work here, don't you?"

"Of course!"

"Ya know about real actin' don't ya?"

"Well, yes, I guess."

"He ain't know about real actin', he's just a guard," Jewels said.

"He ain't just a guard—I know guards when I see em,"

"Me too," Jewels muttered.

"Nah, this guys it, he got director status. He knows em comin' and goin'. When they get up to his gate, he can spot em, can't ya fella?"

The guard starts puffin' his shoulders back.

"Well – yea actually I can. Ya know, I was the one who spotted Barrymore."

"Of course ya did! And when you let em in, you know if they're gonna make it or not."

"Exactly."

"Then why wouldn't you know Henry Caville? He's one of your biggest stars on this set, he's a free agent, he's butler three!"

Jewels laughed.

"Yeah but —" the guard looked confused, "butler three?"

"Yeah," Jewels said, "the funny one."

"Oh."

"You must have seen him, big brown eyes and that hair what flops from side to side, just made for pictures he is. They're callin' him the next Buster Keaton."

Now this old bastard Jewels is squintin' and laughin' so hard he's almost ruinin' my con.

"Oh yeah, yeah I did see him, I did spot him," the guard said.

"And you know he's destined for greatness he is, ain't he?"

"Of course!"

"So, would ya please let us in, sir?" I asked sweetly.

"I mean, I guess I can let ya in, but are you takin' your father too?" he asked.

Now that old Jewels starts scowlin'.

"Yeah I guess," I nodded, "he needs to use the powder room pretty badly."

"I ain't usin' no powder room," Jewels is spittin'.

Guard looks at Jewels then looks at me, then back at Jewels and then back at me. I'm smilin' so hard it's hurtin' and I can't keep up the facade much longer.

"Yeah, alright I guess," he said.

Easy as pie. When he let us in and the gate closed behind us, I felt this sort of urgency to get to Henry, but I didn't even know where he was or where to find him.

"So, what do we do now, genius? What's your next bright idea?" Jewels asked.

"Ah, shut up ya old fool, let me think."

"Ya don't even know, do ya?"

"I'd know if you'd hush up and let me think!"

I'm looking round for some sort of clue, but I'm all confused and that old man wouldn't let me think. It was my first time in a studio and all I saw was dancers and people dressed up in all sorts of wild outfits and big burly men carryin' set decorations. All this spinnin' in circles lookin' round for Henry was makin' me dizzy—throwin' off my balance. All of a sudden, in the midst of all the chaos and the runnin' round crazy in the studio, I hear yellin' and that old bastard Jewels beat me to it.

"I think we should follow that," he pointed.

The yellin' got louder and took us all the way to Henry's set pretty quick. I turned and there was this very, very big man in the director's chair bellowin', wavin' his script around. He was shoutin' towards my Henry, who was lookin' cute in his butlers outfit, but had tea spilled all over the front of it.

"When it says to spill the tea—you spill it on *them*, not you! Can't you follow the simplest direction?!"

The guy is yellin', and he's real rough talkin' and everybody's frozen in their places like he's yellin' at all of em, not just my Henry.

"You're wasting everyone's time!" The director shouts again, "let's get another guy in here, pronto! You're through butler three! I want you out and off of my set!"

"I'll try it again, I'll be better next time, I swear," Henry pleaded, "please don't fire me."

I'd never heard his voice like that, like he were a little kid, all cowerin' down to this big fat guy in a chair. For all the grief he'd given me about butler three, it was like the role was gonna make or break him now. The director stands up and he's even madder cause Henry ain't leavin'.

"You know how much it costs to film? You know what it takes to get everybody together, to keep cleaning that costume? No, of course you don't, you no talent hack! Get somebody else in here that can read, can act and can appreciate the importance of time! We don't have all this time to waste! They gotta keep splicing that film everytime ya mess up! You know what splicing does to the film, huh? It's not a moving picture anymore, cause those pictures gotta fit together and make some sorta sense!"

He looks round and then spots Jewel's, who's been leaned up against the wall with a cigarette in his hand.

"How about you," the Director askes, "can you act?"

"Who...me?" Jewels' lookin' real confused.

"Yeah you, ya speak English?"

"Maybe."

"Ah, never mind,"

He sits back down in his chair and takes a sip of his water, but I'm sure startin' to think it ain't just water the way he's shoutin'.

"let's take five, or ten! Yes, let's take ten!"

I run up to the guy on break, cause he don't look like any kinda special to me, but everybody's watchin' like I'm gonna get my head chewed off for disturbin' him.

"Excuse me sir, but I think your whole picture got some flaws."

"And just who are you?" he asked.

"I'm your audience—I'm the masses!"

"Oh yeah?"

"Yeah and another thing, you got three butlers right? And the first two are all dressed nice and neat, and so what if you leave the tea stain on Henry's—I mean on butler three's shirt. See, it's funnier my way cause that means he spilled on himself 'fore we even saw him on camera."

The directors thinkin' about it and sippin' more water, so I get closer to him cause he's hearin' me out at least. This time I'm so excited, hoverin' over his shoulder and readin' the script with him, pointin' out more stuffs I see.

"And change the *tea or tea* thing, just have him offer em tea, then when they drinks it, it's not tea it's hooch, cause he thinks that's the kind of tea their serving and sure he spilled it all on hisself earlier, cause he's already two sheets to the wind and all!"

The director finally laughs and he lets out that type laugh that I know he ain't kiddin' about. He looked at me with some type of big, surprised smile.

"What's your name?"

"Cece."

"Cece what?"

"Just Cece."

He laughed again.

"That's great, Just Cece, you want to act?"

"I'm Henry's – I mean *butler three's* coach. I don't have to act, I already got a job," I smiled.

"His mother more like. Alright well, let's roll it again, with *Just Cece's* corrections. Let's see just how bad it is," he said, "and you stay here, you stay right here. You're real pretty, you. You stand right next to me."

Henry's lookin' at me real serious and I don't know if he's mad or nothin' that I was buttin' in, but he went back and redid the scene, and everybody were laughin' cause he did such a great job with my buttin' in.

"*Just Cece*," the director smiled, "I'll remember that."

Henry looks at me and waves me in his direction. I walk over real slow like I'm in some sorts of trouble.

"You know I should slug ya for comin' here," he said in a low voice.

"But..." I smiled.

"But nothin'," he said.

Then he grabbed me and kissed me real smooth and it was all worth it I swear.

"*Who is that?*"

A man, about Jewels old age, with clothes that looked much more for sleepin' than workin' came rushin' out the door of the studio and when he walked, crowds parted and the cast stood straight. Even the director took notice and put his cigarette out on the ground. The man was important, I thought, and so I straightened Henry's piney.

"I asked, *who*, is that?"

This time he's comin' straight towards me, the tall British guy with grayin' hair.

"What's your name dahling?"

"Cece," I said.

"By jove you've got the accent, the face, that—"

When he looked at my hair, his face scrunched up like he smelled somethin' bad.

"—well that hair can be changed, but look at you! Harris!"

The director stood and rushed towards us as everyone else looked on.

"Yes sir?"

"You get this woman over the script, that new one I feel like – *To Hunt or Be Hunted*. Get her prepped and ready, that starts filming in a month or so, but I want screen tests."

"Yes sir."

He turned to leave like now it was law.

"Excuse me, sir, I ain't no actress," I called.

He turned back towards me in disbelief.

"This is the chance of a lifetime," the director said.

"Aren't you here getting extra work?" British asked.

"No, this is my guy, my Henry," I presented him in all his glory, "he's the one acting, Henry Caville—Butler Three."

"I saw that script, butler three. That was good work, good work I say," he told us, "Henry Caville—Henry Caville, I'll remember that name. Why's it so familiar? Aren't I meeting with you later? Aren't you Bonnie's friend?"

"You're Vincent? Oh, it's so nice to meet you sir," Henry stuck his hand out.

Vincent looked down at it then back without shaking it.

"Hmmm," he started, "why don't you come along too—Cece? Bonnie's told me a lot about you, now that I think of it."

He set his eyes to Jewels who was pacin' by the grub table, lickin' food off his fingers.

"Now who's that?"

Jewels couldn't answer, cause his mouth was full of potato salad. All we could hear was gurgles.

"Oh, he's nobody," I spoke up, "he's with us."

Vincent peered at him again, still inspectin' anyways.

"Yes, he is very familiar, yes *very* familiar. You bring him along too and don't be late about it!"

12

Being a Slimeball Agent

'To Hunt or Be Hunted' was a big production, with some huge type of budget set aside for it. Vince said the government wanted this picture made and they was givin' some heavy duty cabbage to the studio so's they could produce it. It was one of them pictures they wanted the whole country to see—a lesson to learn type of film. *'To Hunt or Be Hunted'* was about a two-bit mobster on his way to the top and nothin' could stop him, short of his enemies and the fuzz. It was supposed to warn folks, I guess, of the dangers of bein' somebody like me and my family.

Henry had made his plea to Vince and it were a good one. It was his sad comin' of age story, his truth—the fact that his father was a boozehound who owed money to the mob and died cause of it. He didn't go into details for sure, *thank God*, but it was enough to have Vincent strokin' that fuzzy gray beard of his and sippin' his drink, thinkin' of all the publicity. Henry made enough of a case for hisself and he was in, but where he would fit was still in question.

We'd choked down a strange dinner at the Henson's that night, caribou meat that Vince grilled hisself and more drinks mixed by Bonnie. We smoked cigars in his study and looked over slides from their recent trips. Henry sat in awe of their spacious home, with more money in antiques and collectables than he'd ever seen in his life. Jewels and I yearned for meatballs in sauce and weren't too impressed by the money ourselves, cause we was thinkin' just how much taxes he would pay for it all. Jewels and Vince paired off, as so did Bonnie and myself, all hoverin' round poor Henry who sat at the foot of the dining table while we stared on. He waited and we talked, all mullin' over his future in the Henson Brothers studio. For nearly a month, two goons who knew nothin' about makin' movies, *Jewels and myself*, attempted to carve out some type of actin' role for Henry Caville.

First, he was gonna be a g-man extra, gonna give him a crew cut hairstyle and make him look like a gentleman. Then Vince said no—he wanted to keep his hair floppy and slick it back with some oil. He liked that look for a mobster, so pretty soon Henry was playin' one of the goons with one or two lines and a toy gun to run around with. Far as he told me, Henry just wanted a speakin' part and he would be fine with it, but I couldn't take that. So, we kept workin' til' we was hammerin' out a deal of a lifetime—that maybe, *just maybe*, Henson Brother's might take the chance on a newcomer and give him the lead, but it was a long shot. It would probably take a few more dinners, winin' and dinin' with the Henson's and some shoppin' trips with Bonnie 'fore good ol' Vince would give in. They liked the sound of newbie's makin' debuts in pictures, but Henry just couldn't get his act together enough, regardless what kind of yarns Jewels and I tried to spin.

Screen test after screen test he'd blow it. *Didn't photograph well,* they said—those big wigs in Hollywood. He *didn't move well on camera* either, they told him. *Not very believable as a mug,* they said. Lucky enough Vince liked us quite a bit and his late brother had been named Henry, so maybe he thought it was some sort of fate to give my Henry a try, but we could only go on fate, hunches and dinners for just so long. Pretty soon Henry Caville would have to come with some talent in his pinky. Truth be told, Henry weren't a very good actor, but he were cute and he were mine, so maybe he'd survive in that town on those qualifications alone, so's long as he had me with him.

"Boy's got to get himself an agent," Vince said one night over another caribou dinner.

"That's all?" I asked.

"That's all. And they're a dime a dozen out there, so be careful."

"What—a lotta slimeballs?" I asked.

"Yes Cece," Vince laughed, "there's a lot of slimeballs. You've got to know the difference."

"Oh, trust me, I know."

Now I'd been interviewin' mugs for my pops organization for years. He taught me real slick. I knew how to separate a slimeball from a professional, no problem. But a few days of lookin' and searchin' and I came up with zilch.

Of course it had to be Jewels who did it first. That old bastard beat me to it and found one and he ain't even been tryin'. Jewels, the one who'd made fun of Henry day and night as he tried to learn lines and run scripts and comb his hair this way and that. Jewels, the one who'd talked like he didn't believe in Henry, like he'd just wanted the free steak dinners on Vince's dime and all the talkin' 'bout old times like old men like to do, and one false move from them studio heads, Jewels warned we'd all be back in New York and he'd been itchin' to do so. *Still couldn't hear the fights right on that old radio*, he'd complain. *Good luck Vince likes goin' to the dog track*, he'd say. Good thing he met a pal like Vincent, he'd warn, or he'd be back to the East and couldn't come back without me cause, well, what would pops say? But for all that tough talk, it was Jewels who'd stuck his neck out to help my Henry.

"I got ya somethin,"

He's lookin' all proud of hisself, standin' in the apartment eating peanuts, throwin' the shells on the floor like an animal.

"Jewels, whatd'ya do?"

There was a man in our kitchen, all tied up in a chair and gagged. He was lookin' confused and squirmin' round for his life.

"I was helpin' ya," he said while he was chewin', "Henry needs an agent, Vince said so, and you were comin' up a whole bunch a nothin', so I had to find,"

The guy's still squirmin'.

"this fella's an agent and all."

Jewels and I hadn't had no conversations since comin' out West about leavin' our past behind us, but I figured maybe it was time to, especially now that he had an agent tied up in our kitchen. Yes, he was a professional con man. Yes, he had bumped up against the odd body or two walkin' the streets and I did find some empty wallets of people I didn't know and didn't ask about sittin' on the coffee table, but this was different. It weren't no taking bets and lettin' old fools like Vince Henson lose their money playin' casino. It weren't no lettin' Bonnie's purse lean over and takin' a fin or two. This was different, this was serious. This was kidnappin' and weren't no Tony here to tell us no California law, but I just knew we'd swing for it!

I said, "now what gives you the right to tie this man up? What gives you the right, I say? Why can't ya do anything doggoned normal?"

"Ah, I thought you'd be thrilled. Shoulda known, yous a woman. Ya ain't never been thrilled a day in your life! All ya do is nag, nag, nag. Need an agent, can't find no agent, nag, nag, nag, so I find ya an agent and what ya do? Ya nag, nag, naggin' still!"

That old man's really standin' there all sauced, gettin' angry that I'm readin' him the riot act 'bout this.

"What if Henry was here? What if he weren't at his screen test? What would he think?"

I pointed to this guy still squirmin' and sweatin'. Jewels shrugged his shoulders and finished eatin' his peanuts.

"Henry's a ninny. That's his eighth screen test in two weeks. Hell, good old Vince even offered me a part in that dumb damn movie, and I passed mine just like that."

"Henry's not a ninny and I'd pass too if all the actin' I had to do was chewin' tobacca and bein' my old bastard self, wearin' the same old shoes I come in with cause I had years of playin' con!"

Jewels puffed his chest out.

"This guys cream of the crop," he said, "Henry weren't gonna get no top agent any other way. Not failin' screen tests, he ain't. He were gonna get some guy what sleeps on park benches or somebody you found down the flophouses, but this guy, he's the real deal."

"Hmm...never thought of checkin' flophouses."

"And you ain't never checkin' flophouses, not while I'm down here with ya."

"Oh really?"

"Yeah really!"

I'm lookin' this guy up and down as he's squirmin' and he's all kinds of cute and well dressed and groomed. So *cream of the crop* he said, okay well maybe he had some type of point. I let Jewels continue his story.

"So I saw him travelin' round with some big players, ya know? I trailed him for days, I did. Lots of work I did. Spotted him down the tracks and it was fate. Heard him sayin' he was packin' his bags, gonna take a trip out to Raleigh. Had to pounce on him then, didn't I? Had to strike while the iron was hot!"

Sometimes Jewels did have a point.

"Ah, that's real swell of ya,"

I took the socks from out the guys mouth. He sighed relief.

"I'm Cece, nice to meet ya."

"Nice to meet me?" Guy's huffin' and puffin', "untie me! Untie me right now!"

"Not so fast," Jewels said and he pointed a peanut in his face, "you won't run away now won't you? If I unties ya? And ya won't do nothin' like try and slug me like ya did earlier, right?"

Guy's lookin' mad like he's gonna spit in Jewels face and I'm just smilin' waitin' for it.

"You won't take that pistol out on me like ya did earlier, right?" he mocked.

"Nah, nothin' doin'," Jewels answered, "I just wanted you and Cece to be able to get to know each other, that's all. Maybe you get to know each other for a time and then I'll unite ya, deal?"

The man looked up at me like maybe I was gonna help him, but Jewels and I stayed stood hoverin' over him with identical expressions. Now 'fore ya start gettin' on me too like Jewels did wrong and maybe I should have let him go, the thing about it was yes I wanted to help Henry and Jewels were right, he weren't gonna get no cream of the crop agent no type of other way then this. We'd done a lot for my Henry to get him where he needed to be by that time, but this was the next thing, yeah? Good ol' Vince, head of Henson Brother's Studio said our Henry needed an agent so that's exactly what we was gonna do. It was just business, ya know? Nothin' personal. No pride in business.

"Maybe I'll call the authorities," the man started.

"Yeah? Maybe I'll break your legs," Jewels said, real calm like.

"He ain't gonna break em'," I assured.

"Cece, he been following us too, I forgot to mention."

"What?"

"He been followin' us all around—me and Vince while we was at the tracks and we was wonderin' why we was being followed."

"Why was ya followin' em?"

"I don't have to answer to either of you."

"Yeah well maybe he'll break your legs then you'll answer," I got right in his pretty face.

He started squirmin' again.

"We heard you callin' in to the studio sayin' you's an agent," Jewels said, "did I get that correct or was you some type of *other agent* I should know about?"

Now the guy's back trackin'—less squirmin' and more back peddlin' in his talkin'.

"The studio? Yes, I am an agent, a – oh yes I'm a talent agent – and that's why I was, uh, following you."

"Good that's what I thought, you're lucky cause I was gonna break your legs for followin' us or maybe better yet just put a bullet in ya, but good ol' Vince said I shouldn't put a bullet in ya, maybe just break your legs. Break your legs, then hear ya out. Maybe you'd be good for Henry and all. Henry needs a good agent."

"You weren't gonna put no bullet in him and ya weren't gonna break his legs," I said.

"You ain't my mother," Jewels said.

"Where am I?" Guys askin'.

Jewel's patted him on the back like it were all in the past.

"You're in the deal of a lifetime—go on, you kids talk business and then we'll untie ya, okay? Just as sure as we got some type of agent for Henry Caville so I can stop hearin' agent this and that, savvy? I'll be in that next room, Cece, just the next room over if ya need."

He looked at fella like it was a warnin' and slinked his old self over to his newspaper and then we heard static, like he was tryin' that radio again.

"Sorry to meet like this, he ain't mean nothin' by it, he's just an old fool is all. No manners where he comes from."

I looked at the guys legs, all cramped against the chair uncomfortable like. He was much taller than he seemed, with a real strong build. No wonder Jewels looked proud of hisself, a man of his age tyin' this guy up with all his muscles. Confusin' really, why a guy like that would have willingly been tied up by the likes of Jewels. Jewels musta been tougher than I thought, I was sure of it.

"Want somethin' to drink?" I asked.

He shook his head no.

"You sure? Ya hungry? I can whip up some eggs for ya."

"Your friend forces me here by gun point, ties me up and puts his old dirty socks in my mouth, and then you offer to make me some eggs?"

"Yea, ya want some?"

Guys lookin' at me in disbelief, but I weren't gonna let him go hungry. I weren't into no torture and starvation of men. Couldn't never bear them guys bein' tied up and waterboarded, couldn't never see it—always had to cover my eyes and look away. Guy finally gave in cause his stomach was rumblin'.

"Ya know what, yeah sure, what the hell."

"What's your name?" I asked.

"Why?"

"Cause you know mine, so how's about I know yours? It's only polite."

He's shakin' his head again and sighin'.

"I'm Raphael."

"Then just stay there Raph, I'll have them eggs done in a minute."

"It's *Raphael*."

"So what? I like Raph, so 'll call ya Raph. Want a little coffee?"

"No."

"You sure?"

It was percolatin' and smellin' the kitchen all up, so his stomach started growlin' again.

"Fine."

"Good," I smiled.

"I'll take some eggs too and maybe some bacon while them pots are clangin'," Jewels said from the other room.

"Who asked you old man?"

"She must like ya Raph-e-elle, cause that's the most non-cookin' woman I ever seen in my life," he said, "she ain't even cook for Henry, I'll bet."

"Ah blow it!" I'm sayin', "don't listen to that old fool, he's crazy!"

Raph started smilin' at me all sly and now my face were all red, cause yes maybe I did like him a little. But if anybody were to see him, they'd have understood why. He had this strong, handsome face and these light brown eyes that I just got lost in. His skin was a milk chocolate hue, with his hair a low military-style crew cut and the way he looked at me, well, it made me kinda wish he'd look at me more often.

"Maybe I should loosen them ropes."

"Maybe?"

"If I do, you gonna run?"

"Not from a beautiful woman making me breakfast," he smiled again.

I reached over and untied his hands. That bastard Jewels did a tight knot, some sorta figure eight on him, the type that he weren't gettin' out of too easy. It were funny how I didn't do nothing but unloosen it a bit and Raph were out, his hands on the table reachin' for his knife and fork real easy. I got real nervous when he was outta them ropes so quick, like he might wanna touch me or somethin' and I was waitin'.

"So, you're an agent, right?"

"Right."

"Well my friend's in need of one of them and all, but it seems all you agents talk is a bunch of hooey."

"The old man said he was your steady."

"Yeah, that's what I said, my boyfriend Henry."

"You didn't say boyfriend. You said friend."

"Well—"

"—I'm just kidding with you, calm down," he said, "why are you so nervous now? You're the one who kidnapped me, remember?"

I'm breathin' all heavy and I don't know why cause Romeo Romello's daughter don't breathe heavy for no man, so why was I doin' it? He kept on talkin' and his voice was real smooth like butter on bread, I swear it.

"Agents are all different, with different styles and so's mine. My approach is unique."

"Like stalkin' people?"

"No, not stalking, not even following—"

"So why *was* you followin' us? Why didn't ya just ask us outright?"

"Well, I was going to, but I thought – well you don't just go up to Vincent Henson of Henson Brothers Studio and tap him on the shoulder. And I saw you all together all the time, I assumed you already had representation."

"Representation...what's that?"

"It's when somebody's gettin' jobs for ya," Jewels interrupted.

"Yeah okay, well we're talkin' here, so *butt out*," I snapped, handin' Raph his cup.

"He's right. I thought that there was already a contract—no milk or sugar I'll drink it straight, thanks."

No other man that I knew cept' my father, *tough as nails*, drank his coffee black. I liked him more. Well maybe that Jewels drank it black too, but his taste buds left him years ago, so he didn't count.

"No contract, not yet, and the way I sees it, Henry deserves that main part, ya know? Nothin' less than the main."

"Oh, you misunderstand, I was thinking for you."

"Me? Oh no, not me no, we're talkin' bout for Henry. Henry Caville."

Jewels piped up, "Raph, let her know she could have a part. Good ol' Vince already wants her in that film. Good ol' Vince likes the look and shape of her."

"Good ol' Vince has good taste,"

Raphael smiled this sly smile. *I didn't know if we was talkin' pictures no more, saavy?*

"We're talkin' Henry," I assured.

He toyed with his coffee cup, "I can try and help him. I'm already representing another member of the cast. She's a lead."

"Go on and tell her—tell her who it is," Jewels ordered, "Cece you'll be proud when he tells ya."

I handed Raph his eggs and he lifted the fork to his mouth like he ain't eaten in days. I liked to watch him eat, he had such strong hands holdin' his fork. He barely breathed between bites, but enough to utter the name.

"Jane Pearl."

"See, I told ya he's the real deal. Cream of the crop I told ya," Jewels shouted.

"Jane Pearl? From the silent pictures?" I asked.

"Yeah and with that voice of hers, I'm surprised they let her in the talkies. She's old hat," Jewels said, "Cece you could have that part soon as lookin'."

"I ain't want that part and don't be talkin' about her like that. Jane Pearl's Hollywood royalty!"

"Ah fooey,"

Jewels come into the kitchen and was standin' over Raph like he was gonna start threatenin'. Raph looked up.

"yeah I bet an agent could get Cece a lead role—just like that."

"You mean Henry?" He asked, not breakin' a sweat.

"Yeah, yeah I meant Henry, that dumb cluck Henry," Jewels corrected.

"Sure," Raph shrugged, "if he's any good."

Jewels clicked his finger in Raph's ear, but the guy didn't flinch.

"Good is subjective. Just like I have a good feeling, a real good and strong feeling that you's can help us," Jewels answered, "and if Henry needs help in the actin' department, well just maybe you can help with that too."

Now I knew and Raph knew there was a switchblade at his back, but I'd had enough of that cause there come to a point where I didn't want to play them type games no more. I left that life for a reason. Hollywood weren't like that, ya know? And if I couldn't convince Raph of representin' Henry on his own merits, then I didn't want no representin' for Henry, cause that type of business weren't right. Maybe in the old days it were all threatenin' this one and that one, but I couldn't stand by and let him put a knife to Raph's big strong back. I saw Raph, not even flinchin' just eatin' his eggs, not scared of no switchblade or some old bastard Jewels. Henry would have been tremblin' in fear, I just know it, but that Raph, *that Raphael*, he were just sittin' sippin' his coffee and eatin' his food, tough as nails. I liked him more, I swear it.

"Untie his legs,"

Jewels is lookin' at me all confused and then I'm shoutin', *"that's an order!"*

All my life Jewels been forgettin' who's a real Romello and who's just acquainted. Yes, he raised me. Yes, he was Romeo's right hand, but at the end of the day I were blood. I was Romeo's seed and Jewels had no choice but to answer to me. I'd never used that fact against him before, but this time I felt I need to, and his eyes told the story of what he knew to be true. Jewels cut his rope and now Raphael was sittin', enjoyin' his breakfast a free man, stretchin' his feet out on the floor, showin' that he was taller than tall.

"So now I know who's runnin' things," Raph teased.

"I think we should talk—just you and me," I said, "about Henry's future representation."

"Or yours," he said.

And that's when that Raph was lookin' at me all googly-eyed like them men down the speaks and even Henry hadn't looked at me like that in a while. It was like respect almost, respect that women never got no way. He didn't even know I was a Romello, but he respected me. He took a fork full of egg and put it towards me. I ate it real slow, smilin' back.

"Ah fooey," Jewels grumbled, turnin' away all mad cause he knew he couldn't stay.

Raph and I carved a deal, a good deal, and it took some convincin' but who was convincin' who was the question. It was one of them deals, like my pops called it, in a way only a pretty woman could really get the point across and Raph let me keep tryin' and tryin'. He held out for a while, *oh yes he did*, and he was a very good sport about it, he really was.

By the end of our day, Raph was convinced that Henry Caville was the next big thing and that he could make him a star. He told me he would see about gettin' him a lead part. I was also convinced that maybe I ain't want to marry Henry Caville no more, cause how I was gonna get all tied down with a marriage when there was men like Raph out in the world and I ain't even know it!

13

Being Hunted in Hollywood

That good ol' Vince Henson had an *'Everything Room'* in Henson Brothers Studio. It was a place where them big studio fat heads could run around slantin' glossies of promisin' young stars and starlets. They'd be smokin' their expensive cigars, drinkin' giggle juice on a mission for who's goin' where and who's goin' nowhere. They wore cream colored waistcoats with matchin' jackets draped over chairs and their panama hats, with their shiny shoes pacin' around the table. More hollerin' and carryin' on happened in that room than probably my pops and his clan could ever dream of and these palookas was just makin' a movin' picture! They weren't carryin' out no hits or gettin' no dock deliveries or plannin' no soup jobs—no they was just talkin' how this one and that one looked in the face and was a payin' audience gonna like em'?

I would laugh when I heard Vince for the first time talkin' like that's how deals was done and I ain't say nothin' about it to him, but *I knew deals,* real wheelin' and dealin' and these weren't real to me. What I liked about the pictures were it was all make believe, ya know? It was like dreamin' and that's what brought me to start likin' it. I was even likin' it enough to take them glamour shots with Raph.

He really ain't have to twist my arm, we just did it. When I seen my face all done up and painted professional, I really couldn't believe it was me. My tanned skin and hazel curls was comin' off well in black and white glossies—eight and a half by eleven frame. So much so, that I ain't even recognize myself. I'd taken pictures before yes, years before with the family and I was always hidden in the corner or squeezed in between taller folks. Even when the newspapers snapped pictures I didn't look clear, I was all blurry and washed out with my bleach blonde hair lookin' fake. Nobody back home woulda ever recognized me now, cause I ain't look like the Cecelia Romello they knew, no sir!

That's when one day Vince told me it was my picture in that pile of pictures they'd be decidin' on and don't tell me how my headshot got itself into that room. Maybe it were Jewels, that sneaky bastard, cause he were the one goin' on and on about that shot for days like I just needed to be on film. I must confess I thought it would be worth it for pops and my brothers back home to see how well we were all doin', so I liked the idea of all three of us bein' in a mob movie. And yes, Jewels was still gonna be on camera but just a small bit part. He'd be leanin' on a street corner goin' '*huh?*', but he didn't care what he said—he'd still make a fin for it.

"You look beautiful,"

That was Raph standin' and gazin' them eyes and he'd told me I was the most beautiful woman in the world a hundred times since we met and I ain't never been tired of it. For all the nervous I was standin' around waitin' for them big men to judge my face in a sea of faces, Raph had no doubts of what they would say. When good ol' Vince finally came outta that meetin' with my picture in his hand, he had a smile on his face big as life and it weren't no put on. It was one of them smiles what ya try to stop smilin', but your face won't let ya.

"Henson Brothers Studio presenting... Cece...in her debut picture!"

From then on it was all toastin' champagne and funny cigarettes bein' passed around in our excitement. Bonnie wanted me with her friends, sayin' I'd be in pictures. Vince wanted me learnin' lines. Raph wanted me goin' to dinners with him, signin' contracts. Jewels wanted all our gang back home to know when they could go to the pictures and see Cece's face on the screen. The one person I'd hoped would be prouder than ever of me and joinin' in our little celebration was Henry and I just wanted to see him and hug him and tell him I'd made it.

"Kiss me!"

I was grabbin' his hands and gettin' up real close to him, almost on my tippy toes, tryna steal a kiss. Henry found hisself a little corner to stand in with his champagne glass half full and that stem nearly broken 'neath his fingertips from pressin' so hard. He turned his face from mine quick as he could, fakin' like he were allergic.

"What's wrong?" I'm askin.

He had his mouth all turned down with his bottom lip poked out, showin' the biggest pout I ever seen on a full-grown man, I swear it!

"Sometimes a guy just don't want to kiss, see? Don't make some federal case of it!"

"Yeah, alright."

"And don't give me those eyes!"

"What eyes?"

"Those crazy eyes ya give me. How do you expect a fella to wanna kiss ya when you're givin' him those crazy eyes?"

"I thought ya liked my eyes? Ya liked em before!"

"Yeah well, maybe that was before all this."

"Before what?"

I tried to kiss him again, but this time he raised a hand and it ain't connect with my face but if it did—there was gonna be a whole East coast gonna hear about it! He lowered it slowly.

"Before I pinned you for a snake."

Henry Caville knew, even in them times, that he could say things that hurt me and for as much as Raph was callin' me beautiful and them studio heads were sayin' it too, Henry's words meant more. And why he'd say it then, when they was all lookin' for me to be one of them majors, not a lead, but with a important part with lot of lines and only a few weeks to learn and lots of rehearsing to do it in. Why'd he say it when he knew I was nervous as all hell? And who was he to say it? What right did he have, *callin' me a snake*, after all I'd done to help him! You'd think he'd talk a little different to the so-called love of his life. As a Romello, I was taught from an early age that all we've got is our word in this life, and if we don't go on our word, then we ain't mean much and I was nothin' if not a woman of honor. I weren't no snake and if my pops ever heard him talkin' like that, he'd have heard an earful from a double barrel shotgun, ya better believe it!

"Snake?!" I'm yellin'.

"Yeah, snake!"

Fact of the matter was it were just jealousy, that's all. He was just jealous cause there was another glossy picture bein' talked over in that *'Everything Room'* of Henson's and it weren't gettin' the same warm welcome that mine got. Henry Caville failed screen test after screen test, but he'd had plenty of walk on roles to practice, just like when he got the audience laughin' playin' butler three. He'd had a few speakin' parts where he played some type of cab driver or waiter or just somebody with a couple few lines here and there. His face had been on the screen whereas mine hadn't even hit celluloid yet and I don't know who he thought got him them roles with all my talkin' and manipulatin' and pipin' him up, but I guess it were that old snake in the grass Cece!

Vince told me they didn't like Henry, them big guys in fancy suits. They didn't like his face, it were too pitiful. They didn't like his voice, too whiny, and not tough enough. He walked on his toes, they said. Why's his hair so floppy, they asked. Why'd he squint on camera, couldn't he see? He wore glasses in real life, but couldn't he fake it? Worse than anything else, he started gettin' mean to everybody. Worse than anything else, he started on the booze like his old man.

"And if you'd lay off the sauce—" Jewels would say.

"Ah, blow it out your ears!" He'd answer.

Then they'd get into it too, that Jewels and my Henry. I'd witnessed so many arguin' matches in the apartment that'd just go on for hours. Henry would ruffle some feathers with his tough talk, gettin' in Jewels face, but all that old goon had to do was cock his gun and warn he'd be playin' target practice with my Henry's head to get him to stop. Henry would scream, scared, hidin' behind dressers and lamps and chairs, just wakin' up the whole apartment buildin' with his yellin'.

"Shoulda never let her rope me into this one! Shoulda called it quits when they said we had to bring you, ya dried up old prune!"

"You're a boozehound, just like your old man! Ain't no good, I told em, ain't no Caville that were any good!"

Jewels would report all our drama back to pops, you better believe it and Henry'd say he didn't care what no mob boss had to feel about it—no guy what gave his father the bump off. But it started gettin' to Henry, the drinkin', and I don't know what type penny hooch he was findin', but pretty soon he weren't even showin' up to work. Good ol' Vince started phonin' up askin' where he was and why he couldn't make it here and there, makin' us all look bad.

Raph tried, but even he'd had enough of him, so he set his sights on me full time—which Henry didn't like no way neither. Raph started becomin' my rock and all, 'specially when things were gettin' harder with me and Henry. I tried in those days, I really did, but he weren't makin' it easy showin' up on sets drunk or makin' a fool of hisself out in town.

The one person that saved him and to this day, Lord is my witness, I couldn't tell ya why and probably Henry couldn't either, was Jane Pearl. Jane Pearl, the one they'd taken straight from silent pictures to star as lead in her first talkie and carry the heavy behind her name— it was she who set her sights on Henry soon as lookin'. Then she'd throw her weight around the studio, tellin' Vince Henson and the boys that she wanted Henry. *Wanted him for what*, he asked, and *never you mind*, she answered. I ain't too clear on what happened next, I just know she took my Henry on a trip, ya see? It was a week that they was gone, and then they come back sayin' he'd swear off the booze, he had a new agent and then that Jane Pearl's insistin' he stars lead with her in *'To Hunt or Be Hunted'*.

Now Vince weren't really havin' it at first, cause it was his film, but she's all talkin' like it's hers, like she's leadin' things. Now I didn't know nothin' about films, but I knew about organizations and the chain of command, but maybe Jane Pearl didn't. Not no-body liked the idea of Henry leadin' the film, *not even me*, and he had a bad reputation in tinsel town already, so there weren't really much of a case. Would it be so bad if Jane Pearl walked, Vince asked, and at the end of their meeting they'd found that yes, it would. It would be real bad for them and the investors. It would be real bad for the picture and that payin' audience. The lesser of two evils was to put Henry's ugly mug up in the movies, Vince decided. They'd slap a lot of makeup on and maybe that character would have less lines than usual. Maybe the promotional stills would come out and maybe the ladies wouldn't think he were too unfortunate lookin', Vince said, yeah maybe it might work and all. I was happy for Henry when I found he was makin' the lead, I just weren't too happy that Jane Pearl got her mitts on him, just when he was comin' off the booze. I also weren't too happy about his new agent, a *real slimeball*, and for as much as Raph weren't no slime, this Louie fella was double!

Louie, Louie, Louie, that was his name, Louie Harris. He were a rotten bastard, but Henry Caville didn't know no better. He didn't grow up spottin' frauds like I could, and his pops didn't teach him neither. We all tried to tell him, to warn him, but he stuck his nose up at all of us and all we heard was Louie this, Louie that—Louie hell! He'd wine and dine Henry, he would, and sometimes I'd tag along for support, but them days was few and far between. It was during them times when Henry found he was thinkin' of bein' sweet on me again and makin' amends, which was confusin'.

Louie took us to a real ritzy restaurant on the beach, force fed Henry caviar and eels, with his big fat lips a flappin' while Henry soaked up every single word like they was law. Now my brother was a lawyer, so I knew law and Louie weren't talkin' no law. By this time too I had an agent of my own, Raph, and he ain't never fed me no bullshit like I was hearin' that night comin' from the mouth of Louie. He was spewin' poison, he was, but Henry took it like Louie was some sort of guru, so I just kept my mouth shut. I did the same growin' up when pops would drag me to them fortune tellers lettin' em damn near run his businesses with their mystical advice he took as gold. I learned at an early age when men were talkin' crazy with others actually listenin' to it, just be quiet and eat my soup.

"You ain't talked much," Henry said.

"For a woman! Maybe she ain't no real woman," Louie laughed, "I'm jokin' with her—gotta relax little lady—now what part you playin' again? Brown-Eyed Waitress?"

Louie was loud, rude and wrong. He were one of them men what wore expensive suits on loan and smoked half the cigarette, then put it out and stuck the rest in his pocket for later, cheap bastard. He were the fella who went out to eat for a big lavish meal, then stuffed the rolls in his pockets and asked for the other table's leftovers. He had a big, bravado type attitude and pops always warned me about those types, ya know? He warned me of the type of guy who wants to be seen without earnin' nothin' to be seen for. That was Louie and if my pops met him he woulda spit in his eye soon as lookin'.

"What's your problem?" Henry asked when we was alone.

I'm crunchin' crackers into my soup and shruggin' my shoulders, just keepin' to myself.

"I don't got no problems."

"That's a lie. You're acting sore, so spill it."

"Nah, I ain't sore, I just don't like him."

"You don't like Louie?"

His eyes went all wide like he weren't really payin' attention to the expressions on my face for thirty minutes.

"No, can't ya tell?"

"No, I thought you was just bein' rude—just plain rude cause he ain't your precious Raphael."

Then Henry's all besides hisself and puffin' his shoulders out all jealous. I gotta admit one thing, one small little thing that I ain't too proud of, cause it was during a time when Henry and I was tryin' to patch things up and all. Yes, he did caught me kissin' on Raph, but it were only a little kiss and it was one of them celebratory things, ya know? Nothin' serious, savvy?

"You stuck on him?" Henry asked.

"Course not!"

"You still a cherry and all?"

"Yes Henry of course," I said, "and why you talkin' like a goon now? You may be playin' a thug, but you sure don't gotta talk like one on the daily."

"You talk like one too, maybe it's from hangin' around you all these months. You and that old man ya brought with us. Why'd he have to come anyway?"

"Cause you wouldn't marry me."

"Oh yes, precious Romeo Romello and his rules. One rule for his daughter, one for the rest of the world."

"At least my pops gives a damn about me."

"My pops gave a damn about me too! You didn't know my pops! I'm tired of you keep bringin' him up!"

"Didn't have to know him to know about him, trust me."

Then it's Louie comin' back to the table and Henry and I are both stewin' and as much as I didn't want to see no Louie again, he caught us right in the middle of what mighta been a big embarrassin' fight—so I was glad to be interrupted.

"You gonna eat that?"

Louie points to my pork chop with his big fat finger.

"No," I snapped.

"Good ya don't need the calories,"

Now he's reachin' over and grabbin', chompin' on the bone real rude. Low class he was, just low class.

"it's easier for women than men in this town,"

Louie's sayin' with his mouth all full.

"truth is it ain't so much to be pretty for men, men gotta be good performers too."

"What's that supposed to mean?" I asked.

Louie is laughin' and carryin' on and I'm just wishin' he'd choke on his meat.

"I'm just saying–"

"—yeah he's just sayin' so don't be sore at him," Henry said, "he knows the way and he's tellin' the truth, you just don't want to hear it."

Now I'm eatin' faster, cause with every bite I ain't sayin' what I want to say. I'm workin' on keepin' my mouth shut and all, but Henry ain't satisfied with all that. He wants to bring up *and another thing*.

"And another thing, I got Louie now so you can quit tryin' to help me! All of you can quit trying, Vince Henson too. From now on I'm number one, okay? You focus on yourself. I'll get in the hard way and you get in just using bein' a woman."

He said it and those words cut me worse than if he'd have taken his steak knife and stabbed me in the heart with it. How dare that damned Henry Caville and his fast talkin' Louie?!

And all I could say was, "yeah, alright, swell."

"Alright? Swell?"

"Alright, swell!"

I pushed my soup to the side. I was through eatin' and talkin' and all of it.

"They got some nice washrooms in this place,"

Jewels comes up chewin' on his tobacca and pullin' up a seat next to me.

"What you doin' here for? I thought you was waitin' in the car?" Henry asked.

"Yeah, well, I got lonesome, didn't I? I ain't no dog, I ain't waitin' in no cars for ya."

Jewels is grabbin' for the bread in the middle of the table and he's lookin' at my soup like he ain't ate in a year, which was a bold-faced lie. They was a depression goin' on somewhere, but it weren't affectin' him none. He'd been out with us for a year and he'd grown a nice big belly cause of it.

"Go ahead and eat."

I push my bowl towards him and he starts goin' for it with all his might.

"What's with her?" Jewels asked Henry like I weren't sittin' right next to the old bastard.

"I'm just lettin' the men do the business," I said.

"Awe hell," Henry shook his head, "now listen—"

Louie's interruptin'.

"So, we were thinking,"

Louie starts, sittin' back down and continuin' to stuff his face.

"we were thinking of enterprising. We were thinking of pursuing this Henson brothers contract, even though the money they offer is nothin' but peanuts. We'll do his crummy movie, that *To Hunt or Be Hunted*. You got plenty of time to go over the script, Henry, and Jane's there to run lines with you no problem."

"Yeah plenty of time," Henry nods, "Jane and I was runnin' lines last night, she's really helping me."

"Ha!" I laughed.

Louie and Henry looked at me, but I didn't say another word, so they ignored it.

"There's this one little thing Henry. We gotta do some advertising for the movie, ya see? Gotta do some publicity."

"Publicity how?" Jewels askes, his mouth full a my soup, the old bastard.

"More sightings with Jane Pearl and a little less with these two," Louie says like we ain't sittin' there, his sights on Henry only, "so what's your livin' situation?"

"I'm livin' with these two."

Louie smiles and finishes his drink, lettin' out a loud chuckle.

"Well then, ya gotta move. No offense, but an old man and a colored woman, I mean it's really no way to be seen."

I'm standin' up mad, but Henry ain't budging.

"If that's the way it's done," he says, *real* innocent.

"Chemistry," Louie says, "we always start with chemistry. If you and Jane can't get along when the moonlight's hittin' you just right and the music's low, with the drinks flowin'...well then you don't get top billin' with her. Ya understand boy? Course ya understand, you ain't no dummy."

He's askin' Henry, but he's lookin' my way. He'd been lookin' me up and down all night like there was some chance I wanted the big fat slimeball agent in my bed. Henry's just sittin', noddin'.

"And *you* understand," Louie keeps lookin' at me, "why Henry can't bring his broad with him."

"His steady," I corrected.

"Whatever he calls it," Louie smiles.

"Guess I'll have to wait in the car too," I said.

"Maybe you and I can wait in the car *together*," Louie says.

"You watch your mouth," Jewels is growlin'.

"Maybe without your old man," Louie laughed.

I look at Henry like maybe he was gonna say somethin'. Then I felt the slimey fingers of Louie Harris tryna travel up my skirt.

"I'll knock your lights out you son-of-a-bitch!" I yell.

"Cece please!" Henry looked angry.

"You didn't see what he did!"

"You gotta start actin' right if you want to stick with me," Henry barked.

"Actin' right?"

"Yeah! Act like a lady!"

I realized then and there that Henry weren't payin' no attention to me and my pain. He was lookin' around at all the high society mugs takin' interest in our drama, watchin' me fly off my handle.

"Come on Cece, I told ya, ain't no Caville was any good. Let's scram."

Jewels stood up, finishin' his bowl of soup on the way. Louie smiled this grim smile that I ain't never seen before and would never want to see again.

"I'll be at *our* home, if it's still our home by the end of the night" I said, "have fun with your Jane Pearl and your Louie Harris."

Then that Louie starts pipin' up again.

"Oh, and you can let our old friend Raphael know from me," Louie says, "that Jane Pearl's signin' with Louie Harris. He don't have to worry about it anymore. Ain't no negro agent gonna steal business over Louie Harris, that's for sure."

"That's good, cause he's gonna need all his attentions on me instead!" I said.

"I'm sure he'd like that," Henry's face is all wrinklin' up mad.

Jewels and I were stormin' out the restaurant, hearin' that big mouth Louie Harris laughin'. That's how loud that man was—so loud we could hear his voice down the steps, out the door and all the way to the street corner, I swear it!

14

Being in Love

Jane Pearl and Louie Harris, *the terrible twosome,* carved out a Henson Brother's Studio contract for Henry that were far better than anythin' me or Jewels or Raph coulda come up with. He was to be the star of *'To Hunt or Be Hunted',* which meant he was gonna need star quality dough, like an upfront on his contract and a big allowance for spendin'. Henry took what he made and rented a rancher, a real nice house near the studio and he got hisself a small car and new threads. He kept up goin' to the barbershop, gettin' his hair cut on the sides only, tellin' fella to keep it floppin' up top cause the ladies liked it. He was lookin' real spiffy in those days—bein' a brand new man nearly every time I was allowed to see him. When we met up, they was supervised visitations by Louie and there was not a camera or another person in sight for miles.

Henry took to takin' me for walks on the beach at night and I was confused I admit, but I maybe started fallin' outta love with him. Whenever we talked it was *Jane this* and *Louie that.* One of em said he would start havin' to dress this way and walk that way and maybe they did have a point he said. They was schoolin' him plenty, he said. Pretty soon Henry ain't had a thought of his own in his head and maybe he never did. And all them times we was walkin' and talkin' and I was strainin' to hold his slippery hand, he never once said he loved me. He never once said I was beautiful. The moon was shinin' and glistenin' on my face and the sparkly dress I'd picked out just for him was taped to the curves of my body, but he never commented on the fact that I were so dolled up. He never once said I looked pretty. It started gettin' to me, ya know, 'specially when I was hearin' it from others and not from him.

Jewels was gettin' real sick and tired of hearin' about Henry and our walks and my askin' if he loved me. Jewels was insistin' I tell good ol' Vince I wanted my money upfront too, or maybe even talk to pops about settin' us up proper in somethin' nicer than a motel apartment. It was all well and good to ask Vince, although I weren't nothin' too special in the movie so I was sure he couldn't swing it, but askin' my pops was another story. With askin' him I had my pride, see? So what if I was seein' the same four smoke stained walls with the paint chippin' off em' every day? So what if Jewels had to sleep on the couch and was complainin' of his bad back cause there was only one bed and it folded up into the wall? *Better than sleepin' in the bathtub, ya old coot*, I'd say. It was the fact I'd done somethin' with myself outside of my pops shadow that I liked. It was that I didn't need no more family way and no more Romeo Romello's rules. Out here in the wild west, I could mind my business and pops could talk through Jewels all he wanted to, tryin' to get to me. I was livin' my own life and lovin' it, savvy? Weren't nothin' or no-body gonna get me to change that, not in them days, and 'specially not Jewels!

"We gotta pack up and go back to New York," Jewels said.

"Alright, well see ya later."

"Didn't ya hear me? I saw *we*. Both of us gotta go."

It just happened to be the day before the big day—the day we was finally gonna start filmin'. Production started with no hiccups, Vince said. There was no more upchuckin' director, no more company runnin' outta dough, and no more other films to produce with *'To Hunt or Be Hunted'* playin' second fiddle. We was surely gonna start filmin' on Tuesday and Monday this old bastard Jewels comes to me talkin' about goin' back to New York. I waved him towards the door, cause he had another thought to think if he wanted me goin' with him.

"Nothin' doin'. I been rehearsing for weeks! Vince needs me!" I said, steamin' mad.

Jewels is rollin' his cigarette all calm, "Vince'll be fine. The movie's still gonna get made without ya."

"But—I got the role of a lifetime!"

He's all lookin' at me like he did when I was a kid, his eyes lowered like he knew he was gonna get his way eventually if he kept on talkin'. But, this time was different, see? This time I weren't no kid, I was a star!

"You're playin' secretary, *ya got ten lines.*"

"Yeah, but I learned all them ten lines!"

Jewels is slow clappin'.

"Good job."

"Good job nothin'! That was hard work!"

"Yeah and for all your walkin' round here repeatin' them ten lines, they're burned into my memory bank. Hell, I could play secretary now too if I shaved my legs."

"You ain't hearin' me right, I ain't goin! I'm gonna be a star!"

"Don't matter. Romeo Romello's callin' it. I guess your acting career just got cut short. Sorry Cece."

Now I'm crying. It weren't cause I had ten lines. He was right, I was a secretary without even a name in the movie just, *'secretary'* but it weren't no secretary two or three, there were only one and it was me! It was a place to start. It was a chance to be seen. Plus, good ol' Vince Henson liked me. Bonnie liked me. Raph more than liked me. *I had it in*, they said, the men round the table were lookin' at my picture with dollar signs in their eyes, Vince told me. When all was said and done, I was just hopin' them men in that big room would say *'we liked her playin' secretary and so did the audience, now let's give her, her own picture'* and women like Jane Pearl could be tossed in the waste bin as old news. Maybe I could be a leadin' lady one day and then I could be makin' all the demands and gettin' allowances and budgets—new clothes and a house in the hills for myself. I'd do it on my own too, with no help from my pops or my brothers. Nobody in this town would need to know I was a big, bad Romello!

"Jewels, I can't leave," I pleaded.

"Ya gots to. He called it."

"Yeah well, maybe he just needs you. Maybe he didn't mean me."

"He needs his whole family. He's called it."

"I need more time."

"He's given you plenty of time," Jewels said, "things are bad back home. He can't handle it hisself no more."

"He's got my brothers."

Jewels laughed.

"He can't concentrate with you out here so far away and he needs me by his side. I'm his right hand."

"Then *you* go back. Ya got my blessing."

"I can't come back without his daughter—not unless I want a bullet in my head."

"Yeah, well, what's it gonna take for me to stay?"

"You bein' married, and the way that Caville kid is goin—"

"—he's still talkin' about it."

"Yeah...sure he is."

Jewels is shakin' his head and smokin' his cigarette, lookin' real smug.

"And every time my pops says jump, we all just have to say how high, don't we?"

"Oh, so you gots ten lines in a talkie, and all of a sudden you're feelin' your oats? You ain't even been talkin' to your pops in months,"

Jewels is scrunching his face and spittin' on the floor.

"but don't worry, I would never tell your pops what an ungrateful, spoiled brat his daughter is. It would break him."

"Go ahead and tell him!" I'm yellin', "you tell him how ain't none of us can have lives of our own cause of him. You tell him how everything is always about him. You tell him I finally ain't no Romello out here and I finally ain't havin' to pass myself off like his daughter all the time. Now finally, just finally, I can be Cece without the last name bein' tagged along at the end."

"You ain't just Cece. You're always a Romello, and just cause ya hide it don't change the fact. You're always gonna have your duty, a loyalty to your family!"

"Ain't no duty! Ain't no loyalty!"

"I ain't hear that."

Jewels started walkin' away, but I caught his arm. Now I'm pleadin'.

"He promised me top spot, Jewels, *the* top spot! I wouldn't be standin' right here if he'd been honest about that. All my life I waited and all my life I planned and then what? What was it all for? It was just lies from a professional liar. That's all my pops does. He uses us and he lies to us. He's been lyin' to me for years."

"Ain't no woman gettin' no top spot in the mob," he said, "and you was a damn fool all them years believin' it."

"Maybe I was a fool," I said, "but I'm a fool no longer. A fool would be returnin' to somebody who never wanted me to be anythin' but his lap dog in the first place. He just wanted me to play along to his little game. Pops was wrong for raisin' me to want to be the best, cause now I found somethin' that a woman can be top spot in and I'm not gonna lose that chance."

Jewels was already packin' his couple of shirts and pants in the old knapsack he brought with him.

"Listen, people like us—we ain't got nothin' but family," he said, "and when all this goes wrong, yes all these pictures and the Hensons and this Hollywood, when it all goes downhill for ya, your gonna be on that wire to your pops and you better hope he's still got all the dough he's tryin' to save now to help you then."

"I don't need savin' and I don't need helpin'."

"Then you're even more daft than you look," he said, "there's a mornin' train and you better be on it."

"I won't."

"Then I'll tell ya what I tell all the men that try to run from Romeo Romello, all the goons who think they're clever enough to hide from the mob. When Romeo Romello gots to come lookin' for ya, your life ain't gonna be worth lookin' for."

"What's that supposed to mean?"

"It means maybe you're his favorite daughter today, but maybe you'll learn quick that Romeo Romello ain't really got no favorites."

Jewels had his gun, his .45, and he was tuckin' it under the shirts in his bag, lookin' real pitiful.

"Pops ain't really gonna put a bullet in ya, if I don't come with ya?" I asked, "He wouldn't do it to you—not his right hand."

He let out a breathe of air, a sigh, longer than I ever heard come outta that old man's lungs.

"Like I said, Romeo Romello ain't got no favorites."

Jewels was already packed by the end of the day and was gettin'
a good nights sleep for the morning. I was out the house by sunrise
and *good luck findin' me*, I thought. By the time I got back to the
apartment he was gone and Raph came callin'.

It was the big day, the first day of filmin' and I had to be in
hair and makeup by ten. When Raph came up I was cryin', like this
big curtain of guilt fell over me and I ain't never refused a Romello
orders before. I ain't never said no to my pops and I lived my whole
life goin' by family rules, so why couldn't I just do my own thing
for once and stop feelin' guilty cause of it? Why couldn't I stop
picturin' Jewels with a bullet in his back?

"What's wrong?" Raph asked, "where's the old man?"

"He's gone," I said.

"Oh," he smiled, "so...we're finally alone."

He tries to grab hold of me, but I'm refusing.

"It ain't like that," I said, "I should've gone with him."

"Gone with him where?"

"Back to New York."

"That's crazy! We start filming today."

"I know."

"So, what are you talking about? What's happened?"

Then I'm cryin' and lettin' him pull me close in his arms and I
felt safe in em, I really did.

"I got to tell you somethin' Raph and I need ya to understand—I
need you to hear me."

"Sure, I'm listening."

"Cause ain't nobody really heard me my whole life."

"Don't worry, I'm listening."

I took two deep breaths, then two more. Then maybe three.

"My pops," I said, "he's Romeo Romello."

I paused, only cause I was used to the shocked look of a person when I said it. But Raph was different. He ain't say nothin' or looked no special sorta way. We was sittin' on the couch and he had my hands in his, but he were just lookin' at me plainly, starin' into my eyes.

"Didn't ya hear me?" I asked.

"Yes," he nodded.

"Do ya even know who Romeo Romello is?"

He laughed.

"Of course I do."

"Well, you ain't say nothin'."

"I'm listening. You said you want me to listen to you. That nobody's really heard you your whole life. So, I'm listening."

"Oh."

He's rubbin' our hands together real gentle and waitin' for me to continue.

"So, tell me. It's okay," he said real soft and I believed him.

So, I told him my whole sorry tale. It started with the bassinet in Harlem, with Regina and my pops. It started with all the promises. It started with the hidin' and the locked doors and them passin' me off with my bleached hair. I told him everythin' about my five brothers. Told em about the times that George was sneakin' in my room and all the fights and the deals bein' made. I told him about the charges for tax evasion and all them times the Romello family ended up in court. I told him about the Santini's and the pact and everything I could til' I couldn't say no more. I finished with the events of that morning—me not answerin' my pops call for help. How could I be a woman of honor, I asked him, when I was lettin' my own family down. That old bastard Jewels had a point, I said, and when they came lookin' for me it wouldn't be hard cause my face would be right in the pictures, so they'd come lookin' real quick.

"*Wow.*"

Raph's eyes went wide, cause it were a life's worth of information and I'd spoke it real fast. I'm sure he ain't catch half of it even, and my lungs was fillin' up with cold hard air from not takin' breaths. He's tellin' me to exhale and calm down, cause I were shakin' and tremblin' almost. I was havin' some sorta panic attack and he was just holdin' my hands together tryna keep me steady.

"I get it if ya want to stop representin' me. I get it if ya want to stop bein' by my side—"

"—I love you," he said.

It took me by surprise, cause I was wonderin' just how I could tell him my problems and everything about my mob family and then he spits out *I love you* so casual like nothin' changed from my little speech.

"I love you Cece," he repeated.

"But, you can't."

"Why not?"

"I just told you, my pops—"

He let out a laugh, a loud snortin' laugh.

"I'm not afraid of no mob boss," he smiled, "and trust me when I say...I have a lot more to lose than you do."

And then he did it. He took a small box from his pocket and he's all on one knee with hisself, so I couldn't bear to watch it. He was really openin' it and exposin' the shiny diamond ring inside. It weren't nothin' big, nothin' extravangant, but it was beautiful and it was bein' held by Raph's big strong hands so calm and sure.

"Marry me Cece," he said, so matter-of-fact.

And I don't know why I said it. I don't know why I said it— it was just something I'd been kicking myself the rest of my life for sayin'. Raph was lookin' at me all wide-eyed and wantin' to kiss and love on me and I'm just sittin' there like a fool, thinkin' of a million reasons to say yes in my head, when all I could say was...

"Henry."

After all the vile, dirty deeds he put me through, I'm bein' dumb and sayin' his damn dumb name. Raph is on his knee proposin' and I'm mentionin' that snake in the grass Henry Caville.

"Why?" Raph asked.

"Cause I made a promise to him. I said I was gonna help him."

"Ha!"

"I'm serious—and he promised me he was gonna marry me."

"He's never going to."

"He sure is gonna and when he does I can't tell him no, not after I waited, I waited all this time for—"

"—you're just stubborn!"

"Excuse me?"

Raph got up and smiled real wide, throwin' the box at me. I caught it, just lookin' at it real careful.

"He said he would marry you, so you damn sure have to see it through to the end. You have to call his bluff, see if he was serious."

"No, I'm not! I ain't stubborn!"

"Yes, you are. You're just stubborn and spoiled!"

"You watch your mouth!"

"Oh yea?"

"Yeah!"

And then he kissed me, and this wave fell over me like everythin' was gonna be fine. It was like all my problems weren't really problems, like my whole life made sense in that moment. Promises were promises and they still stuck, but there was this kiss and all. There was this strong man who was much stronger and wiser than Henry could have ever been and he wanted to be my husband.

"You're gonna be late for curtains," he said.

"Don't ya want your ring back?" I asked.

"Nah, you'll be wearing it one day soon. Real soon."

Raph left and I was thinkin' I probably shouldn't see him again, cause if Henry Caville did marry me, there'd be the problem of Raph. Maybe me and Raph would be out sneakin' over here and over there and stealin' kisses and that weren't no way to start a marriage to Henry, so I'd be sure to keep my distance. And all them nerves didn't help for the first day of filmin' and all. I needed to think, forget about this family and just breathe and exhale like Raph instructed. He was so smart, that Raph.

But then there was Jewels, old bastard Jewels, who was on a train half sleepin' and half-stewing over the fact my seat was missin' and he had to go back to pops and face him alone. He had to tell him the truth of what happened and the reason for me not bein' there. I couldn't stop picturin' Jewels standin' in front of my angry pops, bein' interrogated. Jewels practically raised me all my life—committed nearly a year of his own just to come out here, followin' me to California so I could help Henry and live out my own dreams. I knew Jewels hated Henry Caville and he could see through snakes better than anybody livin', but he stuck it out only cause he cared about me. And that's when I saw on my pillow that note. It was a note and Jewel's .45 caliber handgun. I were cryin' and smilin' cause I weren't his daughter *'praise be to God'*, but he sure always treated me like one. It was the worst handwritin' in the world, but when Jewels wanted to get his point across, well, he damn sure did it...

Sometimes ten lines mean you got more to prove than being in somebody else's shadow. See you on the silver screen Cece – give em' hell!

15

Being Engaged to Assistants

I knew my pops put one of them gypsy curses on me. That Tuesday my life started bein' ruined out of nowhere, for no reason at all, so's what was to blame but him and his damn gypsies. He were already wise to the fact that I weren't on the morning train with Jewels, cause he phoned me up at the studio askin' around. Now my pops ain't never used no blower, not once, cause them feds had our house line bugged. He wouldn't use no booth neither, cause he swore them operators were listenin' in on conversations, so it must've been somethin' serious for him to drop a dime. He ain't used no names, but I knew it were my pops cause of him wipin' the sweat from his forehead with a rag too close to the receiver. His voice were all muffled and cracklin' with his heavy breathin' and stallin' his dumb old code words.

"*Little Birdie flew the nest.*"

"Who's birdie?"

"Little Birdie fly home," he said, "fly home if your wings work."

"Whatcha mean?"

"Red dust. Emergency."

"Ain't happenin'."

"Little birdie flyin' too close to the sun! Emergency! Emergency!"

His words was cuttin' off and the operator was comin' back on the line tryna say she's lost him. I hang up the phone real quick cause I knew. All his red dust talkin'—he been over to see that Madame Josephine days before and she probably tipped him off that I weren't comin' back and now they was gonna do me dirty, they were. I knew what his red dust meant, and she'd set some curse in my name from way down in the trenches.

I remembered Josephine from bein' small and she'd scare me, lookin' like a wicked witch with her broomstick in the corner. She worked from a tiny room in an alleyway what ya had to shoo the beggars and stray dogs away from the door 'fore ya could get in. She'd have all this powder and different colored dust and her scary lookin' cards with bags of seeds and marbles. She'd be shakin' em round and makin' em rattle. Pops would be mystified, sittin' in the chair sweatin' his can off while I'd be hidin' my face in his shirt. There was all black curtains surroundin' us and then a little light comin' down from the ceiling, so she'd flick it on and off real furious when she had the urge. She'd lean over top of us from across her round table, with her eyes full of mascara and liner real heavy, makin' the whites go wide.

If Jewels was pops right hand, then Madame Josephine was his left and he were at her place sometimes two or three days a week gettin' his palm and tea leaves read. The scary part about Josephine was that damn near everything she told him were true, startin' with me. *Your baby is in the belly of a young girl, a dancer. I draw a card, the letter C.'* She knew about Romeo Jr. goin' mute too, *'Your eldest son—his voice box will be broken.'* And she predicted Regina's death, oh yes, she'd spotted it years before, *'Your wife was born in the bathtub and that's where she shall die.'* To be so right about all them things in pops life, well, I knew if she had powers like that, she could put a curse on me quick. I didn't doubt it, not once!

The first day of filming started and all them weeks of rehearsin' lines were ruined, all cause of her curse and a mohair sweater. It were itchin' me somethin' awful. I couldn't concentrate or say my lines cause of my stingin' skin. I kept messin' up my que and gettin' nervous, scratchin' myself with the pencil prop they give me. Good ol' Vince kept checkin' on me and that director was tryna be sweet as pie, but I could tell it were workin' their nerves and messin' up their whole operation. I tried my best, but it was no use so they called a break—a long, long, long break. That curse had a hold of me, and it were just startin' there.

The *'To Hunt or Be Hunted'* promotional still stared me in the face as I made my way back to the dressing rooms. It was a huge photo decoratin' the hallway and I saw Henry's mean mug on the poster next to that has-been of Hollywood, Jane Pearl. She was, by the looks of it, hangin' on to his bare chest like my Henry was a jungle gym. My plan was just to say hi, ya know, cause I hadn't seen him all week and I wanted to wish him luck on his big break. They said he was gettin' ready to film his first scene, so he was dressin' and I didn't want to disturb him, really. I just wanted to take a small peek and maybe have a kiss on the lips for good luck. But then I seen Bonnie runnin' towards me all outta breath, actin' urgent.

"Cece, did ya see it?"

She's clackin' those high heels across the set and shovin' a newspaper in my face. I'm squintin' to see what's so important that she'd come all the way over here, especially after I was all embarassin' everybody with ruinin' my lines.

"See what?"

I'm readin' it quick and skimmin' words and I notice what she's talkin' about is Henry Caville. I'm grabbin' the paper so hard it tore in half, but it was just the half I needed.

"That dirty—"

"Cece, hold on!"

Too late, I was off to his dressing room, speedin' cross the way to Henry's, and I tore that itchy sweater right off my body. My hair was all stickin' up every sort of way cause the sweater got stuck goin' up and over and I got red marks all over my skin that had to be some type of allergic reaction. Now I was runnin' around the Henson Brother's studio set, naked up top except my bra, seein' just as much red as I looked. Bonnie was tryin' to chase me, but she couldn't keep up in them stilts cause my shoes were already kicked off. Pretty soon I'm barefoot runnin' towards that Henry, ballin' my fists up ready to fight!

Now I gotta clear somethin' up real quick. It was the fact that Henry Caville and I had made certain promises to each other and them promises were that we would wait for each other—which was why I gave up that good lookin' Raph and his fancy, shiny ring. He also made the same promises to my pops that yes, we would be married...*eventually*. I assumed it would be when he was makin' big money as an actor and them days were comin' real soon, which is why I always stuck around in his life. And then with them ten lines I had, there was even more of a reason to stay in Hollywood. But Bonnie showin' me that small newspaper article really had just sealed the deal for us in a lotta ways. It made me feel foolish for comin' to California and tryin' so hard to be a good little lady waitin' for a slime like Henry.

"Don't do it Cece."

The only man in that whole place with any balls to get in front of my enraged temper were Louie, that big goon, and he's laughin' that great big cackle of his the whole time. He was sittin' in a chair set up outside Henry's dressing room door, smokin' his cigarette with his legs all out-stretched and comfortable, playin' guard.

"Outta my way!"

I looked down at him and thought if I was goin' to shove that newspaper down his throat, I better do it 'fore he gets up and tries to overpower me. But then again, I needed it as evidence. He leaned back, still lookin' smug like he weren't afraid of no dame, *'specially a 5'3 dame like me'.*

"He don't got time to see ya right now, he's getting ready," Louie said.

"Gettin' ready or not I gotta see him —move," I growled.

"I can't let ya do it, Cece. You know how the papers get. You know how the rumors start. Blow!"

"Get outta my way Louie, I swear!"

I meant to punch his stomach, but my fist went lower. He rolled hisself off his chair and was on the ground, callin' me all sorts of bitches. I went round him to Henry's dressing room door, cause Louie coulda died there for all I cared—I was on a mission. I had that newspaper in my hand and some questions to be answered and damn sure if they was gonna be! I started bangin' real hard on that door with all them producers and actors and starlets watchin' the crazed woman in her brassiere nearly breakin' her fingers. Every strike of that door hurt my knuckles, but I weren't yella, so I kept poundin'.

"Henry! Open this door damnit or I'll break the whole thing down!"

There were a silence behind the wall til' he finally answered. I didn't hear his usual voice but a lower, tougher tone like the one he was using on *'To Hunt or Be Hunted'.*

"It's been open the whole time. What are ya daft?"

Wrong answer! I burst in and slammed that door behind me. Mirrors and bottles and tabletops shook, but Henry wasn't impressed no way.

"Who's daft?" I'm yellin'.

He's all standin' in his shirttails, underwear and socks, with his little olive colored toothpick legs bare. He's puttin' on his tie, smilin' smug in the mirror like I didn't mean a damn.

"You. Whatcha come in here for anyway?"

"I come in here for—"

"—you came in here for what?"

"I come in here to ask you what this is, you son-of-a-bitch?"

"What's what?"

"This!"

I waved the newspaper round, but he never turned to look. He was starin' at his own reflection, still with that stupid grin on his silly face. That's when I realized Henry Caville ain't know the real me, Cece Romello. He ain't know it cause I ain't never showed it to him. He had no idea of me, the woman half them goons in New York had seen the wrong side of. All he knew was me speakin' sweet nothin's in his ear and blowin' kisses. All he knew was *baybee* this, *baybee* that, and me playin' with his flippin' floppin' hair. He ain't never been on my bad side, not til' now. He ain't never heard the rough edge of my tongue, no way!

"You gonna read it?" I'm askin'.

"No, I'm busy."

I wanted him to turn round just so's I could knock his block off! I stuck my fist out and it stopped at the back of his head, real close. He hadn't looked my way, but I knew them corners of his mouth were raised like he thought I was funny. He was feelin' hisself these days, forgettin' the times all my brothers were crawlin' round him, makin' him tremble. Forgettin' the times George had a gun to his neck. How was he of all people in that town gonna forget who I was and where I came from, just cause I had to hide it in them days. Just cause I didn't flaunt it around no more, didn't mean it stopped bein' so. He was actin' like he ain't remember that I was a Romello, so I had to make sure he didn't forget, ya follow?

"Don't worry —I'll read it for ya!"

I held the newspaper up to my face, my sight blurry cause I was tryna get my bearings. I was good and mad with my hand shakin', but I could still see well enough to read the fine print of that sleezy article.

"It says...Henry Caville, an insatiable lover who was said to manage it at least three times a day!"

He's just laughin'.

"So what the hell's that supposed to mean?" I asked.

"It means—" he started.

"—it means, darling,"

A voice slithered out from the corner of the room.

"if you aren't numbers one, two or three, then you must be missing out. Could I see that publication my dear? Henry you must be holding out on me. Does it include a picture?"

I turned round and I saw her. Must've missed her in all my excitement. It were that Jane Pearl and she looked just like she did in all her movies. She laid on that chaise in the corner lookin' cool and glamorous and sexy like she knew it. With a long-stemmed cigarette in one hand and a bottle of nail polish in the other, she was busy paintin' her toes and then takin' a break and sippin' her drink. Jane had more ice on her wrists then I'd ever seen and even if it was on the studios dime, still she looked like a sheba. I clammed up, nervous, although I didn't have no reason cause Romeo Romello's daughter don't clam up easy.

"I'm sorry, I didn't see you there Ms. Pearl," was all I said, real soft spoken, like a ninny.

If her voice were smooth and purrin' soundin' like a cat, then mine were high pitched squeakin' like a mouse.

"That's certainly alright my dear. I love a bit of theatrics in the morning. We're all actors, made from drama. The show doesn't stop when the curtains drop, they say."

"Oh no miss I didn't mean to —and you're just great —ya know —in the pictures."

"Well thank you."

"I thought ya said she was old hat,"

Henry's soundin' off again.

"and she was too over the hill for the talkies."

"I ain't say that," I lied.

Now Jane Pearl's lookin' at me sideways.

"Aren't you going to introduce us Henry?" she asked.

"Jane, this the girl I told you about – ya know, Cece?"

Jane laughed, "Ah, the infamous Cece. You're dancing in this, aren't you dearie? Playin' secretary, right?"

"Yes," I was all lowerin' my eyes, suddenly shy.

"Show me something."

I shook my head no, too nervous in front of Hollywood royalty, but I were still mad at Henry for tellin' my tales.

"You never told me how pretty she was. I'm feeling very jealous," Jane said, "Would you like a drink Cece?"

"No, she doesn't want a drink, she was just leaving," Henry answered for me.

"Well, I want to—"

"—You want to what?"

Henry was glarin' at me and I didn't know what to say, I was so caught off guard and all by all Jane Pearl's starin' at me like she liked women. She spoke next.

"She's trying to figure out what I'm doing here and if she should either punch me or ask for an autograph. I'd advise against the first as I'm on the studios insurance, you know, but if it's the latter, there's a pen right over there my dear. I'd be happy to oblige."

I grabbed for the pen and nervously handed it over.

"Henry, weren't you saying something earlier about little Cece. Something about her being your fiancé, *your fianca'*," she mocked and scribbled somethin' on a piece of paper.

"Never officially..." Henry grumbled.

"Well if not official, it must be serious. We females rarely make a scene if it's not serious," Jane said.

She handed back the pen and paper and continued paintin' her nails.

"Yea well," his voice trailed off.

I looked down and saw her name Jane Pearl in lovely cursive handwritin', then the note after: *nice breasts*. I looked up and I met them eyes piercin' into my soul. She started laughin' real hoity toity.

"Just a small joke," Jane said.

"Small?!"

"I have a fiancé too, Joseph Bottane, have you heard of him?"

Joseph Bottane were a popular star, a real actor. He'd studied in England, done Shakesphere on stage, ya know? He ain't just been picked up and carried round like Henry. He weren't no fake like Henry. Joseph Bottane was wildly popular and extremely attractive. He weren't no son-of-a-bitch like Henry!

"Sure, I heard of him," I said, "surprised he weren't up for the lead."

"You're engaged?" Henry asked her, a concerned look on his dumb face.

"He was up for it," Jane said, "but things go south when the producers are too cheap to pay big money to two leads. Pity though. He'd like actin' with you very much."

"He would?"

"Yes, and that's saying something because he's doesn't think much of negro women."

Henry saw the look on my face and Jane's baitin' me, so he stepped in real quick.

"Jane, could ya give us a moment?"

"Of course, of course," she winked at me, "look me up dearie, I might have a part for you."

"In what film?" I asked, real naïve like.

"Oh, it's private," she's smilin' and givin' me the once and twice over.

Jane left the room and Henry gave me a look like he did on *'To Hunt or Be Hunted'* and I felt like I wanted to just punch him —oh I was so mad.

"Now darling, Cece, I know you must be upset."

"I must be upset —yes I must be must I darling?" I mocked.

"Why don't you sit down, you want a drink?"

"I'm not sittin' down or nothin'. You've been actin' strange for weeks now, actin' like I could live or die."

"Don't say that —no —you know you mean everything to me Cece."

"Then why don't you call me baby no more?"

"It's not good for press. We aren't married."

"What was that article about?"

"Just rumors, that's all, just rumors," he assured.

"Well if it's all rumors then marry me. Marry me Henry!"

"What?"

"Marry me today!"

"I can't today, I have rehearsal."

"This week then!"

I went over to him and put my hands on his head, tryin' to shake him up, sure, but maybe shake some sense into him too.

"I can't this week, there's promotional stills and shootin' and I have to go with Louie to go get fitted for my suit for the award show. Can't it wait?"

"No," I cried, "it can't wait cause if somethin' is important it doesn't wait. Aren't I important Henry?"

"Oh, stop whinin'. You know you are."

"I don't want a big wedding, just something small, ya know? Or somethin' just at the courthouse. Ya know a lot of women would take you for all you've got. They'd get all that money and they'd make you do a lavish wedding, a big wedding, with all the cameras and paparazzi there and they'd make it a big deal, but not me. I just want somethin' small, just at the courthouse that's fine, anything to just be married to you Henry."

"Stop naggin' me."

"We can do it anytime, Henry, just think about it okay? Doesn't have to be some church wedding, although my pops would kill me if he found out we didn't have it at the church, but it's okay I'll take the chance for love—"

"Cece!" Henry yelled.

I realized my hands had moved from his face to his tie and I was tightenin' it round his neck as I was talkin' in circles. He grabbed my hands and loosened my grip on him, pushin' me away. He was lookin' like I needed to go to the looney bin and maybe that day I did.

"Why don't you sit down?" He asked tryin' to calm me.

Hysterical still, I sat down and grabbed for a glass with Jane's lipstick marks on it, thinkin' it was straight water, but realizing soon enough it wasn't. I coughed up her gin and tonic, but choked it down cause I were that upset and Romeo's daughter wasn't gonna be told she couldn't hold her liquor.

"I want to say something," he started.

This time he knelt down in front of me and put both hands on my knees. I opened my legs like I was playin' but no dice.

"Cece, you are a lovely woman, you are the most important person in my life," he said, "I owe everything —where am I today— to you,"

Then I'm waitin' for the but...

"but...and I didn't want to say this before, cause you've also been such a great friend to me, and a great help to me through this whole thing..."

"Yeah?"

"I need you to go back to New York."

"Why? I want to stay here with you—I won't get in the way Henry, I promise! And I've got my lines to say and all. They're talkin' like I'm gonna get a redo tomorrow."

"No. It's not that. I just don't think you could stay here knowin' that I'm engaged to somebody else."

"Who else?"

He sighed one of them long sighs like he was too much of a coward to say the truth out right. Oh, I wanted to punch him so bad!

"Who is it? Who is she? Do I know her?" I'm askin'.

"You know the lady that picks out the clothes?"

"Which one?"

"The brunette."

"The asian?"

"No, no, of course not. She's English, her ancestors came over on the Mayflower."

"I didn't see no brunette broad comin' over from the Mayflower pickin' out clothes."

"No, she brings the dry cleaning. Ya seen her?"

"Oh, wait...*the assistant?!*"

"Yes."

That's when I lost it. I really lost it. If he thought I had lost it before well I damn well did then. I stood up this time and started walkin' round the room all in circles. My mind went nuts and he stayed kneelin' on the floor, not sure like if he was just waitin' or prayin'.

"I'm thinkin' the whole time you're running round with actresses, big name stars, and the whole time it's assistants? People who fetch dog soup?! The one that got me in that damn itchy sweater? It was a plot I tell ya, I knew it!"

"Weren't no plot. She's trying to get into pictures too. She's good, she's gonna be a star, I told her I'd help her. She's got big dreams, like me. That's when we met and started talkin' about her big— dreams."

"Met? When? When did you met her?"

"Yesterday."

"Yesterday?"

"Yeah, she brought my dry cleaning."

"Only yesterday?"

"Yes."

"And you love her already? You want to marry her?"

"Yes."

"Let me guess, did the studio say—"

Then he got up, fightin' mad.

"—it's not the studio sayin' it's me sayin'. That's why I'm through with you Cece, you never let me have a say, it's always this way or that way, it's gotta be your idea. Sometimes a guy has to make his mind up for himself, see?"

"Why're you talkin' like that?"

"Like what?"

"Like a mug!"

"I don't know."

"You don't know a lot of things, like why you're cheatin' on me with assistants now."

"Cheat?"

"Yes —unfaithful! Adulterer! After all I done for you and I made it a point to wait til' we got married, but it was one or two careless nights yes, too much to drink, okay. But it was alright to slip up cause you had designs to marry me, so I said the hell with it waitin' but—"

"—You can't be unfaithful to someone who's not your wife, somebody you never proposed to officially."

"Oh, now who told ya that?"

"Louie. He also told me that I should be hangin' around with dames, sorry women, like Norma, women who ladies—"

"—oh so not like me then?"

"No, not like you. Norma's family, they are plenty educated, and they raised her right. She wouldn't be doin' this assistant stuff if it weren't for she's really trying to get into pictures. She could have had her old man call up to one of those studio heads and they'd put her in just like that, they'd have to cause of who he is and he's real respectable back in her hometown, but she wants to make a way of it herself. That's admirable, I think. They also have a boat I think, yea she told me they have a boat and their own private dock, ya know—"

"—so, throw yourself from it!"

"Oh, don't be like that Cece, just don't. You've never been the jealous type."

"You've never given me a reason before."

"Yea but you know what Louie says—"

"Since when is Louie tellin' you things? That Louie, he's changed you, he's the one. I knew when they said they'd send ya somebody over from the studio to try to teach ya things—ya don't need nobody from any studio teachin' ya nothin'. When I get my hands on that Louie, that no good son of a—"

"—Cece,"

He shook his head no again, this time lowerin' his eyes and lookin' at me all serious.

"I'm askin' you to go,"

I know I shouldn't of, but I had a tear in my eyes I couldn't hide.

"nothing against you, it's just, well I've outgrown them old times and I feel like ya just mean a time in my life where—I've just got to grow up and move on."

I composed myself cause of the lady I were and I didn't need it gettin' back to the family back home that Cece Romello was a dumb dora cryin' over some Caville kid in the middle of a Henson Brothers studio dressing room at 11:30 in the mornin' in my under garments.

"I'm gonna to tell everybody that *I left you*," I said, standin' by the door, my hand grippin' the knob til' my bones was burnin'.

"That's fine."

"And I ain't leavin' til' I've done my duties here for this film and if they pick me up for more, then they pick me up, but only if not am I packin'."

"That's okay, I'll pay for everything if you need more time at the motel," his voice was smooth as silk.

I were still grippin' the handle like it were about to break off. All I could think of was the sacrifices I made for that rat faced son of a boozehound.

"And I never want to see you again, Henry, I swear it. I wouldn't see your picture or any of your pictures if they were the last pictures I could ever see."

"Goodbye Cece."

"And that Norma, I hope she's crawlin' all over you for your money. I hope you waste it all on her and you're left penniless on the side of some road in some sorta of bad way on account of some badger game she's playin'."

"*Thanks.*"

"And if you change your mind and come to your senses I'll be at the La Royale hotel across the street for the next two days and it's gonna take a big ring and a slew of flowers to get me back in your good graces, I swear."

"Sure."

"But knock first, cause I might have visitors."

"Yeah, I know them type visitors you have. I hear he's six foot two and all muscles, keepin' ya warm at night."

And then Henry's lookin' real mean and he didn't have no cause to talk about my Raph that way cause he weren't doin' nothin' but holdin' me. I was bein' true when I said I'd waited for Henry all that time and that's the biggest reason I was kickin' myself that day cause of all that holdin' back and bein' a prude didn't get me nothin' but heartache.

"Yeah well, I get cold!"

All that time I was waitin' for the top billed actor Henry Caville to propose to me officially and nothin'. All that wasted time by his side, all that keepin' my mouth shut and bitin' my tongue round him. All that hidin' and sneakin' with Raph and turnin' down a real proposal, for what? All for that no good Henry Caville, a man who was apparently comin' three times a day, but never once came to me!

16

Being a Retired Prize-Fighter
with a Face for Pictures

I remember bein' dragged away from Henry's dressin' room door by two big burly men and damn near carried back across the set. They wasn't discreet about it one bit and I ain't help matters much with my hollerin' and carryin' on. No big dumb galoot was gonna carry Romeo Romello's daughter across a picture set mid-mornin' without a fight! The one with his right hand round my mouth got bit—yes I ain't ashamed to say I clamped down on his flesh, tastin' metallic blood and he let out a yelp bigger than life. But he kept on draggin' me kickin' and screamin'. We was travelin' to the head of the Henson Brother's Studio, which sat in the corner of the lot. We was goin' to good ol' Vince Henson's *Everything Room* and I knew that this weren't no pleasure trip.

People was watchin' and speakin' in hushed tones and raisin' eyebrows pretendin' like they ain't never seen nothin' like me. I heard them flashbulbs clickin' too and those men who get paid to take pictures of famous people—well they was all gettin' their shots in and writin' lots of scribble into their notepads. They was all just busybodies anyway, good for nothings with nothin' better to do on a

Tuesday then to watch me bein' carried off set. When they dropped me in to see Vince and shut the door, it was dark, but I could hear somebody whistlin' some sorta western tune as the smell of cigar smoke filled the air.

And then there was good ol' Vince Henson starin' me down. He was sittin' at the head of this long table with a few other mugs I didn't know and who weren't too important to me at this particular time. There was too much cigar smoke in too little space makin' me cough and through all the fog and the darkness, I seen Raph. He was sittin' at Vince's right hand side with his expression kinda hurt since the last time we spoke I'd turned him down to go chasin' Henry Caville.

I was lookin' at him sittin' in his nicely pressed suit, starin' straight at me. I knew I was wrong—dead wrong for still choosin' Henry over him. It was when I saw he was the type of man that didn't shy away from folk's eyes that I loved it. Tough as nails like my old man. Maybe in his mind he were wonderin' why I was runnin' round the set like crazy in just my brassiere and bein' carried by big men and spittin' and cursin' all over the place, but he held his cards. His expression was blank, and he ain't never show what he was thinkin' and maybe if he didn't think I were no lady no more, he still made sure one of them goons pulled my chair out for me.

"What's the meanin' of this?" I asked.

I was lickin' my fingers and smoothin' my hair down, cause I knew it looked a wreck. Them men was just starin' at me not sayin' nothin' til' Raph handed me one of his button up shirts so I could cover up.

"Somebody say what's goin' on?" I asked, pleadin'.

"Cece, this is bad," Vince spoke and his voice meant business.

I finished puttin' the shirt on and braced my chair, my hands grippin' both arms.

"You can't go off, running around the set, yelling at lead stars and biting members of security staff. Especially nearly dressed."

I met Raph's eyes and I couldn't tell but I think he were disgusted.

"Well I—"

"—and another thing," he interrupted, "we are taking you off the film."

"Off the film?!"

"Yes."

"But – you can't – I gotta contract," I looked at Raph, my eyes pleadin', "don't I?"

This time he looked away. One of the big men sittin' at the table got real huffin' and puffin' mad.

"She's nuts!" he said.

"She's a liability," Vince added.

"A what?"

"She's crazy!" the other guy said.

"Haven't you seen the papers?" Vince asked me.

He was passin' it towards me down the table, the other half of Bonnie's paper I'd ripped off.

"The reporters are swarming with news, it's not good for any of us. How can we make a picture about the dangers of mob if we've got a bonafide mobster playing a part in it?"

Bonnie had shown me the papers that morning, but I only seen Henry's clippin'. I missed the bottom of the front side, the important stuff, the stuff about me!

Cece Romello tries her hand at acting...

Henson Brother's Studio hires the infamous Cece Romello.

Cece Romello—Hollywood's feared baby!

In my excitement goin' over to Henry, I missed the headline. And then, worse thing about it was there was a whole front page story with my sorry mug in the frame, my glossy picture, the one I'd been so proud of and a big X coverin' my face.

"How could this –"

"—I'm going to ask you a question," Vince said, "and I want you to be very honest with us. And I'll give you the benefit of the doubt since papers like to lie."

"Yea sure Vince, anything," I nodded.

"What's your name?"

"Cece."

"Cece what?"

"Just Cece."

"She's stupid!" guy yelled.

"Ah, shutup!" Raphael commanded.

Vince stayed calm, calm but still focused on me.

"What's your last name Cece, your family's name?"

"Oh – that," I'm squirmin'.

Raph's sittin' there real still, but now I see him lookin' like he's about to crawl out of his own skin.

"Well?" Vince asked again, so I'm startin' to stutter.

"It's, it's Rom—"

"—*It's Romello! And what about it?*"

"Who let this man in?"

Vince is fightin' mad now cause here my brother George is bargin' into his office, in all his glory. He's fresh from New York, we could still smell the train on him. He's all cut up and scarred, but he's got a big, bright smile on his face and he's high as ever.

"I'm George Romello, I don't get let in places, I show up places. There's a difference,"

George said as he's leavin' the door open,

"and I brought our lawyer with me, so don't try nothin' funny neither."

"Unhand me sir!"

That's Tony with his briefcase and his notes. Some big bouncer caught him in the hallway, the one with my bite mark on his hand, and he's tryin' to rush behind George. George Romello gives the fella a look and the guy's lookin' back, real confused like maybe his job ain't worth it. Vince knows he's gotta give my clan the room, so he makes em calm themselves.

"Just let him go," Vince sighs an order.

Now the only one in that whole room that were standin' toe to toe with George Romello was Raph and they was squarin' up like they was gonna fight just cause Raph is starin' and no Romello liked no man that stared em in the eyes for too long.

"Now, who's this chump? Ya wanna get rough?"

George is in full fancy garb and all his jewels, but he's still raisin' his fists like he's gonna duke. That crazy Raph puts his fists up too like he's gonna knock out Georgie Boy who's undefeated thirty-seven to nothin'. It's enough to make George smile and he pats a confused Raph on the back real swift, puttin' his own fists down.

"Hey, what's twenty-four times thirty-six?" George asked him.

"Eight hundred and sixty-four," Raph answers.

George turns to me smilin' sly. I nodded.

"Did ya'll come here for some arithmetic classes?"

That big one with the cigar chompin', the one that was callin'me nuts and crazy, is chirpin' and chimin' all ways. George turns and sits down next to him, slidin' over makin' him nervous. George had this way about him, that he was always makin' guys nervous, so he's lookin' in the guy's eyes real calm and sideways.

"Don't I know you?" George askes.

"Nah, you don't know me," fella shakes.

"Nah, I do know you. We did some time together, didn't we?" George askes.

"Nah I ain't do no time," guy says.

"Nah, ya lyin'," George laughs, "never could tell a good lie, Pudgy. It was all in the past Pudge, good ol' Vince Henson not gonna put it against ya. Already did trial. Domestic dispute was all – sure maybe that wife of yours deserved it for not cookin' your meal right – not sure if your daughter deserved a plate to her head though for standin' up to ya. What was she, five?"

"Wrong – uh – fella," Pudge says.

"Ain't never been wrong yet with knowin' who I was in the lock up with,"

George was movin' closer to Pudge and that cigar was fallin' out his mouth,

"nah ain't never been wrong about that – cause when your locked up with a mug, you got twenty-four hours a day seven days a week for three hundred and sixty-five days a year together. And we had three years Pudge – *how many hours is that, guy?*"

He's pointing to Raph.

"Twenty-six thousand, two hundred and eighty."

George winked at me.

"So, you're in the lock up with a guy for twenty-six thousand two hundred and what he said – so believe me, you remember every wrinkle on his face and every ugly hair on his head, the smell of his breath in the mornin' and the way he bites his fingernails and hums that silly tune, that old western number."

Pudge is lookin' real guilty and the other guy motions to him, "*it was you wasn't it?*"

"But we didn't come here for no reunions and no arithmetic classes," George says, "we come here cause you doin' Romeo Romello's daughter some disservice interrogatin' her without an attorney present."

"This is not an interrogation," Vince said.

"I'll be the judge of that," Tony pipes up, "Anthony Romello, attorney at law."

He stuck his hand out to shake Vince's but Vince ain't havin' it so Tony shrugs and takes his hand back. He's opening his briefcase and starts grabbin' some papers with nothin' on em'. He starts shufflin' the papers on the desk and then all of a sudden he slams em down on the table.

"Who's running this organization?" Tony demands to know.

"I am," Vince folded his hands.

"I need to see the contract – where's the contract between my client and this studio?"

Vince laughed, then handed it over. Tony looked at it, skimmin' the pages and then turned to me.

"Aha!" He shouted, "Cece McAllister—not Romello. Must prove the Romello name in court – otherwise this could be slander, defamation of my client's character if you're wrong."

"The law," George nodded, sittin' down next to me and sprawlin' his feet out on top of the table.

"Aha – and if I'm right, which wouldn't take long to prove in a court of law, then this document is a fraudulent misrepresentation for monetary gain and I can countersue her for falsification of records," Vince said.

"Can he?" George asked.

"He can," Tony looked scared.

Vince smiled, "I went to law school too, you know. Oxford. Good school."

"Great school," Tony raised his eyebrows, impressed.

"Let's do us a both a favor then, huh? Let's agree as a whole that this contract is null in void."

Vince didn't break a sweat, this time he hisself put his feet up on the table.

George sat low in the chair now, his mind buzzin', eyes lookin' like he was really puzzled. Tony scratched his head and walked round the room, touchin' the backs of each chair as the guys swung round to watch him. He started stretchin' his suspenders out like he did when he was up to somethin'. George caught on and started mimickin'. Tony started gabbin', cuttin' the silence.

"Just seems funny—"

"—what's funny? You?" Vince smiled, "yes I agree, you're a joke."

"I've been called a joke before, nothin' I haven't been called before, right Cece?"

"Right," I nodded.

"No, what's funny is the name Henson," Tony said, "you know –the name Henson really makes me think."

"Is that so?"

"Yes it is. And I did a little – digging as it were, into some of your own – falsified records."

Good ol' Vince kept his poker face, but I noticed he took his feet off the desk and sat up a little straighter.

"And I'll tell you, big chief," Tony smiled smug, "your falsified records could get you in a lot more trouble than my client's, since all she wanted was just ten lines in a bad moving picture,"

Now Vince is sweatin' and so are the men in the room, all cept Raph.

"you, however, have a lot more at stake. A couple houses, bank accounts, a company – a hell of a lot more contracts signed as...Vincent Henson of Henson Brothers Studio. And an old man somewhere in England thinking he's found his long lost son."

George's face lit up like a lightbulb went through it, smilin' crazy.

"The Brit..." he said.

"The Brit," Tony repeated, *"ain't it nice to finally meet you."*

There were a few stories about *The Brit* and one in particular I'd grown up hearin' in the speaks. The other mugs talked about him in the underground like he were some sort of King. My pops even loved him, respected him, and feared him. The Brit didn't care, he had nothin' to lose and everything to gain. Thought he was untouchable, The Brit did. He was a con man, a guy from Hells Kitchen same as my pops and Jewels and all them startin' from scratch.

They called him Vinny, Vinny Hanson from the start, and he went to prison for killin' a mug so he was out there diggin' holes for years til' he ran, ran and ran and jumped on a ship, sailin' to England. Started using a british accent, grew a handlebar mustache, callin' hisself Vincent Henson and then found there were a real Vincent Henson out in Britain and he killed him. He put a bullet through that poor fools head and buried him on the Henson estate. It was a good thing the guy was estranged from his real family so Vinny could work a real good con on the real rich Henson's. Made his way back to America, but went west cause he couldn't go to no New York again, not with the feds on his tail. Lucky for him California was a great place to build an empire in them days and he started it. 'The Brit' they called him and when everybody back home was worryin' about runnin' speaks and bettin' horses, he was out there makin' pictures and livin' it up in Hollywoodland. That was The Brit for ya, he was one of a kind and untouchable...til' now.

"Jewels, that son of a bitch."

Vince shook his head and he ain't have his british accent, more like a New York slang.

"Good ol' Brit."

Jewels stood in the doorway with all them guys mean muggin' him. Jewels and him were out diggin' holes together all them years ago in the lock up, probably why they liked each other from the start. Probably why I got whatever I wanted outta Vince too, even if

I didn't deserves none of it cause that old bastard Jewels were gonna make sure I had what I wanted, the sweet old bastard.

"I ain't pin ya for no snitch," Vince said, cuttin' his eyes at Jewels.

"Jewels ain't no snitch," George defended, "but you always remember when you was in the lock up with a mug. Never forget."

He poked Pudgy in the side fat and Pudge giggled then put his cigar down and coughed like we ain't notice.

"No I ain't no snitch, ya been good to me," Jewels agreed, "I just remember things is all, remember all them years ago, I ain't snitch on ya then and I won't snitch on ya now."

"Thanks," Vince smiled.

"Don't mean we won't," George said.

"We're the biggest snitches ever lived," Tony said, "and if you don't want the news on you about it—"

Vince gettin' all hot under the collars again.

"—Then what? You want money? House? Car? What?"

"We want ya to give her them ten lines back," George said, "should be easy enough for ya. Brit."

Vince thought about it for a second, then looked at me and nodded.

"Yeah alright," he sighed.

"Nice doing business with you."

Tony stuck his hand out, this time Vince shook it. George ran over to him to shake his hand too.

"Ah Brit, I'm so glad to finally meet ya – *heard so much about ya* – I'm such a fan of your work."

George is talking over hisself and Vince is laughing and I never seen George get all googley-eyed and fawnin' over a man before, but he did for Vince.

"Yeah, okay," Vince is smilin'.

"You tough son-of-a-bitch! You're a legend! I bet you could tell so many stories!"

"Tons," Vince smiled, "you know what son, you gotta face for pictures, you know that?"

"Don't be sayin' that," Jewels piped up, "I'm finally gonna get to bet on a fight of his and win!"

George smiles that signature smile of his and they're laughin' but the whole time I'm lookin' at Raph. His hands are reaching into his pants pocket and I had been round long enough to know that somebody was reachin' for his gun when I saws it.

"Hows about a part for old Georgie?" George asks, "Hows about a part for a retired prizefighter with a face for pictures?"

"George stop," I'm warnin'.

"I see it," Vince nodded, "I can make it happen. Maybe not for this picture, but definitely the next."

"Ah, who you got as lead now?"

"Henry Caville."

"Ah, that guy? That no good loser with a father who was a boozehound? Nah, you're connin'."

George and Vince are rappin' and Tony's puttin' his papers away as Raph stands.

"There's not going to be any picture," he says and then they're all lookin' confused at him.

That's when the bracelets came out and pretty soon Vince was in handcuffs. Raph was slappin' em on him and showin' the real con, a double agent. From then on it were all big shiny badges and them goons outside the door was g-men too, shufflin' good ol' Vince and my brothers and Jewels with em.

"What cause do you have for arrestin' me?" Tony's yellin', "Just what cause?"

"Aiding and abetting," Raph said.

"Can he do that?" George asked.

"Yes, actually, he can," Tony said, stumped for the first time.

Raph's readin' rights and cuffin' our gang and his voice were real gruff when he did it. I'm just sittin' there all googley-eyed, I must admit, cause even for a copper he were some sort of magnificent. Tough as nails he were, just tough as nails and when he said he weren't afraid of no mob, he weren't kiddin'!

17

Being the Infamous Cece

Two days had gone by and I ain't do nothin' but lay around in my underwear and think. I did a lot of thinkin' in two days; sittin' and thinkin', smokin' and thinkin', drinkin' and thinkin'. I couldn't hole up in that apartment for the rest of my life just cause there weren't no prospects or film deals for the infamous Cece Romello. I'd been listenin' to the radio playin' sad jazz tunes, the ones that matched the pitiful feelin' in my stomach cause there was nothin' left in Hollywoodland for little ol' me.

The newsies wouldn't give me no rest neither. My picture and my brothers' pictures were all front page news next to headlines of The Brit and the stories lyin' sayin' the feds had caught up to all of us. We weren't no gang, I told em. *We ain't know nothin' bout no Vince Henson of Henson Brother's Studios bein' no Brit,* I told em, but they never believed me. Weren't no use explainin' myself to all them flashbulbs what kept me prisoner in my own room, cause none of em' ever listened to reason, so I'd wait. Two days later they all got sick and tired of waitin' or me to emerge from my tomb so they up and left, but by then I had more important problems besides. I had to finally make up my mind of what I were gonna do with the rest of my life!

With Vince Henson in the slammer, Raph's case was over, which meant so was production. It were all finished, they said. The government seized all the assets, paperwork, set props, trailers, scripts, and they was over there gettin' it done in double time. Bonnie's cryin', hysterical, whinin' that they took everything from her. They come to strip the houses and take everything, even the ring off her finger, they did. Nabbed all her cars and all that fancy furniture and even claimed they was gonna send them horses to the glue factory. For as awful as I felt for Bonnie and myself, I felt even worse for Henry. He had just got hisself a new house that he couldn't afford without the picture starting and a fiancé who didn't want him, cause he weren't gonna be no big star after all. The news hit him harder than any of us and it hurt him real bad—bad enough for him to start drinkin' and carryin' on down the speaks, just like his old man. He was ruinin' the little bit of reputation he had left in that town with his loud mouth and his startin' fights and chasin' women.

Two days and I'd finally got up the energy to open my suitcase and start fillin' it with the clothes I'd thrown around the room. Two days and I'd got myself put together, ready to skip town and answer Romeo Romello's call, so Birdie was gonna fly home. Two days and I'd fallen outta love with that lyin', cheatin', double crossin' Raphael and I didn't say his name without wantin' to cry or spit at him. Two days and I'd had enough of their tinsel town, enough of my big dreams of bein' an actress or at least a secretary with ten lines. That place had chewed me up and spit me out for the first and only time, cause Cece Romello weren't gonna be no city's tobacca!

I were slippin' into my furs and my kitten heels and doin' my hair up real nice for the train ride back to New York with my brothers. No way was I gonna go back home lookin' like no failure who's

Hollywood career ended for it even started, no sir! I weren't even gonna bleach my hair blonde again or try and cover my tan with clothes. I was gonna return as glamorous and beautiful as I'd been on my glossies and they was gonna like it too. This was gonna be the new and improved Cece Romello, and I'd dare them goons had somethin' to say about it!

"Cece," there were a knock at the door, *"Cece let me in. Please."*

"Nothin' doin'."

"Come on, I gotta talk to you."

"I don't want to see no liar."

"Please – I brought you some flowers, can't stand out here all day with em'. This vase is too heavy."

"Oh boy!"

I unlocked the door and opened it, threw myself into his arms with a huge smile and it weren't til' I smelled some sort of cheap cologne and scotch whiskey or felt some rough stubble against my forehead that I knew it wasn't my Raph. I pushed away from the man and looked up at Jewels who were starin' at me with a big smug grin on his stupid old face.

"What's the idea?!" I asked.

"What'd ya mean?"

"What's the idea of lettin' me hug ya like that? You knew I thought you was Raph!"

"I didn't know no such thing. I thought you was happy to see any man after you been cooped up in this apartment like a shut-in. 'Sides, I thought you swore off that gumshoe?"

"I did."

"Thought ya told him it was through? Thought ya clocked him in the face on the way to the station, tellin' him ya wouldn't never be able to trust him or look him in the eyes ever again, so as long as you was livin'?"

"I did!"

"So why was you throwin' yourself in his arms—cause he bought ya some flowers? Cece Romello can't be bought with no flowers, can she?"

"Of course not! What'd ya come round for anyway? Come to give me the third degree?"

"No, I come to get ya."

"Yeah well, I ain't gonna fight ya this time old man, grab my bags. I'm already packed and headed for the train. Get me the hell outta this state!"

"Good to hear."

Jewels is strugglin' with my bags and then there's another knock at the door, this time somethin' fierce.

"Cece, let me in!"

"Oh boy,"

This time Jewels is groanin'. He's puttin' my cases down and sittin' on em, crossin' his arms and legs.

"well open it, ya know ya want to."

"I ain't want to."

"Yes, ya do," he's noddin'.

So maybe I wanted to. I throw the door open, another grin, but it ain't my Raph, it's that Henry Caville and he's drunk as a skunk.

"Oh, Cece I missed you! I should've never left you!"

I smelled the liquor on his breathe as he tried to come in for a kiss and I'm scrunchin' my face up real tight, duckin' him.

"Cece I wanna marry you! I got to marry you! I just got to!"

"Yeah well too little too late and you're drunk!"

"Nah, it ain't too late. And I'm sorry Cece. I did ya wrong, I did ya dirty!"

"Sure's hell ya did," Jewels is sayin'.

"But let me make it up to ya, I promise. I gotta let ya know my plans,"

Then Henry's gettin' all dramatic like he did in *'To Hunt and Be Hunted'*. His eyes are goin' all serious and his hands are wavin' all over like he's playin' a part. Weren't nothin' I could do but stand there and watch him make a fool of hisself, cause I weren't gonna take him serious no more.

"things ain't over for me out here cause of Louie —Louie said he's gonna get me a role, he's got plenty lined up. The guys, the big guys at the other studios they all like me and they feel plenty sorry for me too cause of that dirty trick, that Vince Henson and his lies."

"Hey! You have some respect for ol' Brit," Jewels is warnin'.

"Yeah, have some respect," I said.

"*Ah fooey!*" Henry is spittin'.

"That Louie's gonna keep feedin' ya lies and your gonna keep bein' daft believin' em," I said, "I just don't have the time no more."

"Nah Cece, it's different now, just hear me out. All them screen tests and pictures I took, well they have em and they want me to run some lines over there. Louie says so—it's all Louie! And I can keep my house and my car and I'll be able to make something of myself and provide for ya! I'll make ya real proud of me I swear! Proud ya you were in the old days. And I think I...well I think I'm proposin'."

"Proposin'?" I asked.

"Yeah. That's what I'm doin'," he said, "I'm proposin'."

"Ain't down on one knee," Jewels is sayin'.

Henry's mad, "Shut your head, old man!"

"Nah he's right," I agreed. This time my arms is crossed too, "you ain't down on one knee, so what gives? And where's the box or the ring? Where's the diamond ya owe me?"

"*Well I...*"

"Well you what?"

"What's the matter Cece? Why ya actin' different? Why you expectin' so much?"

"I ain't actin' different, I just got standards now that's all."

"Standards? Whatcha mean by standards?"

"She's a lady," Jewels is join' in. I nodded.

"Yea and a lady don't get proposed to without a ring and a fella gettin' down on one knee doin' it. So, if ya ain't gonna do them two things, you can as good as scram!"

I'm pointin' to Jewels to get my bags, we were out.

"No, no, I'm proposin' but, well not right now—"

"—that's another thing I ain't have time for," I'm sayin', "ain't that somethin' Jewels? Well if I had a dollar for everytime this goon said 'not right now'."

"It'd be a nice chuck of change, it would," Jewels said.

"Wouldn't it?" We're laughin' in his face.

Now Henry's fightin' mad and it's gettin' worse cause he's on the sauce. He's all in front of the door tryna stop me from leavin'.

"I'm tryin' to explain," he's yellin', "it's not cause I wouldn't propose to ya, I'm just waitin' till I got something to give ya! I'm tellin' ya, day after tomorrow I got an audition. I'm tellin' ya they got me lead in another gangster film at that studio."

"What studio?"

"Kingdom Pictures, I think it is. And that Jane Pearl's gonna get me in too, she's leadin' lady. It's one of them love scenes, ya know? One of them romantic pictures. It's gonna be great Cece, we're gonna be rollin' in dough and havin' a good life! I even cashed in the rest of my checks down the bank, the rest of those checks Vince Henson owed me. Weren't it smart Cece? Cashin' them checks 'fore they froze his accounts?"

"So, where's the ring?" I asked.

"I told ya there weren't no ring!"

"You cashed them checks in, so where's the ring?" Jewels asked.

"Yeah, so where is it?"

"Ring, ring, ring—is all you mugs care about is ice? Can't a fella propose to a lady without all that glitz and glam? Can't a guy just promise to marry a gal without goin' overboard with some bendin' knees and fancy jewelry?"

"Sure he can," I'm noddin', "but not to Cece Romello he can't. Not no more."

"Why not? What makes you so different, huh? You think you're so special? What makes you more special than them other dames walkin' around what would be honored to have *the* Henry Caville spendin' time with em and promisin' em things?"

"They ain't special, they just stupid. And if I hadn't already been there once, well, I guess I'd be stupid too."

"But, don't ya think I want ya, huh? Don't ya think I'd have to love ya to want to be stuck to ya for the rest of my life?"

"Stuck to me?" I asked, "See that's the problem—I don't want no man who thinks he's stuck to me. I want a man who wants to be with me. Don't say you're stuck to me, makin' me feel like some ball and chain!"

Henry's glarin' and runnin' around crazy.

"You're a spoiled brat, you know that Cece? Just cause your pops never give ya what for! Just cause you were runnin' round with mobsters, ya think you know better with all your fancy talk, your fancy clothes and your big house. Well guess what, ya ain't so special, ya ain't so tough and you ain't so fancy! And ya definitely ain't no lady! You're just a spoiled brat, ya are. Just a spoiled bitch!"

"You watch your mouth!"

This time Jewels is standin' and now he's takin' Henry by the collar and he's draggin' him towards the door.

"I've had just about enough of you!" Jewels is sayin.

"Oh yeah?"

Henry's tryna act tough, but he's tremblin' underneath Jewels fists all balled up around his shirt. He's shakin' in his boots he is, while Jewel's got him up with his feet swingin'. That old man was stronger than he looked, no doubt.

"I been sittin' around this place with your sorry mug for a year and you ain't never said a word of thank you or an I love you to Cece and she ain't no waitin' woman. She ain't no lady that deserves bein' at your beckon call when you decide you wanna quit runnin' around with this dame and that dame. You ain't deserve no better than bein' a washed up actor and the son of a boozehound what's stuck on the sauce hisself!"

"—but I—"

"—but nothin'! Your pops didn't know no better, so you need to wise up or you'll end up just like he did."

Henry's scramblin', twistin' his words and stutterin' all wide-eyed, cause that lovely old fool Jewels got him by his shirt and he's 'bout to carry him out hisself.

"Is that a—is that a threat?"

"Yes, it is a threat. It's a threat if I ever did say one. Sue me!"

Now Jewels is openin' the door, about to toss Henry out on his rear, that sorry excuse for a man. That Henry Caville—I couldn't stand the look of him, so good riddens! But then all I see is my Raph, with his six foot two muscles fillin' the door frame and his holdin' flowers and chocolates with a smile and a black eye, wonderin' *whats goin' on* and *what's Jewels doin' with Henry Caville all up in the air like that?*

"He's stronger than he looks, isn't he?" Raph's sayin' to Henry, "what's happening?"

"This one called Cece a bitch and all," Jewels said.

"Oh, did he? Excuse me."

Raph's handin' me the flowers and chocolates and pushin' his suit jacket sleeves up like he was gonna take out the trash hisself.

"Be my guest,"

Jewels is handin' Henry over like he's as good as garbage so Raph can take him nearly in one hand and carry him down the hallways to the waste bin, throwin' him in and wipin' his hands off on the way back. I'm busy eatin' the chocolates and smellin' the pretty flowers he give me as Jewels is all commentin' on his big strong figure and *'fuzz or no fuzz, that's the type of man ya need to marry'.*

"Oh, clam up," I said.

Now Raph is back and he's all sweet talkin' and *'baybeee'* and kissin' me on my ear. I'm not givin' in not even one bit, but it was nice and all cause I missed him and a girl can only take so much sweet talkin' and kissin' til' she gives in a little, but who could really blame me?

"I just mean, why didn't ya tell me? Why didn't you tell me the truth?"

"Would you have still been with me if I did?"

"Well, no."

"So that's why."

"But – but – no don't kiss me, get off me! What am I doin'? Ya arrested my family!"

"So? They were out on bail the next day. Your family was not my target."

"But they're my family Raph!"

"Yeah but," he's lookin' confused, "they're mobsters. I should be the one with the problem with you, not the other way around."

"He's got a point," Jewels said.

"Well that ain't good enough."

"I thought it would impress you," Raph said.

"Impress me?" I asked.

Jewels is laughin'.

"You really are somethin', ya know that?" I'm sayin', "You take them chocolates back and all —I mean why would it impress me? Why would such a smart guy think somethin' that dumb?"

"Cause he arrested the fast-talkin' Tony Romello," Jewels said, "ain't nobody been able to arrest that man in a long time. Not even tried it."

He did have a point and even if the charges didn't stick, it did ruffle his feathers a bit and maybe that hoity toity, thinkin' he was better than everybody else, callin' me 'Ceceliaaaa' pretty boy needed to be cut down a peg. Even if he was out on bail, he spent at least one night gettin' his suit dirty in the slammer.

"Yeah so, so you were lucky with Tony cause we don't get along very much, but what about George, huh? George is my favorite. Ya really did wrong arrestin' George!"

Raph's showin' me his face, his cuts and bruises.

"Yeah but George, he didn't go down easy," Raph said, "as soon as we got him to the car, he's finding his way out of those hand-cuffs and sparring with me, but I got a few good hits in. He was so impressed that he got back in those handcuffs himself. Jewels, you saw for yourself, didn't you?

He's lookin' at Jewels and he's noddin'.

"Even George said you should marry that man," Jewels told me.

"You're connin'. You're both really connin'."

Raph is shakin' his head no and tryin' to come near me again.

"We ain't connin'," Jewels is confirmin'.

"Yeah but—"

"—oh, just kiss him," Jewels sighed.

"You got somethin' else to say old man?" I ask.

"Yeah I do," Jewels said, "I spent a lotta time gettin' yous two together, so I want to see some action!"

"What?"

Raph's eyes are pleadin' with me and I couldn't bear no more of it, I swear.

"Jewels figured out early that I were workin' double agent, but he didn't spill the beans."

"Why not?"

"Because he knew I wasn't after the Romellos. And he knew I wanted to meet you,"

Jewels smiled, the smile that showed he was missin' teeth. He reserved that smile for special occasions only.

"It was Jewels that picked me up," Raph explained, "he wanted me to meet you and for us to start seeing each other. I thank him everyday for giving me the pleasure."

"But I—"

I ain't even know what to say. Raph smiled, the kind that glistens white teeth. It was better than a George Romello smile cause it were genuine and innocent like.

"He ain't our kind," I'm tellin' Jewels.

"What kind?" Jewels is askin'.

"He's fuzz, and we Romello's don't call the cops for nothin'!"

"Yeah? Well maybe it's time you did," Jewels said, "maybe it's time you got out of the life. I'm not a young man and if there's anything I'd rather see before I die it's Cece Romello just bein' Cece. It's you runnin' away with somebody respectable, somebody like Raphael here and just bein' a normal citizen. And if you were my daughter—"

"—but I ain't your daughter! I'm Romeo Romello's daughter!"

"Yeah don't I know it," Jewels is shakin' his head, then turnin' back to Raph, "sorry, she ain't never gonna learn."

"I love you," Raph said to me, "and I can't possibly be here knowing what I know about you. My whole career's at stake, but I just love you Cece. It's a conundrum."

"A what?"

He laughed.

"A conflict."

"A what?!"

Then he grabbed me and kissed me. And I'll tell ya Raph kissin' me weren't like nobody else's kiss in the whole wide world cause Raphael knew how to kiss. He weren't no sloppy kissin' like Henry or no peck on the lips like Mackie. And his breath weren't all bad and his lips all dry, no sir. It were warm and soft. It was a kiss ya could just get lost in. I didn't even remember where I was or when by the time I opened my eyes again. In his kiss, I forgot we was from two different worlds, two different worlds entirely. I didn't feel no difference between my kind and his kind when we was kissin'. I just felt what was right, what was somethin' I always wanted and didn't know it.

But being Romeo's daughter meant I couldn't be with no federal agent – no guy whose job it was to lock up guys like my old man and my brothers. It didn't matter if what he thought he was doing was right, so there were jails all full of guys that didn't grow up with nothin', tryin' to earn a livin' as best they could. Who was guys like Raph to say what was right and wrong? Who was we supposed to follow? Some government that didn't give a damn about us? Some law built to cut us down—keep the rich richer and the poor in their place? Nah, they were the ones really connin'. I just couldn't believe it and I couldn't stand for it neither. Even with all his kissin' that felt good and his strong arms holdin' me, I just couldn't get out my head that he weren't one of us.

"Things are only gonna get worse for them, now that the Brit's captured," Raph told me, "the Santini's and the Romello's of the world...the law is cracking down on them, fast. Men like them can't possibly survive against law and order. You have to understand that."

"I don't have to understand it," I said, "cause the only ones not survivin' are the ones who don't have no family supportin' em. I'm gonna stand by my pops til' the bitter end."

Raph let me go. He backed away from me like I weren't the Cece he loved and maybe I weren't, but I were through havin' men defining who I was and who I wasn't.

"She'll come around," Jewels said.

"No, I won't!" I yelled, "cause all of ya's want to say what I'll do and what I won't, but don't none of ya know a damn! So guess what—I am goin' back to New York and I'm gonna get what's mine! I'm gonna have that top spot, Jewels, and nothin' you or my brothers or my pops have to say is gonna stop me. It's what was promised to me since I were knee high!"

Jewels ain't say nothin', he's just lookin' at his feet.

"And another thing," I point to Raph next, "if you got some beef, you and your government, with my pops and our kind well just be ready to have beef with me too, cause I'm leadin' things! And I hope the next time I see you, I got a rifle in one hand and a drink in the other!"

Raph ain't say nothin', he's just lookin' at the door.

"And ya ain't gettin' your ring back neither!"

I touched the ring he give me. I'd put it on a chain around my neck, cause it were prettier and meant more to me than any piece of jewelry I'd ever gotten from a man. I was chokin' back tears I was, cause I knew weren't no Raphael gonna want no mug like me, but it were my duty, as a woman of honor. And I was finally gonna get what was owed to me.

"I don't want it back," he said, "I gave it to you because I love you and I'll always love you Cece,"

He's leavin', with his big beautiful broad shoulders walkin' through my door, out of my life forever and then he's turnin' back one last time so he can say,

"I just never thought I'd be using my own ring to identity your body."

18

Being a Lady

Dr. Edwin Billingsly, as he so politely introduced hisself to me, were an eloquent man of color with tight dark brown curls and an immaculately trimmed beard. He were in his forties it seemed, with skin smooth as silk, the color of milk chocolate, and glistenin'. He were prominent in social circles in Harlem and had two kids at home waiting to be tucked in by their father after a long trip out West for a medical conference. He were one of them doctors what dealt with the mind, as he explained it, and him and those other big wigs he ran with were lookin' at cures for somethin' or other. Four days from California to New York on a sleepin' train car service and he'd introduced me to the other folks as his wife. We traveled back together, innocently enough, as *Dr. and Mrs. Billingsly*.

"My apologies sir, I didn't realize," the conductor said, when he was corrected.

When I met the doctor he had instructed I take Raph's ring from around my neck and slip it on my own finger 'fore the conductor took our tickets. When they came round wonderin' just who I was and why I was travelin' alone, Dr. Billingsly took the matter in his stride and immediately wrapped an arm around mine. We was married and that was that. It shut all of em' up to the fact I were so young, so female and so alone, or so they thought.

"What's the idea?" I asked, "why were they so upset at me?"

"There's certain protocol my dear," he said.

Dr. Billingsly was very matter of fact with everything he did and said and he knew a part of me were just a little more than naive. Sure, I'd joined my brothers and Jewels at the station, but when it came to boarding the traincar I got stuck. I were immediately separated from the rest, shuffled to the back of line, to this unspoken colored section. My luggage were long gone, stolen I'd guessed. He'd been so sweet and paid for my meals and helped me along. I didn't look like no promiscuous woman, no woman wantin' somethin' for nothin', so he were willing to help me. He just wanted to know why I'd been comin' along by myself so far from home and where I was goin' when I got there. My story fascinated the family man who'd had his head stuck in books for all of his life. We dined together that mornin' and he found the way I ate my food what he called *'laughable'*, with my elbows on the table usin' my knife to knaw away at breakfast sausages, slurpin' up my eggs and coffee.

"May I?" he asked, so I nodded and then he showed me.

Use the lace napkin, carry it 'cross the body, drape on knees for me, on left knee for him. Eat, sip, wipe mouth. Never let my fork and knife lay back on the table. Always position on my plate, with knife secured by fork. When eatin', cut, then drag to back of fork, lift to mouth. Focus on my dining companion. Take small bites. Chew, chew, chew. Never talk with my mouth full. Visit the powder room after. Wash hands, wipe mouth fully and reapply makeup as needed. I ain't learned so much as I learned that day about bein' a lady and it was from a man, no doubt!

We settled in a private compartment shortly after, lettin' our food digest and takin' advantage of velvet covered cushions and the elaborate designs on the ceiling. I ain't taken in the beauty of it the last time I was on, only cause Henry, Jewels and I had been two sheets to the wind on our homemade hooch from the flasks we snuck in our pockets. This time, my eyes were opened. With Dr. Billingsly, it seemed the whole world looked brand new.

"I have a wife, Alma," he said, "she's the light of my life."

Doc took a picture from his wallet, a fine embroidered leather-back with his initials. He showed me a photo of a woman, whose beautiful curls were pinned back on her head. She wore a pretty lace dress with stockings and shoes all neat. She had on a simple row of pearls, no extravagant ice like Regina. Her makeup was not overly done and her eyes sparkled still, even in a now aged photograph. She wore a smile I knew he'd put there on purpose.

"How about your kids? Let's see em'." I asked, but he had no photos of em'.

"I keep Alma to my heart," he explained, "she keeps the kids to hers,"

I just stared at him, confused.

"but they are fine kids," he said, "they should be more than I am."

"How can ya be so sure?"

"Because time will allow them to be."

We spoke on so many things, me and the doc. He were amazed with my pops, my stories of growin' up in New York and my wantin' to be so much in the life. He weren't somebody I'd think of as tellin' tales outta school. I knew he wouldn't be no snitch on me. I could tell from an early age about people who wanted to listen just to gossip and who wanted to listen to help, and he was the latter. I just kinda looked at him as a protector on that trip, ya know? This man I'd never met before in my life who took it upon hisself to be so sweet and kind to me, just when I was losin' control.

"You know, it's just fascinating, I've been studying the psycho-logical ramifications of war. So, you say your brother hasn't spoken in years?"

"Not a word."

"And even he, the son of a –well I'm sure he saw some form of combat even before he went overseas. For it to leave such trau-matic scarring to someone like him, someone almost groomed for war based on his upbringing, it's just very interesting. I'd be very intrigued to observe him."

"Pops says he needs to man up."

The doc looked very seriously towards me.

"Post-traumatic stress is not a lack of strength. *How dare he?*"

I ain't say nothin', but I wanted to look out the window, any-where that weren't his eyes.

"Why do you bite your nails when I challenge your father's beliefs?"

"I don't know," I shrugged.

"Look at me," he ordered, "when you're talking to someone you look at them, you look them in the eyes. Don't be afraid of their reactions."

I turned back and he were still focused, leanin' into me and all.

"Do you believe your father is a good man?"

"Yes."

"How?"

"Cause...well...cause he..." I couldn't think, "because he always took care of me."

"Took care of you how? Monetarily?"

"Yes...and protection."

"He had to protect you. He had no choice for this. The life he built around you was what needed protecting. You and your broth-ers, you are assets to him, no good to him vulnerable. No good to him exposed to his enemies. He has to protect what is his, as a good business man would, that's what you do you protect your assets."

"I'm his daughter."

"Worse!" Doc shouted, "for a man whose life has been lived in total masculinity, teaching men to be men and believing strength is based on testosterone levels only, it would be a worst case scenario for him, in his own mind, to have to be responsible on his own for a daughter,"

His eyes, his expressions lit up while we talked like he were exposing truths and realizing it hisself as the conversation went on.

"so when his wife died, he knew he had to lock you away, as an asset, because he knew at that moment he'd be totally and solely responsible for you and he knew nothing more than to put you away like a, like a—"

"—like an object."

"Yes," he nodded, "an object. Nothing more, nothing less,"

I ain't say nothin'.

"and this was the biggest offense of all, to someone who had from an early age, in her own words, stuck by his side and loved the attention, the 'heavy behind the Romello name'. But you understand it wasn't respect given freely to the Romellos, it's never been. It was fear, infamy, and no one should be feared to be liked. You must come to terms with the fact your father and your brothers and that Jewels, they have kept you safe, but only away from a plethora of their sins. It's those sins that brought the respect and attention you adore. It came with a price. That life always does."

The words he said I understood, but I were angry by them and I had every right to be. He saw me, the rage buildin' up. Who was he to think he knew all the answers to my life, my family, my pops? Doctor or no doctor, he weren't gonna analyze me to death, not sittin' there for four days. I just weren't gonna take it.

"You don't know nothin' bout my pops."

"I'm sorry Cecelia, I just see him differently than you do, that's all."

"Yeah well, you ain't see when he was out there feedin' the poor in Hell's Kitchen. You ain't see when he was givin' money and food to folks who was needin' it. You ain't see when he was bringin' them men up from nothin', helpin' em feed their families and buy houses for their kids to sleep."

"So, he's a modern day Robinhood," he nodded, "that's admirable."

"Exactly!"

"Doesn't make him a good father, it just means he's resetting his bad karma."

"He's a great father."

"I'm glad you think that."

"Good, cause I do. And nothin' nobody says is gonna make me change my mind."

"I'm not trying to get you to change your mind, Cecelia. I just want you to understand that your father...he's only human. Understand there are parts of him that aren't so great. You must understand it and process it. It will help you."

"Help me how?"

"It will help you to not repeat his mistakes in your own life."

"Ain't no mistakes to be like him. He grew me up to be like him, and that's just how I see it."

"Well then we see different."

"Well then we just gonna see different."

I turned my head and crossed my arms and when Cece Romello's done talkin'—she stops.

"And we should," he smiled, "we're perfect strangers. Why wouldn't we see things differently and why shouldn't we have a dialogue about it? That's how we learn both sides of a story. Too many people want to shy away from conversation and refuse to learn about each other. That's what I'm fighting to change."

I'm keepin' my mouth shut and my lips pursed together. I'm sneakin' peaks at him out the corner of my eyes and the smile never left his face.

"You know what? I just realized something about you. You're too agreeable. You don't like confrontation of any kind, not really. It makes you uncomfortable and that interesting, for a Romello. You must be an anomaly in your own family."

"I ain't yella!"

He laughed.

"So why don't you speak your mind? Why do you hide yourself from others?"

"Because it ain't worth it! Ain't nobody ever listened to what Cece had to say!"

"All your life?"

"All my life!"

"Then don't let it go any further! They hid you away, locked you away, bleached your hair, and made you up to be someone you weren't. You should mad at this. You should fight against it!"

The porter came over. Guess cause we was gettin' loud with our voices and I looked down like I were embarrassed, all red in the face.

"Everythin' okay?" he asked.

"Yes, George it's fine, we are fine," Doc said, embarassed himself.

Doc had been so good to me and he weren't bein' disrespectful, just askin' me questions, but ain't nobody asked me questions before, not really.

"Okay, well if that's all..."

"No actually, that's not all. George what's your real name?" Doc asked.

The porter looked around so's to make sure weren't nobody else near.

"Sam."

"Samuel?"

He nodded.

"Thank you, Samuel. Yes, everything's fine here."

The porter left with a big grin on his face and I'm askin' Doc why.

"All the colored porters are made to look the same, so all their names are George and I find it nonsensical. If his given name, his birth name, is Samuel then I'll call him Samuel and you'll do right to call him it as well. No George, no Sam and no boy. Respect is given with a full name only."

"But nicknames are easier."

"No, they aren't. Too much familiarity. You aren't Cece. You are Cecelia. You deserve respect and you have every right to demand it," he said, "just as I am a doctor and because of the length of my education and the cost of my degree, no one has any right to call me *'Mister'* for the rest of my life. No *'Mister'*, no *'son'*, no *'boy'*. Why should you not be given the same respect?"

All them years bein' mad at Tony and Regina for usin' my full name cause I thought they were bein' disrespectful. Did I get it the wrong way around the whole time?

"So, if nobody listened to you for all of those years, what's stopping you from saying what you want now? You are an adult, Cecelia. Part of growing up is making yourself seen and heard. What do you want, what do you really want?"

I told him I had to think.

"Think long, think wrong," he smiled, "You already know what is it. You've known what it is for years."

He was right and I was just itchin' to say.

"I want to be married."

The words came out of me real quick, so quick I ain't even see them comin'.

"That's fine, that's perfectly fine. You want to be married, you want to be protected, you want to be loved. You had a wonderful man who proposed to you...why didn't you accept? Why did you put his ring around your neck like some sort of trophy? Why didn't you say yes when he bore his soul?"

I felt the ring on my finger—Raphael's ring. I saw him in my mind, big and strong and handsome. Why didn't I accept, I thought. Why didn't I really?

"He weren't gonna want me in the life. He was tryin' to take me away from my family."

"That's marriage. It's a partnership. Your partner comes before everyone, including your family, including your kids. Til' death do you part should be an unbreakable bond. That's loyalty, that's everything you've been taught to believe. Why do you fight against it?"

"Cause he wanted to change me!"

"He didn't want to see you get hurt. Why wouldn't you want that in a husband? A protector? He doesn't understand why you are still in this life you speak of. Everyone in your family, your father included, have been trying to push you out and you still stay. And frankly I don't think you even know why you stay anymore!"

"But —he's the fuzz! I'm a Romello and we don't call the cops for nothin'! No matter how handsome they are!"

"That's your father talking, that's not you talking. Try again."

I'm steamin' mad now and he knew it.

"I want my pop's spot. It was promised to me and it should be given to me too! My pops, if he's a man of his word, will keep up his end of the deal and keep mine. If I'm demandin' things, then I should go back to him demandin' that. And Raph—Raphael didn't want no parts of it, so I told him to scram!"

"That's not what you said at first. I asked you what you wanted and you said you wanted to be married. It's the first thing that came from your conscience. That 'top spot' didn't come from your mouth, not once."

"Well I thought it and then you started talkin'."

"Hmm, so if you want to be married and you also want to stay in the *family business*, we'll call it, then your wonderful, strong, charming Raphael will have to be out. He will truly have to *scram*.'"

"Well, that's just fine with me," I lied.

Doc looked at me like he knew.

"I guess you'll have to settle for a man like Mackie Jones, or—"

"—I ain't settlin' for no Mackie Jones!"

And if we weren't in no traincar together and I weren't tryin' so hard to pretend to be his wife, to be a lady, I swear I woulda spit. Doc settled back in his chair and he crossed his arms, smilin' smug.

"Why not? That's the only kind of man that will want you."

"Who says?"

"My apologies, let me rephrase. That's the only man whom will be able to stand by and watch you make a complete and utter fool of yourself."

"A fool?"

"Let me rephrase again,"

His smile faded, he leaned in closer.

"he's the only man who will willingly sit idly by while you slowly kill yourself."

"What?!"

"It's no slight towards you specifically, Cecilia. It's just what this kind of life does to a person. It was your stepmothers' end and it will be your end too, if you persist."

"Liar! You don't know nothin'—you're just a—just a quack!"

I stood up, doctor or no doctor, payin' for my meals or not, I couldn't take him no more.

"Excuse me, but I'm goin' to bed!"

"So early?"

"So early!"

He stood up, politely, like the gentleman he was, and I was just tired of him bein' so right and so polite, the bastard!

"Of course. Goodnight, Ms. Cecelia."

"Yeah, yeah goodnight to you too!"

The next morning, I woke, dressed and went to breakfast. Doc sat a few places down from me with his coffee and his newspaper. He was bein' all silent and still polite and I still couldn't stand it.

"Not dinin' with your husband this morning?" Samuel asked and I shook my head no, "well that's just fine, sometimes you need a break. Sometimes a break does the marriage good, makes ya miss the other person more."

"Are ya married Samuel?"

"Yes'm," he said.

His eyes looked sad, but he's keepin' a smile on his face like he's strainin' and his head's down as he's rearrangin' the dishes and glasses on my table.

"How long you two been, on a break?"

"Eight months," he said, "Eight months, two weeks and two days to the day."

"I'm sorry, Samuel."

"Don't be," he said, "weren't makin' any money where we lived. Now she's got the best of everything and that's keeping a smile on my face. She's a good girl. She deserves every penny of it."

"Don't ya miss her?" I'm askin.

"Somethin' terrible,"

And then he's kinda frozen at the table and don't wanna move no muscle to arrange no plates no more, cause his hand's tremblin'.

"and this way she can have her wallpaper the way she wants and keep the beds all nice and neat not wrinklin' her sheets. Ain't nobody in the kitchen makin' a mess and liftin' the lids on her pots spoilin' dinner."

Dr. Billingsly looked at us from across the way, then put his newspaper back up real quick so I didn't see. I took my linen napkin and my pocketbook and brought myself over to him.

"Do you mind if I dine with ya, husband?"

He looked up like he weren't bothered.

"Of course not,"

He stood and pushed my chair in for me as I sat down across from him.

"Samuel, Mrs. Billingsly would like her coffee here please, if you don't mind."

Samuel's smilin' and bringin' it over, fillin' my cup.

"Course sir, of course. Glad you two are back together again. Real glad. Life's too short, ya know? Too short indeed."

"Yes, it is," Doc said.

Before Samuel left, he slipped him a napkin and I knew the shape of spinach when I saw it. The stack had to be a about three or five hundred. That coulda tied him over for a good long while and now I'm wonderin' just how Doc got all that money, but I wouldn't dare ask.

"Go see your wife, wrinkle those sheets," he said, smilin', "go make a mess."

Samuel's all teary eyed and he nodded, lookin' away real quick cause he didn't want to make a fool of hisself cryin' in front of us. Doc had that way about him. He weren't makin' no big show of hisself, but he were a good man. I thought about how many people he coulda helped and maybe he could help me and all.

"I want to find my ma."

I said flat out and I knew there weren't no other way to bring it up, so I just came right out with it. He were finishin' up his breakfast 'fore he answered.

"Alright."

I could tell he had his doubts.

"Whatcha thinkin'?"

He sipped his coffee and put his paper down.

"It's just been my experience that people who stay away do so for a reason, and most times that reason is that they don't want to be found."

I'm pleadin' my case to him.

"It ain't for her, it's for me."

"Good," he said, "that's the only reason to do it."

"Why?"

"Well, this way you won't be surprised or upset if she doesn't take your visit for the sentiment that it is."

"Oh."

"And how do I know this?" He's askin', "because my own long last daddy slammed the door in my face after our reunion in my twenties. I'd come home thinkin' I was some war hero and that I'd make a difference to him. But he didn't even want to know me."

"Really?"

Doc had some far away stare and then he shook his head, turnin' his focus back to me.

"Why don't you tell me about her. What do you know?"

I started talkin', about the name Cookie Johnson, the hoofer, but he drew a blank.

"I don't frequent many speakeasies, so I wouldn't necessarily know how to help you. I'm sure if you asked around, someone somewhere in the city would know of her, or at least where she works. Finding her is probably much easier than you think."

Then I'm tellin' him all about my pops and her and how they got together and I really didn't want our meetin' to end, but I knew it would. He took his pocketwatch out, real gold, real hinky, and he's lookin' at the time. We didn't have much longer we'd be off that train and we'd have to say our goodbyes.

"She's in Harlem. Aren't you goin' that way?"

"We're all going that way."

He motioned towards the rest of the passengers and I looked around saw em', all fancy dressed although I hadn't noticed before. They was all like him, all polite, all mannerly and respectable. They all had some spinach in their pockets too, probably doctors, lawyers, professors. Some were travelin' with their wives, some were alone. All had Pocketwatches and expensive suits or frilly dresses and nice shoes, with their hair all done up nice. They was also all people of color.

"I ain't never had a problem before."

"Problem?" Doc asked, confused.

"Well, I ain't never been with folks like you before."

"Folks like me?"

"You know...*blacks,*"

The other passengers looked towards me, then back to what they was doin' like they heard but was too polite to comment. They wore them smug smiles like how dare I say it when I was lookin' just like em', maybe less.

"I ain't mean no offense, it's just – well last time I, um, rode the rails, I weren't with you folks."

He laughed, thinkin' I were some naïve or somethin' and maybe I was in them days.

"Well presumably, last time you *'rode the rails'*, you had two white men traveling with you. One who was most certainly, if not nearly, your fiancé. And another who looked as if he were your father,"

He leaned in closer as if almost at a whisper, but not carin' if the rest of em heard it and they did cause by now they turned to listen too.

"not to mention, you yourself admitted you were passing."

I ain't thought about it much, but he were right. And it were true, everytime I'd looked in the mirror or saw my own reflection in the glass in them windows, I ain't recognize myself those days at all. I were darker from the tan, my once fairer skin turnin' caramel from the California sun shinin' on me for nearly a year. My bleach blonde were all grown out and now I had a full head of dark brown curls flowin' free and frizzy down my back. So, they looked on me and put me in a car with others who looked like me too, not carin' how much we paid for our tickets or what kind of backgrounds none of us had, we was just colored. Who were I to keep denyin' it or thinkin' it were some sort of crime, some sort of slight to be who I really was? Maybe it were some sort of slight for them to think less of us and all, maybe some sort of slight not to ask our names and not to give us no respect, but it weren't no slight to be one of them...one of...

"I'm a negro!"

I said it like it were some sort of realization cause it were and that's when he looked at me, wide-eyed like he couldn't believe I'd just came to terms with it. There was a real big smile plastered on his face like he'd done his duty in four days, and maybe he had. He smacked his forehead with his hand and was laughin' alongside with the rest of the passengers round us just gigglin' up a storm and Samuel with his food tray was snickerin' too.

"Yes Cecelia," Dr. Billingsly exclaimed, "*we are!*"

19

Being Tan in New York City

The noon train brought me back to New York City, but my tired feet got me to Harlem. It were a place I'd never been before and weren't never allowed to go, accordin' to my pops. I walked the streets —covered in a sea of black faces —thinkin' just one of em might be my real ma. I knew I couldn't rest til' I found her, so I stayed til' I did.

Cookie were somethin' of a legend in them days, in that part of the city. There weren't nobody that didn't know her or know of her. They was friends with her or went out to drinks with her or knew where she lived, where she worked, and who she hung around with. Plenty of folks tried to help me find her cause they felt for my sob story and so I'd follow em round, without no luck.

By nightfall I'd dragged myself from one corner of town to the next and I were so worn out from travelin', I damn sure needed a drink in me. There were plenty of speaks and dancers, a whole mess of lounge singers and women what fit the description I'd been searchin' for, but not none of em' were *the* Cookie Johnson. I found one gin joint in particular, just in time enough that I'd needed to take a rest, kick my heels off and sit a while. That's when I found

I were sittin' right at a table in front of Cookie, watchin' her dance and sing without even knowin' it.

Cookie Johnson were a short, plump, little ball a fire! She were singin' and dancin' her heart out like she'd done it all her life and she worked a room sure as a professional. All them goons had Cookie's attention and her audience loved her, women and men alike. She come round singin' her tunes with that jazz band behind her playin' loud and she's usin' all her energy, workin' them vocal chords over-time. She was walkin' through the crowd of folks at their tables and she'd be touchin' backs and sashayin' those wide hips of hers over towards the stage they'd set up in her honor. We all clapped between every song and at the end they'd cheer Cookie on and she'd bow her head, smilin', with sweat glistenin' off her nubian skin. Nobody said Cookie Johnson ain't work hard for the spinach they tossed around for her. That woman had more costume changes than I'd ever seen and I only were sittin' there for an hour! Barkeep said they *only got asses in the seats when they knews Cookie Johnson were comin'.*

Cause Cookie ain't just sing at one bar, oh no, *she was travelin' with her band and she traveled all over the country,* I heard from folks. She'd been singin' in all cities, *'includin' cities no colored folks could go so easy',* they'd tell me. Cookie were welcomed everywhere by everybody, I heard, and all the men loved her, that was no doubt. They talked about everybody who wanted a piece of Cookie, *'if ya knows what I mean'.* That night she just happened to be singin' in Harlem, but she'd been long gone from there, yes long gone and she was gonna make a record, they told me. Real proud, they were, her friends and fans, tellin' me with their shoulders back and puffed out. They said she were makin' a record for Harlem and it were gonna sell a million times over!

It was the beginning of summer, a real hot night, and it were after hours. The bartender was yellin' last call. The band's wrappin' up their playin' and packin' up their instruments, and then there were my ma. She had lovely dark skin and a beautiful face, all made up with mascara and eye liner and blush, almost like a movie star or a model. She had all colorful beads and jewelry on her arms and round her neck, gold rings on her fingers and long painted nails— deep red. When she talked, she moved her hands round like she was tryin' to mesmerize ya. When she smoked her cigarette, she took real long drags as she inhaled and let the smoke fill her lungs without a care, so slow and free. A furry boa draped over her bare shoulders and she'd let it fall seductively over her large breasts. She crossed her legs, puttin' her heels in the air, red to match her nails and sportin' the highest slit I'd ever seen in a dress.

I snuck towards her as the house lights came on and the cleaners were sweepin' up. She was sittin' there with her drink, all alone, pressin' cigarette after cigarette into an ashtray and smilin' to herself. I sat down across from her real slow almost like she were gonna bite me or somethin'. I remembered Doc's words, thinkin' maybe she wouldn't want me. *Who cares? I'm here for me,* I had to keep remindin' myself so's to get up enough courage and nerve not to leave. My voice uttered some type of squeak, which was all I could get out after I gasped for air.

"Miss,"

I'm sayin' real gentle and she looked up slow, eyebrows raised like I was interruptin' her own conversation and thoughts she was havin' with herself. When Cookie Johnson looked at a person, she seemed to be lookin' through em' almost, all up and down and then through.

"Miss Cookie Johnson?" I continued.

She let out a loud laugh deep down from her belly. It filled the whole room almost and it echoed like her singin'.

"I ain't been no Miss in a long time," she said, "who wants me?"

"Well – I –"

"—and if it's about your husband, I ain't have no parts of him. Whatever he told ya, he's a liar. I'll swear on the good book to that."

She's back to lookin' down and payin' attention to her ashtray, swirlin' her finger round the top of her drink, movin' the ice cubes to and fro' with the tips of her nails. On stage, she'd looked so cool, so much that was bigger than life, but now she was just, well, *normal.*

"It ain't like that," I said, leanin' forward, "I just come to talk."

"Ain't got no more room in my band," she said, "I work alone. Just me and the boys, besides I don't need no young competition."

She's noddin' over to the men in their fancy suits puttin' away their instruments and smokin' their cigarettes, talkin' bout goin' to the next diner over for chicken and waffles.

"You comin' Cookie?"

One of them askes, the really tall one that looked like he might have designs on my ma. She gave him a wink and a nod.

"You know I'll be there," she's smilin'.

"I just—"

I reached over and touched her hand and I don't know what made me do it, but when I did, she sure jumped. Cookie sat straight back in her chair and the cigarette fell into a heap of ashes and her drink got pushed to the side by the boa. She's lookin' at me real focused, her eyes glarin'.

"Hey! I ain't no carpet muncher," she said, "not anymore."

"No I—"

"Go on, spit it out. Ya want an autograph or somethin'?"

"I'm Cece—Cecelia, um—"

"Yeah, what ya want me to write it on? You gotta napkin or somethin'?"

"I'm...your daughter."

I wondered for a long time what that moment would be like and if it were some sort of hero's welcome I'd received when I got there or some type of tear jerkin' session between us, but she's still glarin' her eyes and not movin' a muscle, just starin'. And then after a long pause, she shook her head.

"I gotta date and all, I uh," she started, "I don't have time for this,"

She's gettin' up to leave me at the table all by myself.

"we gonna be in Chicago, I'm gonna be makin' a record and,"

She's stallin', playin' with the ashtray, standin' up at the table.

"*you've got some fuckin' nerve*, ya know that?" she asked.

"What?" I'm confused.

"Ain't nobody told ya to come find me, ain't nobody said it."

"But I wanted to."

"To hell with what you want!"

I didn't know what to say and I was cryin' like a kid and I were gettin' up to leave. I'd waited so long and for what? For this, to get Cookie Johnson yellin' in my face, tellin' me she ain't want me. Well I ain't need it, got enough of that from my step ma Regina and I didn't need it from my real ma too.

"Well- I—" I stuttered.

"Well you what?"

"I—"

"Quit cryin' and say it! Speak!"

I couldn't get my words out right, I couldn't find none. She was lookin' up and down at me all judgin' and waitin' for me to talk.

"Go ahead," she said, "say it!"

"I just—"

"You just thought I was gonna get up and hug ya, kiss ya, tell ya how much I missed you bein' in my life and all that sappy mess? Nah, wrong dame."

She's back to her cigarette and lookin' towards the door. I'm pleadin'.

"But I—"

She's smilin' smug.

"But ya wanted some type of explanation, cause you think ya deserve some types? Cause now you're all full grown, you're around twenty now so you think you're a full woman and you're entitled? Cause ya think ya know the decisions of a mother cause you're old enough to be one?"

"No I—"

"Well Cookie Johnson don't owe no explanation to nobody! Daughter or otherwise!"

I stand up to leave, but my feet wouldn't move me. I'm tremblin', I say, my body, my legs, my arms, my hands. I didn't know why I was shakin' so hard. It was embarassin' to say the least and she knew it. I didn't stand much taller than she did, but maybe enough for her to look up at me with them focused, piercing hazel eyes, lookin' like she wanted to fight.

"I ain't want —no trouble."

The words came outta my mouth, but I don't know how.

"Why you stutterin'? Did he teach you to stutter? Why you ain't know how to talk right?"

"I do."

"You don't! Why you talk all that slang? Didn't he give ya no schoolin'? Didn't he give ya no tutor? Stand up straight. Be firm!"

"—he didn't—"

"Just like the bastard," she spit, "can't even get that right."

"Why'd you—"

"Why'd I leave?" she shrugged, "or why'd he take ya from me? Why'd that bastard he hung around with steal you from your crib while you was sleepin'? That dumb damn Jewels. I don't know why. Maybe ask either of them."

"They said—"

"They said he wouldn't want no colored baby! They all said it! Then next thing I know, you're gone and ain't nobody seen nothin'. Magically, you just disappeared. Everybody in the apartment was just asleep I guess. No explanation for me, so why I need to give ya one?"

"Did you go—"

"To the police?" she's laughin', "*yeah right,* cause they'd give a shit about me, a little black teenage girl come runnin' sayin' she gave birth in the bathtub and now the baby were missin'. You didn't even have a name! I find out they got you and they're callin' you *Cecelia.* Horrible name —I woulda never picked that name for you."

I'm findin' my words but they're comin' slow and steady.

"So, why didn't you...come get me?"

She put her hands up like she was done with it all.

"If you don't know, I can't tell ya,"

She's wipin' her forehead with her hand and shuttin' her eyes,

"best thing I did for ya was keep ya with him. Best thing I did for ya,"

And she believed it. *She really wanted to believe it.*

"he took ya from me, so's you'd have a good life! And ya did, look at ya! You wouldn't have had no good life with me!"

"You don't know that."

"To hell with what you know! You ain't know nothin'. Twenty years old think you know it all – what the hell give ya the right to come here, huh? What give ya the nerve?"

"I had to see ya."

"Why?"

"I had to see where I come from."

She slammed her fist on the table and the ashtray went flyin'.

"You come from strong stuff! And don't you forget it!"

Now she's pacin' back and forth and round the table at me and then she says it,

"And ya ain't no Romello neither!"

I gasped and it made her stop pacin' and she give me some wide crazy smile and slid her drink my way.

"I ain't lyin' to ya, ain't no reason to lie to ya now! You ain't no skin off my nose."

I ain't say nothin', but I downed her drink myself. She's still talkin' at me.

"I bore ya once, I don't got no more to do with ya."

"But—"

"But who's your father?" she shrugged again, "only fools know. But he ain't no Romello, that's for sure. Hell —you could be a Dickens, or a Jenkins,"

She thought a little harder.

"or a Braylin, or a Green, but never a Romello. He thought he were gettin' somethin' takin' you, but you weren't even his so what were it for? Just cause his old lady wanted a girl. She wanted you somethin' fierce, well have her,"

She turned back to her cigarette and her drink and didn't look up at me again, not for nothin'.

"what good it done her, drank herself to death, I heard. Ain't no good, playin' pretend. Ain't no good for nobody."

I stood up straight, shoulders back, and I knew I weren't gonna get no more answers from her. It weren't no slight it were the truth. I wanted her to be hurt. I wanted her to feel somethin' for me bein' back in her face all them years later. I wanted her to look at me and think how pretty I turned out, how old I got, how much I'd grown, but she ain't done none of that. And that was just fine with me.

"I guess we're done here," I said, so matter of fact.

She wouldn't even look at me again, she's straight closin' her eyes and hummin' some tune I couldn't place. It sounded almost like a lullaby. I'm gettin' up from the table and excusin' myself like I was taught. Cookie Johnson were gonna see how I was raised. Cookie Johnson weren't gonna turn me outta my character. Not now.

"*How dare you?*" she said.

"What?"

And then a tear fell from her eye, it did. She caught it fast with her long nails but I seen it, it were there and it were real. She sat back down in her chair. I turned back one more time and she had been watchin' me make my way to the door.

"How dare you come back here...just when I was gettin' over you bein' gone."

"How dare you be so sure that Romeo Romello ain't my father...he man who raised me all them years when you were nowhere to be found?"

She let out that belly laugh again, this time through tears. She took a long drag of her cigarette, let out a puff a smoke and sipped her drink.

"Cause that sweaty bastard couldn't never finish."

20

Being from Harlem

I only known of Harlem from what my pops told me when I was a kid. He'd talk about it's dirty, dingy street corners and all the drunks walkin' round and folks fightin'. He'd say the four-floor walk ups had doors and windows broken, with neighborhoods full of run-down shacks. I grew up knowin' that my real ma lived there, but he told me never to go lookin', so I listened. The Harlem I'd come to know that night, the place my ma sung and danced in with all its culture, music and fun, weren't at all what he had described. And the Harlem on Dr. Billingsly's business card, the address where I went callin', had nothin' run-down about it. The streets was quite the opposite, with its houses set up like somethin' out of a painting. I would have never imagined it if I hadn't come seen for myself.

The rows of houses were neat and sittin' pretty with painted windowsills and flowers all round the clean, kept up and swept up sidewalks. The good doctor's house had iron rod railings attached to a spotless cement staircase with a potted plant on every step. Shiny new cars lined the blocks, cars that were expensive and cared for. I could tell there were well-off people livin' here, people like the Doc, and weren't nobody walkin' the streets lookin' grungy that morning *'cept me.* I knocked a few times, tremblin' at his doorway when he finally come to it. He was wipin' the sleep from his eyes tryna remember who I was. I were tryin' to explain I'd just seen my ma. I was tryin' to say what made me come there, with no place else to be. I was scared and confused. He heard me out and then let me in—no more questions about it. Through his front door, I were safe.

"Come in, I'll make some hot tea."

Inside his house everythin' was set nice and proper. I sat at the kitchen table as he's fumblin' round his own cabinets and stove tryin' to find what he needs, still half-asleep. His wife crept down the stairs, peekin' her head round the corner, clutchin' her robe to her body like a suit of armor synched up tight. She's squintin' her eyes towards me cause she ain't know they had visitors. Doc saw her and immediately explained the strange young woman sittin' in their kitchen.

"Alma, this is Cecelia. I was just making her some tea. She's had a long day."

"I'll help," she said, not blinkin' an eye.

She moved round him to fill the kettle and light fire under it on the stove. She easily found the tea, the little cups, and the silver spoon for stirrin'. He kissed her playfully on the cheek and she smiled at him like she ain't never seen a man more handsome or magnificent as he. She asked me, very politely, if I wanted cream and sugar and if I were hungry. She had pastry freshly made the morning before and encouraged me to have one. I nodded as she placed a rose patterned plate my way with the most delicious cherry turnover I'd ever ate. She served me tea in her fine bone china with a lace napkin to wipe my mouth. I practiced the table manners the Doc had taught me earlier and he looked on, quite impressed.

"Cecelia from the train?" she whispered to him, and he confirmed it with a nod, "okay well, don't stay up too late. We have to be at the church in the morning."

Alma looked me over, but the smile didn't leave her face. She kissed her husband on the forehead and went back upstairs. I imagined she'd lived like this for a while, patients comin' at all hours to see her husband, so she took it in stride. It was the life of a doctor's wife, I assumed, with his practice permanently in what shoulda' been their sittin' room. I'd finished eatin' and drinkin' my tea, so we moved in there. The office was all plush velvet couch cushions and dim lightin'. He started a small fire and we sat round it. He looked comfortable in his home, in his bedroom slippers and smokin' jacket. I'm lookin' all guilty like I shouldn't have disturbed him, but he ain't felt no slight by it. He told me to talk to him, speak with him and explain myself fully —so I did.

"...and after all this, I ain't even know where I came from," I'm tearin' up.

"Knowing where you come from is irrelevant now. Where you're going is all that matters. Where are you going from here, Cecelia?"

"I don't know, that's why I come to you. Tell me what I should do, doc. Please!"

"I can't tell answer that," he said, "that's not how I help. I help through self-discovery. You find what is wrong and you fix it. Your identity has been in question all your life, so now you have finally figured out who you are and who you can be. This new level of insight should excite you very much. It should open doors for you that you've never explored before. You're a blank canvas —be excited for that!"

The fire's cracklin' and he's lookin' at me, waitin' for some type of breakthrough, but nothin' is happenin'. I thought he would just give me the answers, but weren't nothin' doin'.

"You interest me Cecelia," he said, "I must be honest with you and confess something. When we met on the train, I did know you and I did know about you. I've been studying your family and the other mafia families in New York for years."

"Why?"

"Oh, not for anything more than theory. I'm not someone who stops organized crime, I'm not like your Raphael, there's nothing particularly courageous about me. I'm just interested in human behavior and I think there are characteristics of gang mentality that are fascinating. You see, it's the ultimate trust and loyalty, that sense of belonging. It's what bonds you all."

"It does?"

"Yes, but for you it was different. Your father apparently ostracized you from the rest of the family for some years and that's had an effect on you as well. The bond you had might have been stronger, if that weren't to have happened. It might have been stronger still if you weren't born a bastard. There are certain factors that kept pushing you further away from the family. First your mother, then Regina, and now Romeo. You keep being pushed away, so you push away first before it happens again. You push good people away from you."

"Like Raphael?"

"Yes," he said, "And that's not to mention the most recent...the promise that was broken by Romeo, this promise of a succession plan with you in it, leading the family. This promise most likely was what kept you locked away happily, without tearing your hair out. It was something for you to look forward to when you turned eighteen. It was that light at the end of the tunnel. Without that promise, you may have gone mad. Or maybe worse."

"Ended up like Regina?"

"Yes," he said, "she was promised a much different life. She realized she'd never get it. So, what more was there to live for?"

"I want to run away," I said finally.

"Where to?"

"I don't know."

"What's on your mind?" he asked, "or better yet, who's on your mind?"

I looked down, nervously playin' with my fingers.

"Don't be scared, you can say it. You've been thinking about your Raphael, haven't you?"

"Yes."

His ring was still round my finger. I ain't have the strength or care to take it off, so I left it on.

"Are you scared that if you go to him, he might reject you?"

I nodded.

"So what if he does?" the Doctor asked, "we must take the chance, mustn't we?"

"Why?"

"Because it's the thrill of life. Never really having all the answers until we've walked into the unknown and come back out the other side of things, completely changed."

"Ya think he'll still want to marry me?"

"I think you'll never know if you don't ask."

He smiled and it were calmin'. I did love Raphael and I did want him to marry me. I'd been stupid to leave him back in California. I'd been crazy to throw his love for me back in his face and I'd hoped he'd forgive me for it. Dr. Billingsly were right, if I weren't really a Romello for whatever reasons, why would I want top spot in the mob and why would I want to take on that *emotional baggage* that weren't even mine to take, he asked me.

"They kept you out of that life, far out of it. You, out of any of the Romello's, have even more of a right to your freedom," he said.

"Do ya think he knows?"

"Who knows?"

"My pops, do ya think he knows I ain't really his?"

"I don't think so."

"Should I tell him?"

"That depends,"

He leaned towards me, as if warning...

"do you think your father is emotionally mature enough to handle the fact that you are not his daughter?"

I didn't know.

"Do you even want to take that chance?" Dr. asked, "for as much protection and love you've had from this man throughout your life, even in the face of stark differences between you and the family, it could all change for the worst. If it's not handled properly, by him as the patriarch, it could mean very bad things for you, Cecelia. And so again I ask you if you think your father is capable of handling this truth? Handling it and relaying it to the rest of the family objectively and honestly."

I thought about it, my pops Romeo Romello, and how easily it were for him to fly off every handle there were. My brothers too, the ones who'd protected me all my life, weren't no ones to be trusted in these types situations either. And if I ain't tell him, I couldn't tell them cause there weren't no real secrets, not between made men.

"No," I answered.

Dr. Billingsly sighed and sat back in his chair.

"Then for your sake, in this particular situation, I would let sleeping dogs lie. Use this as your opportunity to run from the world that's been holding you hostage all these years, a world that formed you yes and made you the woman you are today, but where you go from here – well you have every right to choose that destiny. Don't let the Romello's choose it for you, they hold no power over you anymore,"

He was right. I felt free. I didn't have no burden's bout takin' over the 'family business' and helpin' my pops, well Romeo Romello, or provin' nothin' to none of em'.

"and that's where you'll have to decide, complete alienation or the opportunity to step back in, to have the family you grew up with in your life somehow, to still have them call on you, and potentially frame you in the future. Regardless, Romello or not, you were raised being Romeo's daughter and the world at this moment in time knows you as only as that. There's a stigma that surrounds your family, Cecelia, and you know it's negative. You know the lives your father and brothers' lead are not very happy ones."

"I know."

"So, it's just down to what you want. What will make Cecelia happy?"

"I want this," I looked round at his peaceful home, "I want a normal life. I want to kiss my husband in the kitchen while I'm makin' tea and the kids are sleepin' upstairs. I want to sit in front of the fire night's and talk and laugh and dream our little dreams. I grew up thinkin' somethin' was wrong with that. But ain't nothin' wrong with it, Doc, ain't nothin' wrong with it at all."

"There's absolutely nothing wrong with it," he said.

He took my hands in his and smiled at me, reassuring.

"Go. Get your normal."

I'd been given a nice warm bath to soak in and clean night clothes. Alma gave me plenty of blankets and pillows, settin' me up in their guest room, with a cup of water by my bedside. I felt warm, cared for, properly by these nice people. I wondered what would have become of me if I hadn't been with Romeo and the Romello's.

Maybe I would have stayed in Harlem with my ma. Maybe she woulda put me up for adoption. Maybe I'd have ended up with a nice family like the Billingsly's. I imagined for a second, imagined I was young, little while Dr. Billingsly wished me goodnight and he was off to bed hisself, yawnin'. I imagined I were their little girl with Alma finishin' makin' sure I were comfortable, smilin' the whole way. She tucked me in like a child and I let her. It were nice to pretend for a moment, pretend like they was my parents. She sat on the edge of the bed and leaned over as I made myself comfortable under the warmth of the covers.

"My husband helps all people," she said, "I tell him he's almost too benevolent for his own good."

Her voice changed, her expression grave, and this time she meant business. Gone was the polite type attitude, the smilin' face of the good doctor's wife and the dotin' mother. Her eyes glared at me suddenly like I weren't nothin'.

"I want you out of my house when the sun comes up," she said, "you understand me? I want you out of my house and don't come back here. Don't ever come back here again,"

The look on her face weren't angry, it were more of a warnin'. I might not of understood it before I started imaginin' what a normal life would be like, a happy life with Raphael and some kids in a pretty neighborhood such as that one. I would've understood if not for the dreams I were havin' bout what my life could be.

"just nod if you understand," she said.

I nodded.

She got up and started smilin' again. She turned out the light and shut the door, leavin' a crack in the doorway, I'm guessin' to check on me later. I did understand and I respected her more for sayin' it. Nobody weren't gonna take me and my clan at face value. I did have a father in the mob. These people didn't see no glory in it. These people didn't have no respect for the Romello's or people like us. And maybe they didn't have no reason to. Maybe I didn't have no reason to either, not now.

With that thought, I longed to be different. I longed to be somebody like Dr. Billingsly and his wife, somebody people looked on like they was respectable. I longed to be with Raphael cause he were looked at like a hero for nabbin' The Brit. These people, the people who made the world go round and was tryin' to do something good in life, unlike my family, the ones who just wanted to take from everybody and keep for themselves. Weren't no glory in it. Weren't no respect, neither.

I were finally settled, at peace, driftin' off when my thoughts weren't filled of Raphael and the life we'd have together. I'd closed my eyes, smilin', safe beneath the covers till' I heard it. It were the front door slammin' open, forced by two pairs of strong feet. It were footsteps rushin' up the stairs. It were doors openin'. It were a gunshot and the sound of a woman's scream, Alma's blood curdlin' shriek. Men was runnin' up and down the hall of Dr. Billingsly's nice house, tramplin' through their freshly waxed floors in their squeakin' shoes and I saw em trapezin' all on the stairs and then the carpet in my room. Couldn't tell ya how many men, coulda been two or three, or coulda been more with all the noise they was makin'. I heard the little ones wakin' up and cryin', but I couldn't do nothin' bout it cause them men was blindfoldin' me and carryin' me out the front door. They was wearin' all stockings over their heads so I couldn't make out their smushed up faces or their voices even, just that they was gonna take me for a *'little ride'*.

Out the corner of my eye I got a look at the hand of the man draggin' me along to a car, the same man holdin' a smokin' shotgun, and he had rings decoratin' all his fingers. He's holdin' a gold pocketwatch stained with blood, a watch inscriped with the cursive writin', *'from Alma with love'*. They took the blindfold off my face and it were my favorite brother George drivin'. He had a smile plastered on his face, blood sprayed on his clothes and no regrets.

"How ya doin', Cece?" He asked, kissin' me on the cheek.

The blood, the Dr.'s blood I knew it had to be, got on my clothes and my face and in my hair when he leaned over and all I could do was to scream. On the other sides of me was Joey and William and that Mackie Jones all crammed into pop's car and they was all puttin' hands over my mouth tryin' to silence me.

"Hit the gas George!" Mackie called.

I'm screamin' and gaspin' for air and I -- I ain't never been so scared or so upset in my whole life! I still remember the blood and the – then they was snickerin'.

"But did ya kill him?" I cried.

"Kill who?"

George is askin', had the nerve to be askin' with the blood all over hisself still drippin' down and stainin' his clothes —a stench of rust in the air.

"The doctor! Did ya kill him?! Tell me ya didn't kill him!"

"Ah," George is laughin'.

And then I turn and they all is laughin'...Joey and William and Mackie and George.

"Awe Cece don't cry," William said.

"We ain't in no trouble," Joey assured me.

George smiled sly, "yeah—ain't nobody care about another dead nigger!"

21

Becoming a Made Woman

For hours I was trapped in that Tin Lizzy with killers —my thoughts goin' a mile a minute! I just couldn't take all their laughin' and hollerin' and carryin' on, my own brothers and that bastard Mackie Jones and I'd had just about enough of them murderin' goons! With all their gossipin' like old ladies, I found out we was travelin' to upstate Pennsylvania. Grandpa Dellafield had sold my pops some old shack for cash, but he didn't mind cause we was all runnin'! With our Park Avenue house deserted, we was reduced to a rundown farmhouse out in the sticks. There was candles lit everywhere cause weren't no electricity. Turned a faucet to wash up, but weren't no water comin' out of it —better find a stream! *It was the best place to hide out where nobody could find us*, pops said, and my brothers followed his every word as law!

Pretty soon we were there, in no man's land, and I were stuck. I'm crawlin' out that car, the smell of cigarette smoke, bad hooch and rusty blood coverin' me. I'm runnin' through those woods, barefoot in the mud up to this house that looked worse than they'd described. I'm bangin' on the door with my fists til I realized the door had about three or four padlocks on the inside. I hear keys janglin' and Romeo's sweaty palms gettin' it open for me.

"Cece?"

"Pop's it's me, open up!" I'm screamin'.

My brother's voices are trailin' off and they're all breakin' glass bottles outside, takin' advantage of nobody round for miles so they could shoot off their guns and run round like hooligans playin' in the dark. I ain't have no time to play, damnit, I wanted answers! I kept poundin' my fists like the door was gonna break. It finally swung open and I was face to face with Romeo Romello's blood-shot eyes.

"Cece what's wrong?" my pops is askin'.

Inside, Romeo stood in a room full of his fortunes. The whole place were covered in movin' boxes packed and stacked. He'd been sellin' off properties and businesses for months. He'd been collectin' money from folks all round the city that owed him. Madame Josephine read his cards and told him a close personal friend was threatenin' our family business. He decided it was better for all of us to blow town! Duckie Romello, always duckin' con college, always runnin' like that yella belly he was!

"Get outta my way!"

I'm yellin', rushin' him. I ran to the kitchen where there was some whiskey in a bottle and just downed it all myself, gettin' good and loaded. Then I gone to this bucket for a sink and kept throwin' up til' my stomach were empty of nothin' but my guilt. I knew what my clan did and although I ain't paid much attention to their killin' before, I couldn't think of nothin' else in this moment. To have that good Doctor gunned down in his own house with his wife Alma and those kids runnin' round cryin and carryin' on...I just wanted to drown my sorrows and then maybe myself. My pops, that Sicilian son-of-a-bitch, was just sittin' drinkin' hisself silly in the middle of the room and he's lookin' at me like I got five heads.

"How was it in Harlem, huh? Ya had a nice reunion?" He asked.

"How'd ya know? Just how'd ya know where to come and find me?" I'm steamin' mad.

He's playin' coy, shufflin' his shot glass back and forth.

"I always told ya, there ain't nowhere in New York City you can go without me knowin' about it. Do you believe me now?"

"That's stalkin' that is!"

"Ain't stalkin' what's mine! Quit makin' a fool of yourself and sit down!"

"I ain't sittin'!"

"Would ya sit?" he's upset, "ya been talkin' to that damn crazy mother of yours. Probably fillin' your head with all her lies. Sit down woman!"

"Not lies! She told me the truth! Truth ya been holdin' out on me!"

"Oh yeah? And what's that?"

He's got me good and riled up, so he was gonna hear about it! I ran to him, gettin' in his big fat sweaty face. He's all lookin' me in the eyes with his brows raised like I weren't gonna try him, but he didn't know me then. I was different. I was changed.

"You ain't even my real old man!"

He finished downed his shot and then stood up as I'm glarin'. Pops were a full six feet tall and as he's towerin' over me, but it didn't scare me none. Well...maybe a little.

"What'd you say?"

"I said," now my voice was gettin' higher, quiverin', "I said you ain't my real old man. Explain that!"

I took his empty shot glass and threw it on the ground, lettin' it smash into little pieces. He watched all the glass just shatter to the floor and when it was all done rollin' around and makin' a mess, his eyes met mine again. If I had any ounce of anger left in me, any ounce of regret over goin' to the good Doctor's house that night and bringin' our mess to his perfect, neat little normal family way of livin', then I was gonna lay it all on Romeo Romello's doorstep!

"Well?!" I'm yellin'.

First it was a snarl and then he let out a low growl I ain't never heard before. His whole head was red and sweatin' and tremblin' at me, lookin' like an angry volcano that were gonna burst.

"Ten minutes with her!" He said.

Then he snatched me by my curls, the strength of his hand wrenchin' me around. Romeo Romello ain't never lay hands on me my whole life, but he made the exception and my neck was turnin' red too from hurtin'.

"Pop!"

"—you better never—"

"Daddy!"

"Damn right daddy!"

He's still got hold of me and he won't let go for none of my cryin' or pleadin'.

"You get off her!"

George ran in, yellin' from the doorway full of liquor and snow, which were always a bad combination for my brother. Pops still got his hands round the collar of my night shirt and he's hitched me up in the air so's my feet are danglin', kickin' and fightin' him. He turned to George, darin' him to do or say somethin' more. My brother saw the anger in his eyes and backed up some.

"I ain't lettin' her go til she takes it back!"

"Take what back?" George asked.

"She knows what she said," pops told him, "take it back Cece!"

Now all my brothers are gatherin' in the doorway, but George is warnin' em to proceed with caution. That Mackie Jones is smilin' behind em, tryna slant, til he saw how red my pops was gettin' so he changed his tune. Now Dellafield's comin' out the back bedroom all sleepy-eyed in her robe lookin' for drama and runnin' towards George for protection. Romeo Jr. is comin' down the stairs with his guns at his side and his wife May followin' close behind him, her all tremblin' scared.

"I ain't takin' back and I don't care who knows it!" I'm sayin', "Cookie told me the truth! My ma told me, my real ma the hoofer, said it! I ain't no Romello! I'm a Jenkins or a Dickens or a Green!"

"Ya ain't no Jenkins! Ya ain't no Dickens! And ya sure as hell ain't no Green! Take it back!"

"Nothin' doin!"

"What give her the right, huh?" He's askin', "what give her the right to say them things! And what give ya the right to listen?"

"I'm just the negro!" I yell, "just another nigger like my brothers say!"

He took my head and pushed me. I went flyin' into the wall and slumped down onto the floor in pain. I looked over and there was Sal Santini, all sittin' there eatin' his sandwich real calm, cool and collected. A little too calm if ya ask me.

"Who said that?" Pops is yellin', "ya better get them words out your mouth 'fore I take em out with soap little girl! Don't care what big fancy Hollywood and all them people in Harlem be sayin', you ain't no nigger! You ain't like none of them, you's my daughter! You's a Romello so you ain't like none of em!"

Pops is goin' to grab me again and George were the only one comin' up to him, not scared of him no more.

"Get away from her!" George warns.

"I don't want to hear that! How's she gonna talk like that! How's that woman gonna fill her head with them lies, huh?!"

"Don't touch her!"

George fires his gun and the shot rings through our ears. I'm on the floor already with my hands coverin' em. Romeo's standin' over me, sweatin' over me and he ain't stoppin' from grabbin' my arm and forcin' me up off the ground.

"Ten minutes with her and you'll believe anything that fool woman says! Ten minutes with her and all those years of me carin' for ya and raisin' ya as a Romello don't mean a damn, huh? Ten minutes with her only!"

"You get your hands off her, I ain't playin'!"

George shouts, pointin' the gun right at pop's head. He's still got my arm in a vice grip and he's twistin' and I'm cryin' in pain, but he knows George ain't kiddin'.

"Back off!" George says, so pops does.

"Yeah, alright Georgie alright, don't lose your head," he finally backs down.

Pops is wipin' sweat from his forehead and lookin' nervous. He's pacin' back and forth with his head in his hands and then collapses in his chair—defeated. Weren't nobody George didn't protect me from, including my pops even when the rest of my brothers wanted to be lily-livered and now I'm lookin' round for Jewels cause he woulda saved me too, so where was he?

"I ain't mean nothin', I just," pop's is shakin' his head, "I'm sorry Cece I didn't mean—"

"—yeah you better not a meant," George is angry.

"I just left my home, came out to this dump," pops is ramblin', "my whole life's upside down and everybody expects me to not flip my lid!"

George is helpin' me to the chair across the room. I'm starin' at Romeo with a real hard glare, and rubbin' my arm and the back of my head cause they hurt. Pops is lookin' real low on hisself like he's guilty. The whole family was just standin' round like they's afraid to talk. George pours me a drink and lights me a cigarette.

"I don't like her smokin'," pops said.

"Yeah well, let her smoke!" George yells.

"Yeah well, let her have some blow too," pops shrugged.

"My sister ain't no cokehead," George barked.

I'm coughin' up a lung, but inhalin' the smoke cause I needed it.

"I just – I never wanted ya to go see Cookie cause I knew what she'd say," pops told me, "I knew she'd try to tell ya lies, poison ya. Did she tell ya? Did she tell ya I found that mother of hers was tryna deliver you with a wire hanger? That mother and grandmother, they was tryna have ya killed cause of who your father was? They sure thought I was your old man then!"

Pop's is spittin'.

"And who shoulda been more embarrassed of ya, huh? A man in the prime of his life, with a wife and a family and more money than he knew what to do with, gettin' a colored kid from the wrong side of the tracks pregnant? I coulda had her shot for dupin' me! I coulda had her killed without battin' an eyelash, but I spared her! And all that mother of hers was sayin' was she got pregnant by a wop! She ain't want no parts of me or you then, you better believe it! Half negro yes and they woulda laughed at ya, but half Italian weren't no better neither!"

Pops is pourin' hisself another drink and starin' at the wall.

"That's why I took what was mine! I took you back! Didn't want nobody sayin' you was half this, half that, half hell! You is *all* Romello and they was gonna put respect in your name when they saw ya! No colored this, colored that—none of it! Say them words round Romeo Romello and they all was gettin' cement shoes!"

That's when he threw it, threw the card at me. St. Cecilia, to hold to my chest. I looked at her picture, her face so innocent, with hands praying and light shinin' behind her. St. Cecilia were from a rich family, like myself, a virgin who had angels round her, guidin' her. They tried to kill her somethin' like three times, tryin' to cut off her head cause she were different, but it couldn't be done. She died in three days from bleedin' out, but only from her body given out, not her mind, not her spirit, not her soul. I was given Cecelia and 'St. Cecilia', because of what it meant.

"They'll give up before we do," pops said, "and I'm givin' it to ya cause you're worth somethin'. That's why I wanted to see ya. Initiate ya into the life. I need ya Cece, we all need ya,"

Pops is shakin' his head and bowin' down. My pops ain't never bow down to me before.

"I shoulda done it long time ago, I just, I'm sorry Cece. I wanted to protect ya all them years, but it were no use. Ya are what I raised ya to be, and ya belonged at the seat of this table, same as the men. You proved to me tonight, standin' up to me as you did. You really are as tough as all of em, cause I raised ya to be so."

"Give me your hand before he changes his mind," George ordered.

He initiated me into the life that night, with Romeo Romello and all the rest of my brothers; Tony, Joey, Romeo Jr., and William, and even that damn Mackie Jones with his one eye, watchin' on. George were still covered in the good doctor's blood, all spattered on his face and his hands and his clothes, when he swore me in. He pricked my hand with a pen knife, one small slice drawin' blood from my skin. He put my flesh to his, which was also sliced and bleedin'. We touched and was bonded. The clan looked on like it were probably the most important thing I'd do in my life. Our pops explained how serious this was—that now I were really one of them. I was finally a made woman.

It was what I'd always wanted all my life. I could remember bein' young and imaginin' what it would feel like, all them years alone in my room. I were finally a part of them and despite it all, a part of me should've been really proud. But all I could do was sit back, collapsed and hurt. Maybe all he were sayin' was true —every word of it. So I was a Romello, but so what? That meant I were stuck. It was my family that was the true problem all along. They weren't never gonna let me be. They weren't ever gonna let me have my freedom. I weren't never gonna have my normal, never gonna have my peace. But that weren't the worst thing...cause worse than not knowin' where I came from, *was knowin' exactly where I come from.*

Printed in the USA
CPSIA information can be obtained
at www.ICGtesting.com
LVHW090807131023
760664LV00008B/593